Paul Doherty was born in Middlesbrough. He studied History at Liverpool and Oxford Universities and obtained a degree at Oxford for his thesis on Edward II and Queen Isabella. He is now headmaster of a school in North-East London and lives with his wife and family near Epping Forest.

Paul Doherty is also the author of The Sorrowful Mysteries of Brother Athelstan, the Canterbury Tales of mystery and murder, THE SOUL SLAYER, THE ROSE DEMON, and two novels set in Ancient Egypt, THE MASK OF RA and THE HORUS KILLINGS, all of which have been highly praised:

'Medieval London comes vividly to life . . . Doherty's depictions of medieval characters and manners of thought, from the highest to the lowest, ringing true'

Publishers Weekly

'Vitality in the cityscape . . . angst in the mystery; it's Peters minus the herbs but plus a few crates of sack'

Oxford Times

'As always, the author invokes the medieval period in all its muck as well as glory, filling the pages with pungent smells and description. He populates them with fictional and historical personages. Pomp, panoply and poverty are vividly recreated. The author brings years of research to his writing; his mastery of the period as well as a disciplined writing schedule have led to a rapidly increasing body of work and a growing reputation'

Mystery News

Other Hugh Corbett medieval mysteries

Satan in St Mary's
Crown in Darkness
Spy in Chancery
The Angel of Death
The Prince of Darkness
Murder Wears a Cowl
The Assassin in the Greenwood
The Song of a Dark Angel
Satan's Fire
The Devil's Hunt

Also by Paul Doherty and available from Headline

The Rose Demon
The Soul Slayer

The Mysteries of Ancient Egypt
The Mask of Ra
The Horus Killings

The Sorrowful Mysteries of Brother Athelstan
The Nightingale Gallery
The House of the Red Slayer
Murder Most Holy
The Anger of God
By Murder's Bright Light
The House of Crows
The Assassin's Riddle
The Devil's Domain
The Field of Blood

An Ancient Evil
Being the Knight's Tale
A Tapestry of Murder
Being The Man of Law's Tale
A Tournament of Murders
Being the Franklin's Tale
Ghostly Murders
Being the Priest's Tale

The Demon Archer

Paul Doherty

headline

First published in 1999
by HEADLINE BOOK PUBLISHING

First published in paperback in 1999
by HEADLINE BOOK PUBLISHING

8

ISBN 978 0 7472 6074 5

Typeset by
Letterpart Limited, Reigate, Surrey

Printed and bound in Great Britain by
Clays Ltd, Elcograf S.p.A.

HEADLINE PUBLISHING GROUP
A division of Hodder Headline PLC
338 Euston Road
London NW1 3BH
www.headline.co.uk
www.hodderheadline.com

In memory of Patrick Leonard Graves of Woodford Green and for his wife Patricia and his brave children, Steven and Michelle, Joanne and Nicola.

Prologue

Ashdown Forest, or so they said, was as old as the island itself. The chroniclers, those who prided themselves on this sort of knowledge, maintained that dragons once lived there while the great giants, Gog and Magog, had set up home among its dark oak groves. These ogres had celebrated their bloody feasts, eating the flesh and grinding the bones of their victims. All manner of creatures were supposed to lurk in its marshy, tangled depths. The gossips talked of the woadman, a fearsome, shaggy-haired giant, with one red eye and hooked teeth, who prowled the trees at night looking for prey.

The outlaw, the wolfs-head known as the 'Owlman', ignored such rumours. True, Ashdown Forest could be a lonely, gloomy place but it teemed with life: the badger dug his sett; the foxes had their lairs; hawk and kestrel nested with crow and rook in the branches above; rabbits and hares loped across the moss-strewn glades. Deer, both the fallow and the roe, flitted like golden ghosts through the green darkness. Above all, it was owned by Lord Henry Fitzalan and the Owlman's hate and fear were reserved for him. The Owlman took his name, not so much because of the way he dressed, in dark lincoln green, thick leather boots and tarred leathery hood, but because of his silence: the way he could flit through the trees and make his mark, irritate and vex Lord Henry whenever he so wished.

At dawn on the feast of St Matthew 1303, the Owlman had left his lair to practise great mischief against his enemy. He had reached the edge of a clearing and stared across at the lonely church of St Oswald's-in-the-Trees. Brother Cosmas was sitting outside on a bench, a tankard in his hand. The Owlman studied him fondly from the shelter of the trees. He dare not approach this fiery Franciscan, a man who spared neither himself nor his parishioners. A preacher who could conjure up visions of hell and quote copiously from the Book of Revelations, about the three unclean spirits which sprang out of the mouth of the Great Dragon.

Behind the church loomed the charnel or ossuary house. The Owlman watched the smoke rising from this. So it was true what the forest people said, those parishioners of Brother Cosmas, that he had decided to tidy up the cemetery, digging up old bones, placing them in the charnel house while removing others to be consumed by fire. The church, despite its deserted appearance, was a busy place; it served the woodcutters, charcoal-burners, verderers, poachers, aye, even outlaws who lived in the forest depths.

The Owlman studied the front door of the church; above it the great carved Doom depicted Death surprising a king, his queen, noblemen and bishops. Underneath were the words the Owlman knew well:

As you are, so once were we,
As we are, so shall ye be.

The Owlman grinned, a salutary warning! It was a pity Lord Henry Fitzalan did not heed it. A hard manor lord, Fitzalan enforced the forest laws and demanded his due at all seasons. Lord Henry would not even ignore a crime as lowly as the theft of a farthing. The great lord didn't come here. Like all the owners of the soil, he had his own private chapel or, when it so suited, he'd visit those high-born ladies under their prioress the Lady Madeleine, she who carried her head as if it was as precious and as sacred as the relic of St Hawisia, of which she and her priory were so proud.

The Owlman paused to check the arrows in his quiver. Unseen by the friar, this mysterious outlaw of Ashdown then knelt and crossed himself, quickly reciting his favourite prayer.

'Christ beside me.
Christ behind me.
Christ on my right,
Christ on my left.'

Afterwards a short aspiration to St Christopher. The Owlman pulled down his jerkin and took out the silver cast medal which hung from a piece of twine. He stared at the saint, the Infant Christ on his shoulder. They said that if you looked on St Christopher, just after dawn, then you would not die violently that day. The Owlman would need all the help and protection this saint could give him. Lord Henry, or so the gossips said, had organised a great hunt down near Savernake Dell. He'd fenced off an enclosure for his French visitors, lords and clerks from across the Narrow Seas, to kill the deer which his foresters and verderers drove into it. The Owlman was determined to be present. He wanted to do so much mischief, create so much havoc, that Lord Henry and his guests would never forget this day's hunting.

The Owlman picked up his bow by the cord-grip round its centre and hurried on. He had to be near Beauclerc hunting lodge in order to watch Lord Henry and his guests leave. The Owlman moved quietly, eyes constantly studying the trees and ground ahead of him. He was now part of a deadly game. Lord Henry's foresters and verderers, sly knaves all, would love to trap him, haul him as a prize before their master. Or, worse still, if they captured him, execute the forest law, throw a rope over a branch with the end round his neck; then the bastards would squat and watch him slowly choke to death. The Owlman, however, was cunning. More versatile and quick than any reynard, he knew all their wiles and traps while they would never guess who he really was.

The Owlman paused on the edge of a clearing and scrutinised the ground carefully. It had rained yesterday afternoon but the strong autumn sun had dried it up. He looked for any disturbance, any sign of a pit being dug or a rope being laid or one of those great steel traps, their teeth like razors, carefully concealed beneath a bed of red-brown leaves.

When he was about to go across he heard a sound from his left. He quickly took an arrow from his quiver, notching it to his bow, but then relaxed. A fox, triumphant after his early dawn hunt, stepped out of the trees, proud as any champion from the tourney, a lifeless rabbit hanging on its jaws. The fox, arrogant as a prince, trotted across the clearing and disappeared into the bushes on the far side. The Owlman sighed with relief; if the fox sensed no danger, why should he?

He slipped across, silent as a shadow, and reached the welcoming fringe of trees. Here the ground dipped as it fell down to a forest trackway. The Owlman paused. A busy place this, used by forest workers, travellers and pilgrims to the priory of St Hawisia. Merchants, who lodged at night at the Devil-in-the-Woods tavern, a large, spacious hostelry two or three miles further down the road, also journeyed here. The Owlman listened carefully. No sound, no sight. The early morning mist was now lifting. Birds sang in the trees on the other side. He could hear no warning chatter, no alarm raised by those heralds of the forest who always complained so raucously at any trespass on their private domain. The Owlman regarded such birds as his scouts. After all he had been trained well. He had grown up in forests and knew every bird call, every sound. He could distinguish what was usual and what was threatening, what was old and what was new. Satisfied, silent as the fox he had just seen, the Owlman padded down the bank towards the trackway. The birds above began a clamour but this was usual. Once he had passed they returned to their morning song, their usual matins. He paused. He liked that phrase. God's creatures sang the divine office as well as those haughty nuns in their lavishly decorated priory. Perhaps one day he should pay them a visit, create a little mischief for Lord Henry's half-sister.

The Owlman hurried on. He never really knew what happened. Perhaps it was God's way of showing that pride does come before a fall, that he had grown too confident. He reached the far edge of the trackway when he caught a glimpse of steel in the undergrowth. Just in time he drew back, away from the cruel man-trap hidden there. He picked up a stick and furiously lashed out. The trap shut with an angry iron clang so loud that the Owlman missed his footing, slipped on some mud and went tumbling down a bank. He reached the bottom, his hand immediately going to his dagger, gazing fearfully around. He had lost his bow and saw it lying a yard away from him, so he crawled across, pressing down with one hand. He was stretching out when he felt his fingers go beneath the carpet of soil and leaves, touch something cold and soft, something which shouldn't be there.

The Owlman crouched and, digging like an animal, pulled away the leaves and the veil of soil. A decomposing face stared up at him. The flesh was livid. Now he had moved the dirt and leaves, he caught the tang of corruption; the flesh was putrefying.

'You must have been here weeks,' the Owlman whispered.

He dug again, removing the earth, the leaves, the bracken until the entire swollen corpse was revealed. The nails and fingers were carefully tended and he wondered what the body of such a woman was doing in a shallow forest grave. He moved the corpse and then turned away at the odour of corruption. Parts of the flesh had been nibbled by forest creatures. When the waves of nausea passed he examined the face. The words carved above the door of St Oswald's church, 'As we are, so shall ye be', came to mind. The face had once been comely, even beautiful, with high cheekbones, full red lips and eyes, when open, full of life. Her hair was a darkish brown cut close and the neck was used to wearing some gilded necklace or gorget, not that terrible blue-black wound tinged with a reddish-brown. An arrow wound, he reasoned. The shaft had taken her full in the throat, a quick death! But who was she? And how did she come here?

The Owlman sat back on his heels. He knew the forest gossip. Outlaws and wolfs-heads attacked but they very rarely killed their victims, just took what was valuable and fled like shadows. A woman such as this with a soft skin, carefully tended hands? If such a person disappeared there would be hunting parties, questions asked, rewards posted. The Owlman breathed in. Unless, of course, it was the work of Fitzalan? He liked soft, perfumed flesh, did the great lord. Had this young woman displeased him? Had she been hustled out in the dead of night? But why an arrow to her throat? And surely Lord Henry could find deeper pits and more secret places? And what had happened to her clothes? Her possessions? She had apparently been stripped of these. Where was her horse or palfrey?

The Owlman looked up at the crows circling high

above their nests. What could he do now? Leave her here? The corpse brought back memories of his own; rekindled his nightmares, the hatred he felt for Lord Henry. He couldn't leave the body here, not for the scavengers. It would weigh on his conscience and arouse fears of himself being left to die in some lonely spot, his corpse untended. The Owlman recalled his true calling and, bending down, whispered a requiem followed by words of absolution.

On the early morning air, he heard the distant chimes of the bells of St Hawisia's priory summoning the young ladies to sing their devotions, and smiled. Weren't nuns committed to doing good works? To tending the sick and burying the dead? The forest was safe. Lord Henry's verderers and huntsmen would be down near the lodge, well away from any path he had to take. Yes, that was what he'd do. He dare not take it to St Oswald's, that wouldn't be fair. No, he'd give Lady Madeleine and her good nuns an opportunity to show some charity. He slung his bow over his back, took off the cloak his friend had given him and wrapped it round the corpse, then lifted it up and ran, at a half-crouch, back across the trackway and into the trees.

'Exsurge Domine! Exsurge et vindica causam meam!'

'Arise, O Lord! Arise and judge my cause!'

The good nuns of St Hawisia's priory chanted, as they had been taught to by the choir mistress the Lady Johanna, the opening verses of the office of Prime. They stood in polished, wooden stalls, row upon row of white-garbed ladies, their habits of pure wool offset only by the starched creamy wimples which framed their faces. Black velvet cords bound their slim waists and a silver medal, depicting their patron saint Hawisia, hung round each of their necks. They all held their Book of Hours as they had been instructed to, carefully mouthing the words, fearful of the eagle eye of their prioress Lady Madeleine, who sat in her great, throne-like stall.

A woman of indeterminate age, the Lady Madeleine! Her hair, of course, was hidden but her oval face was unlined, not marked by any seam or wrinkle of age. She had ice-blue eyes, a sharp beaked nose and a mouth thin and tight when her temper flared. A woman of poise and good breeding, half-sister to the Lord Henry, Lady Madeleine ruled her lavish priory as strictly as any baron did his fief, or constable his castle. She could walk like a queen or as stealthily as a cat when she was on the prowl, as the good sisters put it, looking for any misdemeanour or anything out of place. She seemed to have the ability to be in all places at all times, to be all-knowing about their hidden faults and secret foibles. Above all, the Lady Madeleine appeared to have the gift of being able to read her Book of Hours, sing the divine chant and yet scrupulously study each and every one of them. They all confessed to be in fear of her, be it the sub-prioress, the Lady Agnes, or the novice mistress, the Lady Marcellina.

If the truth be known, Lady Madeleine could also keep her thoughts to herself and, although she studied her Book of Hours, listening to the chant and watching her good sisters in Christ, she was also distracted by the words of the Psalm. How Satan roamed like an enemy! Even here, Lady Madeleine reflected. Her priory of St Hawisia might be a brilliant jewel in the green calm of Ashdown Forest, yet beyond the walls lurked outlaws like the Owlman, that fiery preacher Brother Cosmas, the forest people and, above all, her mocking half-brother, Lord Henry.

Lady Madeleine closed her eyes, then remembered herself and glanced at the illuminated Book of Hours on the lectern before her. The painter had drawn, to mark the beginning of the Psalm, a small picture of the devil as a knight dressed in red armour, in his clawed hand a banner displaying three black frogs. How apposite, Lady Madeleine thought. Satan was a fallen seraph, a knight in eternal revolt against *le bon Seigneur*, Jesus, just like her half-brother. Just like many a knight! Madeleine was proud that her beautiful priory was a sanctuary for women against the cruel, iron world of men.

The prioress glanced to her right through the

marble pillars which divided the sanctuary from the great side chapel which bore the blessed remains of the virgin martyr St Hawisia. The saint lay there beneath her polished oaken sarcophagus. On top rested a pure glass case, strengthened with silver beading, the work of a craftsman specially hired from Chartres in France. Madeleine narrowed her eyes. From where she stood she could see the golden hair which lay coiled on the embroidered silk pillow beneath the glass case. The priory's most precious relic, a source of veneration, pilgrimage and, of course, the income it attracted. Now, thanks to her half-brother's recent refurbishment, the shrine was more beautiful. Come spring, the word would spread and more pilgrims flock to pay their devotions. Lady Madeleine prided herself on how famous the priory was becoming, not only as a centre of learning and piety for ladies of good breeding, but a hallowed place of pilgrimage. She glimpsed a figure out of the corner of her eye and turned in annoyance. Sister Veronica, the cellarer, was gazing anxiously up, her thin sour face wreathed in concern.

'What is it?' Lady Madeleine leaned down.

'Oh, my lady,' the cellarer stammered. 'The corpse of a young woman has been found outside the postern gate.'

Lady Madeleine closed her eyes: this truly must be a day of tribulation.

Chapter 1

A few hours later, just before noon, Lord Henry Fitzalan and his hunting party gathered behind the palisade built around Savernake Dell, a natural clearing in the great forest, the most suitable location for the slaughter to take place. In the distance they could hear the braying horn of a huntsman, the shouts and halloos of the beaters and the deep bell-like baying of the dogs. Lord Henry stretched, cracking his muscles, and surveyed the dell. Everything was ready; the makeshift palisade stretched like a horseshoe screening off the trees. If the huntsmen did their job, particularly that varlet Robert Verlian the chief verderer, the deer would stream into here and his hunting party would have good sport. He snapped his fingers and a young squire hurried up with a gold-chased goblet, which Lord

Henry snatched from his hand and sipped. The claret was strong, the best of Bordeaux. The great manor lord handed it back and gripped his stomach; the pains he'd suffered the night before had disappeared. They would spend the afternoon hunting and, this evening, feast on the most succulent venison in his great hall at Ashdown Manor. He looked over his shoulder to where his brother William stood glowering at him, his face full of grievance.

'Come, come, brother!' Lord Henry felt a spurt of good humour.

His brother walked across, his high-heeled riding boots squelching on the soft earth. He threw his cloak back over his shoulder and Henry studied him quickly from head to toe. The tunic was wine-stained, the leggings already covered in mud. His brother was a good soldier but a poor courtier and, above all, a bad loser. Henry's smile widened as he grasped William by the shoulder and pulled him closer.

'Today, sweet brother,' he hissed, smile fixed, 'I enjoy a day's hunting. I entertain the King's guests.' He gestured with his head to where Seigneur Amaury de Craon, the pale, red-haired, foxy-faced envoy from the French court stood quietly gossiping with his own entourage.

'I don't give a fig for the French, brother!' William snapped. 'You gave me your promise that the manor of Manningtree would be mine when I passed my thirtieth birthday.'

'I've changed my mind,' Lord Henry replied. 'Manningtree will stay with me.'

'And me?' William accused. 'Am I to stay with you, brother? Become a hanger-on at your court? Feeding on scraps from your table?'

'You are my dearest brother. You are my heir.' Lord Henry pulled a face. 'Well, until I marry and beget a thousand and one sons.'

'Why can't I have Manningtree?'

'First, because I have said so. Secondly, I need it. And thirdly, brother, I want to keep you close. I don't want you skulking off and plotting with some of my, let us say, disaffected knights. I've given you a choice. You can stay here and, in all things, be my brother. Or I can give you a hundred pounds, two good horses and a suit of armour and you can go and seek your fortune elsewhere. Until then,' his grip tightened, 'you will smile when I tell you to! You will do what I tell you to do!'

His brother broke free and stood back, his hand going to the dagger in the belt around his waist.

'What are you going to do, brother?' Henry taunted. 'Settle matters here?' He stepped closer, his face now drained of any good humour. 'Go on, sweet brother, draw your dagger, let's have it out now. But, I tell you this.' He grasped the hilt of his sword. 'Your head will leave your shoulders before that dagger leaves its sheath. Now, play the man.'

William's hand fell away.

'That's a good boy.' He was about to turn away.

'Who's the Owlman?' William whispered.

'Why, brother, he's an outlaw, a wolfs-head, an irritant.'

'But why does he threaten you? Those messages left pinned to the manor gate or shot into doors and shutters? A good archer, brother, why should he taunt you?'

'Brother, I am a great lord,' Lord Henry explained. 'I come of ancient family as you do. I make enemies, not only among my own kith and kin, but further afield! One day I'll go hunting, not the fallow or roe deer but the Owlman. When I catch him, I'll hang him from my manor gate and that will be the end of the matter.'

'He must hate you deeply?'

'Brother, better to be hated than despised.'

'And the French?' William asked. 'Why have they asked the King . . .?'

'Why have they asked the King?' Lord Henry interrupted, drawing so close William could smell his wine-drenched breath. 'Why has the King asked me to lead an embassy to Paris to represent the Crown at the betrothal of the Lord Edward to the Princess Isabella? Yes.' His eyes rounded in mock surprise. 'Yes, that's what I'm doing, William! Because I am what you are not! I am a great lord, a friend and confidant of the King. I am feared not only here but in places you've never even visited.'

'Aye, feared and hated!' William spat back. 'You threaten me, like last night . . .'

'*Mes excuses*, brother.' Henry drew closer. 'I have only hinted at what I know, so now I will tell you! I know about the catamite Gaveston!'

And, spinning on his heel, Lord Henry walked back to his squires.

'Soon our quarry will be here,' he reminded them. 'Shall we agree a wager, gentlemen? That my arrow will bring the first deer down? That my arrow will go deep into the heart?'

The murmur of conversation stilled. Lord Henry drained his cup and tossed it away.

'Come, come, gentlemen, aren't there any takers?'

'I accept.' Amaury de Craon raised a hand. 'Ten pounds in gold, my lord.'

The French envoy came forward, hand outstretched. Lord Henry clasped it, his eyes narrowing as de Craon held it fast, pulling him a little closer. The Frenchman's dark eyes never wavered.

'And when you come to Fontainebleau, Lord Henry, I can take you hunting in our forests.'

'Seigneur Amaury, your wager is accepted. I will take your gold and my hand back.'

The French envoy laughed and let go.

'In France,' Lord Henry felt the anger boiling within him at this French envoy's impudence, 'I intend to go hunting for more than a deer.'

His enigmatic remark had its effect. De Craon nervously licked his lips and his eyes shifted.

'Oh, don't worry,' Lord Henry reassured him, slipping his arm through that of the Frenchman and drawing away from the rest. 'They know nothing of what I say.'

'You'll come to France, Lord Henry?'

'I will journey back with you.'

'And Signor Pancius Cantrone?'

'My physician doesn't know it, but he will join us.'

'And my master,' Amaury de Craon continued in a whisper, 'will be pleased to see Signor Cantrone and silence his lying mouth. But, how will it be done?'

'We'll journey down to Rye. My household will go with me, including my brother William whom I like to keep an eye on. What has to be done will be done then.'

Amaury de Craon withdrew his arm.

'And isn't the King suspicious that we asked you to lead the English envoys?'

'My dear Amaury, I have led similar embassies before. I own land in Gascony. I am the King's most trusted councillor. Why shouldn't I go to Paris? The marriage negotiations between the Prince of Wales and the Lady Isabella have been ordained by his Holiness the Pope and, in time, will lead to peace between our two kingdoms.'

Amaury de Craon studied this sly, secretive English lord, who was tall and thickset, his black hair swept back. In the florid face, those cunning light blue eyes reminded Amaury of his master Philip IV of France: ice cold, soulless, constantly plotting. Amaury knew why Philip wanted this nobleman in Paris and, above all, why that traitor Cantrone, who had fled the French court, should be brought back.

'Won't the English court object over Cantrone?'

Amaury forced a smile, fearful lest others become suspicious of this hushed conversation.

'Amaury, Amaury.' Lord Henry mimicked the Frenchman's accent. 'You worry about so many things. It won't be the first time, and it certainly won't be the last, that someone dies or disappears in Paris. And why should the English court object? Cantrone is not a citizen of this kingdom. He is an Italian who wanders the face of the earth. It will all be forgotten in the betrothal celebrations.'

Amaury stared up at the overhanging oak tree. He watched a squirrel skip across the branch. He became aware of the liquid song of some bird high in the trees, singing its own sweet carol, oblivious to the treachery plotted below and to the bloody carnage which would break out when the distant hunters panicked their quarry into the killing pen.

'My Lord Henry.' De Craon wiped some crumbs from his red woollen tunic, slipping a thumb into his belt. 'I am not fearful of you, or of your king, or of what might happen.'

'Corbett!' Lord Henry taunted. 'You are fearful of Sir Hugh Corbett. I have heard of the rivalry between you.'

Lord Henry recalled the close, secretive face,

framed by raven-black hair, of the Keeper of the King's Secret Seal, Edward's most trusted confidant. Sir Hugh Corbett who, time and again, had crossed swords with his French adversary.

'We heard he was dead,' de Craon declared testily.

'I wager you did.' Lord Henry laughed. 'And the bells of Paris must have pealed to the heavens.'

'We heard he had been killed in Oxford, an arrow to the heart.'

'He was wounded. He was attacked by an assassin whom his manservant Ranulf-atte-Newgate killed. The crossbow bolt was a hunting one, not an arbalest. It cracked bone but, I hear, Corbett now thanks God for the thick leather jerkin he wore as well as for the royal doctors and physicians. He has recovered.' Lord Henry's grin widened. 'Indeed, he may well come to pay his compliments.'

Dr Craon hawked and spat.

'Is it true?' Lord Henry continued his taunting. He plucked at de Craon's sleeve. 'Is it true that your master has put up a reward on Corbett's head?'

'That's ridiculous!' de Craon snapped. 'If Philip of France did that, Edward of England would retaliate.'

'Yes, yes, he would.'

Lord Henry turned away; the rest of the hunting party were becoming excited. The horns now sounded closer and the bellowing of the dogs filled the dell.

'We should take up our positions, my lord.'

Lord Henry walked across to the palisade, where

a squire came running up and thrust a long yew bow in his hand. Next he chose a grey-goose-quilled arrow. A man who lived for each moment, he had now forgotten de Craon, Corbett, his sulky brother and the vexatious messages of the Owlman. He recalled the lovely, olive-skinned face of Alicia, his chief verderer's daughter, and looked around.

'Where is Verlian? Where's my chief verderer?'

'He has not yet returned, sir,' one of his squires shouted, pointing across to the glade. 'He's probably over there ensuring all is well.'

'The fool! He'll be in the line of fire. He won't be the first to be killed while hunting.' Lord Henry shrugged. 'But he knows the hunt is close, this will be upon his head.'

All around him his companions were preparing their bows, heads craned back towards the forest, waiting for the deer to appear. Lord Henry, however, was still distracted. If only Alicia would give way to him. Was that why her father was so sullen and withdrawn? Lord Henry notched the arrow and waited. In time he brought everything down and in his heart he couldn't care what damage he caused. Glancing quickly around, he noticed William was gone. Where, sulking in the trees? Again came the braying of horns. A crashing in the undergrowth could be heard and a roe deer appeared head up, moving so fast its hooves hardly seemed to touch the ground. The speed of the animal caught the hunters unawares. Bows were strung and brought up, arrows loosed but the deer seemed to have a charmed life. It swept across the glade, glimpsed the palisade and, in one curving jump, cleared it.

The deer's disappearance was greeted with cries of derision. Lord Henry flushed with anger. His arrow, like that of his companions, had missed its mark and he heard de Craon's whinnying laugh. Again the hunting horn sounded, loud and clear. Another deer sped through the trees. Lord Henry raised his bow; he loosed but the deer slipped and this action saved its life as all the hunters' arrows either whistled over or smacked into the ground around it. Lord Henry, beside himself with rage, grabbed another arrow, lifting up the bow. This time he would be ready. He glimpsed a blur just before an arrow took him deep in the chest. Lord Henry staggered back, dropping his bow. He stared in shocked horror, almost oblivious to the pain, then turned, glimpsing his squire's look of fear. Finally he slumped to his knees and fell quietly on his side, eyes fluttering, the blood already spurting out of his mouth.

'Hugh! They thought you were dead!'

Edward of England sat in the great hall of Eltham Palace on the south side of the Thames. Above the hall door hung a great pair of antlers, and on the walls the shields showing the principal knights of his kingdom. In the far corner one of his chaplains had lit a rose-tinted candle and placed it in front of the statue of the Madonna and Child. Edward clawed at his iron-grey hair which fell down on either side of his harsh, seamed face. He refilled his goblet and that of his companion, John de Warrenne, Earl of Surrey. He then sighed and smiled at his Keeper of the Secret Seal who sat at the far end of the table, slouched in a high-backed chair.

'Did you hear me, Hugh? They thought you were dead!' The King grinned.

Corbett's black hair, dusted with a dash of grey, framed a clean-shaven, olive-skinned face. His unwavering dark eyes gave little away: a gentle but secretive face. You are a closed book, Corbett, Edward thought. The clerk had thrown his cloak on the back of his chair against which his manservant Ranulf-atte-Newgate now leaned. Edward's gaze moved to him. Ranulf looked the picture of health with his white, lean face, his red hair, cleaned and oiled, gathered in a queue behind him. Like his master he was dressed in a dark tunic over a white shirt.

'Are you deaf?' De Warrenne took a quaff from his wine cup and glared down the table, his popping, blue eyes even more protuberant than normal. He could never understand Edward's tolerance of this secretive clerk. 'Or,' de Warrenne jibed, 'perhaps you are dead?'

Corbett stretched out a hand. Ranulf sighed, opened his wallet and shook two silver pieces into his master's palm.

'Sire, my apologies.' Corbett smiled. 'But I had a wager with Ranulf that I'd be asked that question ten times before I knew the reason for my summons here.' He bowed towards de Warrenne. 'Apologies, my lord, but you were the tenth.'

Edward drummed his fists on the table and bellowed with laughter. He nudged de Warrenne, who glowered back.

'It's good to see you, Hugh.' The King smiled. His right eye, which drooped constantly, remained almost closed. He chewed on his lip and removed morsels of food from the hunting tunic he had hastily thrown on after Mass. 'Do you know something?' he remarked. 'When I go to Mass and pray to *le bon Seigneur* why don't the priests get on with it? This morning my good Bishop of Winchester wanted to deliver a sermon! I told de Warrenne to start coughing, he soon got the message!' Edward leaned back in the chair and gazed heavy-lidded at his Clerk of the Secret Seal. 'We thought you were for the charnel house, Hugh! A crossbow bolt high in the chest?'

'I was fortunate, sire. The bolt was small and not fired at full force because the assassin was running. It is wonderful what protection a thick calfskin jacket can afford.'

'But you were ill?'

Corbett tapped his chest. 'The bone shattered and healed but the flesh turned putrid.'

'I sent you medicines.'

'And my wife, the Lady Maeve, thanks you, sire.'

'I was going to come and see you.' The King became shamefaced. 'But I couldn't bear to see you die, Hugh. Not lose another loved one. They are all leaving me.'

Don't start, Corbett thought. Don't start weeping and becoming maudlin about the past. He respected his King, with his lean, warrior face, that fertile brain which teemed like a box of worms with subtle plans and strategies. But, if he wasn't a prince, Corbett reflected, Edward should have been a chanteur, a storyteller. He could move, in the twinkling of an eye, from the grieving old king to the energetic bustling warlord, intent on smashing his enemies or sitting in his chancery weaving webs to trap his adversaries abroad. He could be mean-spirited, vicious and spiteful and, at other times, magnanimous, open-handed, forgiving an injury, forgetting an insult. He could sit with the children of his household retainers and roar with laughter at some mummers' play then stride out into the exercise yard, seize a sword and show the young ones how to fight.

Corbett wondered what mood the King was in this morning. Edward, he realised, had a fear of sickness and death. His old friends were dying and Corbett quietly thanked God that the King had not come down to Leighton Manor. The Lady Maeve would have been driven to distraction. Ranulf alone had almost sent him mad, asking him, on the hour, how he felt, how was the wound? Corbett's gaze shifted to de Warrenne, who was used to these long silences with the King, but the Earl of Surrey always wore his heart on his sleeve. Despite his boisterous, florid looks, the good earl looked anxious, staring distractedly into the wine cup.

'I was at Westminster when I received your summons.' He spoke up.

Edward examined his fingers.

'The assassin?' the King demanded, glancing up. 'I understand your manservant killed him?'

'I must thank you, sire,' Corbett deftly replied, 'for promoting Ranulf to being a senior clerk in the Chancery of the Green Wax.'

'Yes, yes, yes,' Edward replied testily. 'We all know Ranulf's a clerk but he's still your manservant.'

Edward became lost in one of his reveries. He'd often wondered whether he could divide Ranulf from Corbett, play them off against each other. Corbett, with his love of the law, his insistence that the courts be all-important. Ranulf by contrast believed in swift and summary execution for traitors, which was the way Edward liked it.

'I killed the assassin, Your Majesty,' Ranulf confirmed. He moved in a creak of leather, fingers going down to the sword he was now allowed to carry into the royal presence.

'Two good blows, I understand,' Edward replied. 'To the belly and to the back. Then you cut his head off, set it on a pole and placed it near the main gate in Oxford? The sheriff and the good burgesses were all alarmed?'

'The sheriff and the burgesses were reminded of the power of the King,' Ranulf said. 'I did what I had to do for the good of the kingdom.' He emphasised the last phrase, the all-powerful permission given to any royal clerk to excuse what he did.

'What do you think of that, Hugh?' Edward asked softly.

'The Church teaches self-defence. And an attack on a royal clerk is an attack upon the King.'

'Yes, yes, so it is.' Edward drummed his hands on his stomach. 'And you are now fit for your duties?'

'As ever.'

'You did, once, hand in the Seals,' Surrey taunted. 'What did you intend to do, Corbett, become a peasant farmer?'

'Your Majesty, if I did, I'd come and ask you for all the advice I would need.'

Edward guffawed with laughter. 'You are bored, aren't you, Hugh? Lady Maeve, she is well?'

'As ever, sire. My daughter Eleanor thanks you for the presents your messenger brought from Windsor.'

Corbett shuffled his feet; he was becoming impatient.

'De Craon's back in England,' Edward announced.

'I heard.' Corbett smiled. 'My spies along the south coast keep me closely informed of his journey into Sussex, to Lord Henry Fitzalan's manor at Ashdown. I understand Lord Henry has been chosen to lead the English envoys to France.'

'He won't be going. Surrey here will have to shift his arse and, for once in his life, do something useful.'

De Warrenne belched and smiled to himself.

'Lord Henry Fitzalan,' the King explained, 'took de Craon and his entourage, his brother and members of his household to Savernake Dell. I've been there, it's a clearing in the forest, a good place to drive the deer in so they can be shot at leisure.' He waved his hand. 'You know how these things are organised. The hunters stand at one side of the clearing behind a palisade and the deer are driven in. Apparently two were but they escaped. Lord Henry was furious. He was about to loose again when an arrow came out of the trees on the far side of the dell, some fifteen to twenty yards away, and took him clean in the heart.'

'A hunting accident?' Corbett queried, ignoring de Warrenne's snort of ridicule.

'Hunting accidents do occur,' the King explained smoothly. 'But not this time. The arrow was not one used in hunting. It came from a longbow, sharp and pointed, fit for war and the killing it did.'

'A good archer,' Corbett agreed. 'An arrow to the heart, that would be difficult to dismiss as an accident.'

The King wondered how much he should tell

Corbett; he was pleased to see the clerk was now sitting up straight, eyes watchful. You are a good hunting dog, Edward thought. I'll let you loose in Ashdown Forest and we'll see what you and your red-haired cur can dig up.

'Lord Henry was a strange man,' the King continued. 'He owned vast estates in Sussex and elsewhere. A soldier, a diplomat and a courtier. I sent him on missions to Avignon, Rome and Paris.' The King paused.

'Why strange, sire? De Warrenne's done the same.' Corbett kept his face straight. 'And the Earl of Surrey is not a strange man.'

'Watch your tongue, Corbett!' the Earl warned.

'Lord Henry was always a rebel,' the King said. 'His father fought with the rebels led by de Montfort but then changed sides, just in time. Lord Henry, well, I trusted him. He was fluent in at least three languages. He could read and write as well as a scholar. He'd even been to the Halls of Cambridge.'

'You did say strange?' Corbett persisted.

'Lord Henry's views on religion . . .' the King paused, 'were, how can I put it, er, quite original. He journeyed to Palestine. He'd stayed with the Templars. Let me just say he found it difficult to accept some of the Church's teaching.'

'He dabbled in the black arts?' Corbett asked. 'There are reports from the Justices, rumours, whispers, gossip.'

'He sometimes travelled into Ashdown,' Edward agreed. 'And consorted with a witch, or a woman suspected of being one: Jocasta, half-Spanish, the relict of some sailor who settled down outside Rye and was driven out of there. She has a daughter, and Fitzalan gave them a cottage in the forest, a plot of land near a well.'

'But that's not all?' Corbett asked.

'No, it certainly isn't. Lord Henry was a lecher. No woman in Sussex was safe from him. He never married and often boasted that he had no need to sip from one cup when he could pick from so many. Now, according to what we have learned, his chief verderer Verlian had a rather comely daughter, Alicia. Lord Henry entered the lists to win her heart and take her body.'

'And Verlian objected?'

The King shrugged. 'He didn't really have to. Alicia did it for him. I met them both once when I was visiting Lord Henry's manor. Alicia's small, dark-haired, with a face like an angel and a body which would set our preachers about their ears. Now Verlian was in charge of the hunt yesterday morning at Savernake Dell but he never appeared. Indeed, he seems to have fled and the finger of accusation has been pointed at him.'

'That would be the logical conclusion,' Corbett mused. 'This would not be the first time an irate husband or father had slain a notorious philanderer.'

'Do you know what that means?' the King teased de Warrenne.

The Earl picked up his wine cup and sipped from it. The King was on dangerous ground. De Warrenne's marriage was the gossip of the court. Edward realised he had gone too far and gently squeezed his companion's hand.

'If you don't,' he urged, 'ask Ranulf there.'

The newly appointed senior clerk in the Chancery of the Green Wax just glanced away, studying the shields along the wall. One day, he thought, I'll have my shield there. Sir Ranulf or even Bishop Ranulf! He was learning his lessons fast from Master 'Long Face' seated beside him: keep your mouth shut, don't respond to insults and, if in doubt, just smile, bow and wait for another day.

'But you don't believe it's Verlian, do you?' Corbett demanded.

'No, no, I don't.' Edward sucked on his lips. 'Fitzalan was a man I closely watched. Too many fingers in too many plots. Too much money. A man ruled by his cock. He should have married, settled down! Become as miserable as all of us, eh, de Warrenne?'

'Marriage can be happy, sire!' the Earl protested. 'As long as you don't share the same bed and house!'

Edward laughed softly.

'I was going to let Fitzalan go to France,' he continued. 'I always wondered why he wanted to go and why my dearest brother in Christ, Philip the King, specifically asked for him.'

'Was he a traitor?'

'He had lands in Gascony, and I believe his mother was French, but I don't think so. Traitors are passionate men, Corbett, passionate for an idea or desperate for gold. Fitzalan had no time for the former and too much of the latter. I think he knew something about the French court. He was going back to trade on this.'

Corbett curbed his excitement.

'So, the French might have resorted to murder? De Craon always has assassins in his train.'

'Not this time,' Edward replied. 'Apparently Fitzalan fell to the ground, and died immediately. Chaos broke out. Sir William immediately rode back to the manor to ensure there was no looting and the treasury was safe. De Craon followed shortly afterwards. From the little I know, none of de Craon's retinue were unaccounted for.'

'So, sire, who?'

Edward raised his eyes heavenwards.

'Sir William stood to gain. He inherits the lot and there was bad blood between the two brothers. And, of course, there's our dear sister in Christ, Lady Madeleine Fitzalan, prioress of St Hawisia's, a well-endowed house in Ashdown Forest. Lady Madeleine was highly critical of her half-brother, particularly his views on religion.'

He paused.

'Anyone else?'

'Ashdown, like all our forests, has its fair share of outlaws. One in particular, calling himself the Owlman, sent warnings and threatening letters to Lord Henry in the months before he died. Brother Cosmas, a Franciscan parish priest of the local church St Oswald's-in-the-Trees, also clashed with our good manor lord.' Edward sighed. 'The list is endless. And there's more.'

The King got up and went to kick the door shut, turning the key in the lock.

'I am sending you down there, Hugh, but you have to be careful. This may be a trap. De Craon might have wanted Fitzalan dead but he may also have come to complete the work of that mad assassin in Oxford!'

Chapter 2

The King filled a goblet and put it down in front of Corbett, whom he studied closely.

'You don't seem worried, Hugh.'

Corbett shrugged. 'De Craon's been hunting my head for years.'

'But this time he may intend it,' de Warrenne put in. 'Philip is meddling in every court in Europe. He's made Pope Boniface VIII his virtual prisoner. We know he has spies with the rebels in Scotland and he would love to interfere with our wool trade to Flanders.' The old earl cleared his throat. 'He regards you as a bloody nuisance, Corbett. You may have won your wager with Ranulf but they truly want you dead.'

Surrey just wished he could shake this clerk's composure, but Corbett had been in the game before. He'd heard the whispers, how de Warrenne dismissed him as a clerk, ignoring the dangers, the plots of secret assassins as well as Corbett's own military service in Wales and Scotland.

'Are you saying, sire, that de Craon killed Fitzalan knowing that you would send me to Ashdown?'

'It's possible there might be another accident in the forest,' Edward agreed.

'It's a pretty theory. But you said there was more?'

'Yes there is. On the morning Lord Henry was killed, the naked corpse of a young woman was left outside the postern gates of St Hawisia's priory. Naturally, it sent the good sisters all a-flutter. We don't know the identity of the girl, where she came from or who loosed an arrow straight into her throat. The corpse was decaying; soil, bits of leaves still clung to it. The nun at St Hawisia's, who dressed the body for burial, believes this young woman had been killed some time ago and buried in a forest glade. The corpse was then dug up and, as some macabre jest, left at the priory gates.'

'And what happened to it?' Corbett asked.

'Lady Madeleine recalled the Corporal Acts of Mercy and gave it burial in the priory's own churchyard before reporting the matter to the local sheriff. So you see, Hugh, we have two deaths by arrow in Ashdown Forest. Is it the work of the Owlman? Are the deaths totally unrelated? Anyway, I am sending you down there, armed with warrants to do what you have to.'

'But you really couldn't care about Lord Henry's death?'

'No, Hugh, I couldn't give a fig if he is in heaven or hell. However, his death provides the opportunity to discover why the French demanded that Lord Henry lead the English envoys to Paris for the betrothal negotiations. I want to see if he is a traitor, and the same goes for his household.' Edward leaned back in his chair. 'In a few years' time the Princess Isabella comes of age. She will marry my feckless son, who will do his duty and beget an heir.'

'And that heir will be Philip IV's grandson?'

'Precisely! Now, I am bound to this marriage by solemn treaty and papal decree. But, if I can find that Philip has broken this truce by conspiring with one of my magnates . . .'

'You will send your lawyers to Avignon,' Corbett finished the sentence. 'And demand that the peace treaty be rescinded. No treaty, no marriage, no grandson of Philip IV sitting on your throne at Westminster.'

Edward grinned. 'You have a marvellous way with words, Hugh.'

Corbett put his hand over his mouth and looked down at the table. The old wound in his chest still ached but Corbett was trying to hide his feelings. Was Edward using him as bait? What happened if he went to Sussex and one of de Craon's assassins struck? Could Edward lay his death at Philip's door, scream for justice and rescind the papal peace treaty? Or worse? What if he went to Ashdown and Edward sent his own assassin? Would the King turn on him? Sacrifice him on the altar of expediency and then blame the French? Corbett looked up quickly. Edward was gazing at Ranulf. The clerk knew that look. Would Ranulf be the assassin? Would his ambitious clerk hold their friendship as something which could be bought and sold for further preferment? No, surely not!

'You seem a little anxious, Hugh?'

Corbett shifted in the chair. He picked up the goblet and held it out. He wanted to show that he didn't tremble.

'What happens, sire, if Fitzalan's death is nothing to do with de Craon?'

'That is possible.'

'And what happens, sire, if I travel down to Ashdown, the cheese to de Craon's mouse? Seigneur Amaury might not be able to resist the temptation of sending one of his assassins after me.'

'Continue.' The King's voice was almost a purr.

'Wouldn't you then turn round and lay my death at his door? Send the most irate letters to His Holiness in Avignon, loudly bemoaning the death of your senior clerk at the hands of a French assassin?'

'Hugh, Hugh, how could you say that?'

'You are being very blunt!' de Warrenne snapped.

Corbett studied the old earl. You are a lecher and

a drunkard, Corbett thought, but I had you wrong. You have a sense of honour. You may not like me but you, too, suspect that the King could be plotting. De Warrenne dropped his gaze.

'I say you are very blunt, clerk,' he muttered.

'I'm being very honest,' Corbett jibed back. 'It is my life. The King himself said that de Craon may be after my head.'

'But I'm not sending you there for that.' Edward's mood had shifted from stricken prince to angry lord. 'Hugh, this is England. You are going to Ashdown Forest. If de Craon lifted a finger against you, I'd have his head! Do you understand me, Corbett? I'd take his head clean off at the shoulders. I'd stick it on a pole above London Bridge so the crows can pick at it like they do the rest of the vermin.'

Corbett began to laugh. At first it came as a chuckle but the more he thought of what the King had said the greater his laughter grew.

'You find this amusing, Hugh? You see a jest where your King does not?'

Corbett wiped his eyes on the back of his hand.

'Your Majesty, I am clerk of your Secret Seal. The master of your secrets, your most loyal clerk but, at last, I do sense the game.' Corbett's face became grave. 'I am not some pot boy in a tavern to be sent on this errand or that. Nor am I some new clerk, his hair freshly tonsured, priding himself on his new robes, to believe everything he's told. So, sire, perhaps we can talk? As royal master and loyal servant, prince and councillor. Or, as you said at the beginning, two friends who have seen the days and the different seasons.

'We are being sent to Sussex,' Corbett continued in a more even tone, 'because you really do want to know why a leading baron of this realm has been assassinated?'

'Correct.'

'You also want us to find out if there is a connection between Lord Henry's death and the grisly offering left outside the priory of St Hawisia's?'

'Agreed.'

'And you want me to keep an eye on de Craon: to discover the true relationship between Lord Henry Fitzalan and the French court?'

'I've said as much.'

'And, finally, you wouldn't weep,' Corbett continued, 'if an incident occurred which you could use to nullify the marriage treaty with France. You hope it wouldn't be my murder but, if that happened, you'd use it?'

'Yes, yes, I would.' The King sighed. 'I love you dearly, Hugh. I'd take vengeance for your death. But this treaty?'

'You must abide by it!' Corbett insisted. 'It was decided in full council. Any attempt to break that treaty would lead to a most savage war and incur the anger of the papacy.'

'You agree with the treaty?' the King asked.

'You know I do, sire.'

Edward spread his hands. 'Then let God decide.' Edward pushed back his chair. 'You must be in Sussex by nightfall.'

The King walked down the hall, patted Corbett on the shoulder, winked at Ranulf and, with de Warrenne hastening after, left, slamming the door behind him.

'You should not have said that,' Ranulf said heatedly. He pulled back a bench and sat next to his master.

'I should tell the truth,' Corbett replied. 'Oh, I know Edward doesn't want me dead but he does want to break that treaty. But I won't be killed, will I, Ranulf, not with my guardian angel protecting me?'

His manservant coloured, green eyes evasive.

'You always blink when you are nervous,' Corbett laughed. 'Like when Lady Maeve is telling me off.'

Ranulf beat his metal-studded gauntlets against the table.

'I'm your man, Sir Hugh, in peace and war. You saved me from the gallows. I owe you my life. No pope, no king, no priest can ever cancel that debt.'

'No, they can't.' Corbett sighed and got to his feet. 'But they can try and you are an ambitious man, Ranulf-atte-Newgate. So it's not back to Leighton for us.' He rubbed his chest where it was still bruised. 'We'll have the clerks swear out the warrants and commissions and, before the day is out, we'll be at Ashdown.'

The door opened, and a retainer wearing the royal blue, red and gold tabard entered holding a white wand which he tapped imperiously on the stone floor.

'Good Lord!' Ranulf mocked. 'It's the Archbishop of Canterbury!'

'Your presence is required,' the chamberlain declared pompously, 'by Edward, Prince of Wales. He's in the tiltyard.'

'Now this,' Corbett whispered, 'is going to be interesting.'

They followed the chamberlain out of the great hall into the courtyard. The morning sun was glistening on the rain-soaked gravel. In that busy place, grooms were leading horses out of the stables, sumpter ponies were being unpacked, carts unhitched. Chickens pecked at the ground, clucking in anger as a palace dog came running up yapping. Servants and men-at-arms milled about. A group of royal archers had taken a thief out to judgement; stripping him bare, they'd lashed him to a tree and were now flogging him vigorously with white willow wands. The man gagged, strained at his bonds, wincing and twisting as the red-purple scars scored his white pimply back.

The chamberlain led them along a terraced walk and into the sand-covered tiltyard, which consisted of a long, dusty rectangle of land with a great wooden tilt fence down the middle. A horseman waited at either end, each dressed in full plate armour. One bore the crest of the Beaumonts of Norfolk, the other, nearest Corbett, the red dragon of Wales.

A trumpet blew a long fanfare, a shrill metallic blast. Both horses lumbered into a canter then into a gallop. Lances came down, swinging across the horses' necks as the riders hurtled towards each other. The Prince of Wales was faster, his horse lighter and speedier. His lance avoided his opponent's shield and caught him full in the chest. The Norfolk knight swayed in the saddle, tried to regain his seat then toppled in a crash and clouds of dust to the roar and acclamation of the onlookers. The victorious Prince dropped his lance, drew his sword and cantered towards his fallen opponent. The latter had more sense than to resist but took off his helmet and extended his hands in a gesture of submission.

Prince Edward dismounted, removed his tilting helm and, with the help of a squire, began to strip off his armour. He then helped the Norfolk knight to his feet, clapping him heartily on the back. When the Prince caught sight of Corbett he walked across, still loosening pieces of armour which he simply threw on the ground for the scampering squires to pick up. Edward was a strikingly good-looking man, tall, well over six feet, with blond, closely-cropped hair, a neatly clipped moustache and beard, and a rather thick-lipped and aggressive mouth. He had an oval face with deep-set, blue eyes, and a ruddy complexion. He didn't stand on ceremony but gripped Corbett's outstretched hand and clapped Ranulf on the shoulder.

'Sir Hugh, it's good to see you. You've recovered? And Lady Maeve?' His smile widened. 'After all, she's from my principality. They say there's nothing like a Welsh woman in bed.' He caught himself and closed his eyes. 'I'm sorry, Hugh.'

'No offence given, none taken, sire.'

'And the noble Ranulf?' Edward tried to hide his embarrassment by punching Corbett's manservant playfully on the shoulder. 'A man much loved by the maidens, eh?'

He turned and beckoned a squire who came hurrying across with a tray of goblets. Edward filled three, although the man had been running so fast the silver tray shook. Once Edward had served the three cups he cuffed the man sharply on the ear, and the squire retreated, hand to the side of his head.

'It wasn't his fault,' Corbett protested.

'No, no, it wasn't.' Edward took a gulp of wine and turned. 'Rushlett!' he bawled.

The aggrieved squire came tottering back. Edward pointed to the three cups.

'I am sorry I hit you. When we've finished, the three goblets and the tray, they are yours to sell.'

His squire retreated, profusely thanking him.

'They are not mine to give,' Edward admitted. 'They belong to the Bishop of Winchester but, by the time he realises, they'll be sold. Anyway, he's rich enough to buy them back. You are off to Ashdown!' he continued in a rush. 'Lord Henry's been killed and the French envoy frets for a replacement. Father's in such a hurry to get me married, eh?'

'You look forward to your nuptials?' Corbett asked.

'Don't play the innocent fool with me, clerk!' the Prince replied. He sighed. 'I suppose I'll have to marry the bloody wench! For the rest of my life I'll have Philip on my back. That sanctimonious, hypocritical, conniving . . .'

'Future father-in-law!' Corbett finished the sentence.

The Prince wiped the sweat from his face and took another sip from the goblet.

'When Father dies,' he added viciously.

'May that day be far off,' Corbett interrupted; even to discuss the King's death was petty treason.

'Yes, yes, but die he must! Anyway, when he dies, Corbett, Ranulf, I want you in my household. I'm going to need you. The nobles don't like me, the bishops cluck their tongues like chickens.'

'It's not you, sire, it's . . .'

'Yes, yes, I know, Piers Gaveston!'

Corbett relaxed, now the name was out. The Prince of Wales' favourite, some even whispered lover, was regarded as a Gascon upstart, the son of a witch who seemed to exercise undue influence over the King's heir. Gaveston was sharp of wit, a born jouster and horseman. A beautiful man, Gaveston played Jonathan to Edward's David. Rumours had abounded, gossip that the two had been found alone in bed and the King, infuriated, had exiled Gaveston from the kingdom.

'I want Piers back!' Edward stamped his foot. 'If I cannot have my friends, what use a kingdom?'

Corbett glanced warningly at Ranulf.

'I may join you at Ashdown.' Edward turned away, watching Corbett out of the corner of his eye.

'You were friends with Lord Henry?' Corbett asked.

Edward waggled a finger playfully. 'You stand there, Corbett, as pious as a nun with those innocent eyes and guileless face. You should have been a lawyer in King's Bench. I had no great friendship with the Lord Henry but with his brother, Sir William, yes. And, as you well know, I have made pilgrimages to St Hawisia's shrine.'

'And you stayed at Ashdown Manor?' Corbett asked.

'There or that tavern on the Ashdown road. There's good hunting in the forest though.' He grimaced. 'Lord Henry found it different, didn't he? So, when do you leave?'

'As soon as possible, sire. Your father has given us orders and to Ashdown we must go.'

Edward nodded. He absentmindedly clapped Corbett on the shoulder and, whispering under his breath, sauntered back to his retainers.

'What was all that about?' Ranulf asked.

'I don't know,' Corbett replied. 'This is a tangled web, everybody's telling lies. Philip's a liar. De Craon wouldn't know the truth if it hit him on the nose. Our King hides the truth while Prince Edward ploughs his own lonely furrow. What hour do you think it is?'

Ranulf peered up at the sky.

'Not yet nine.'

'Pack our belongings. Our two horses, the sumpter pony and make sure you bring my saddle-bags.'

'Where are you going?'

'I'll walk round the palace,' Corbett said. 'When you're finished, join me at the main gate. We are going to cross the moat and walk down towards the village, to a tavern, the Tree of Jesse. Its landlord rents out a chamber called the Star of Bethlehem, supposedly painted by some pilgrim who visited the Holy Land.'

'For the love of God, master, what are you chattering about?'

'Me?' Corbett smiled. 'With my nun's face and holier-than-thou looks?'

Ranulf sighed. He stared across at a page dragging a heavy war saddle from one of the destriers.

'I miss Maltote, master, not just because he looked after the horses.'

Corbett followed Ranulf's gaze, watching the

page stumble away, the heavy harness over his shoulder. Maltote had been their horse squire, a clumsy young man with a gift for horses. He had been murdered in a filthy alleyway in Oxford and his body now lay under the flagstones of the manor chapel at Leighton.

'I really miss him,' Ranulf said again. 'I am glad I killed his murderer. I hope his soul rots in hell!'

He strode away, as he always did, to hide the tears.

Corbett wandered round the palace greeting acquaintances, being stopped now and again by other clerks who shook his hand to welcome him back. He went into the buttery and persuaded a cook to provide bread, cheese and a small pot of ale. He sat quietly and ate, watching the hour candle fixed on its iron spigot near the door; when it was about to reach the tenth red circle, Corbett went down to the main gateway where Ranulf was already waiting.

'I was going to ask you, master, why the Tree of Jesse and this chamber the Star of Bethlehem?'

'I told you.'

Corbett slipped his arm through Ranulf's. They walked under the gatehouse across the bridge and on to the trackway which wound down through the trees towards the village. Corbett loosened his white collar. The day was autumnally warm, the trees shedding their leaves to lay a crisp, golden matting beneath their feet. They stood aside to allow a pack train by, horses whinnying at the scent of blood from the deer carcasses, throats cut and bellies gutted, which had been slung across their backs. The blood-daubed verderers and foresters were in good humour. It was not yet noon and they had only been hunting since dawn to provide fresh meat for the royal kitchens.

'You were going to say, master?' Ranulf wished Corbett would not lapse into reflective silences.

'Well, now we are free of the palace, I'll tell you. Everybody's lying, Ranulf. Now, when I lay in my great four-poster bed at Leighton, being fussed and spoilt by Lady Maeve, I still received reports from spies, merchants, pedlars, tinkers and scholars.'

'You said they provided nothing but chatter! Gossip from the village well.'

Corbett shook his head. 'Most of it was. However, I say this, Ranulf, if I had to stay in that bed for another day, my wits would have wandered. Now, don't misunderstand me, I love Lady Maeve more than life itself. And, as for Eleanor, well, you know how it is?'

'And Lady Maeve is expecting again?' Ranulf asked.

'As full as a rose at midday.'

'A boy this time?'

'A living child is all I pray for. Now, my mind is like any other, you have to keep sharpening it. I know de Craon would have found out about my injuries and probably prayed for my death. We are approaching an exciting time, Ranulf. An English heir is going to marry a French princess. Philip of France is going to see his dream realised, that a descendant of his great ancestor St Louis will sit on the throne at Westminster. Edward wishes to break free. If he does, there will be bloody war. So, I listen to my spies, one in particular: Aidan Smallbone, a lonely clerk from the King's own secret chancery.'

'But I thought . . .' Ranulf interrupted.

'Yes, I know! I hold the Secret Seals. Such messages should come to me, but there's one verse of Scripture our King truly believes in: he does not like his left hand to know what his right hand's doing. Accordingly, certain messages, certain documents, go directly to him. All Master Smallbone does, when they are finished with, is place them in a secret muniment room. Edward is always present when he does that. Anyway, Master Smallbone is a friend of mine. He sent me a letter asking about my health, expressing a desire to see me, and that means he has something to sell.'

They entered the Tree of Jesse, where the taproom was sweet with the smell of hams and haunches of venison all being dried smoked and cured against the approaching winter. The landlord greeted Corbett, bobbing and bowing, and led them up the wooden stairs. Ranulf found the Star of Bethlehem a disappointment. It was a large room, well furnished, but the paintings on the wall depicting the birth of Christ were rather shabby and hastily executed, the gold stars on the blue ceiling faded and peeling. Master Smallbone was a nondescript balding man, with a perpetually running nose which he constantly wiped on the sleeve of his grubby jerkin. Corbett greeted him warmly enough and they sat round the small trestle table exchanging gossip and banter while the landlord served blackjacks of ale and strips of venison. Once he had gone, Corbett bolted the door. Smallbone was eating as if his life depended on it, but when Corbett produced a gold coin, he snatched it and dropped it into his purse.

'Very well, Master Smallbone, the fee is paid. Let me hear your song.'

'The King wants to break the treaty.'

'I know that.'

Smallbone sniffed. 'He believes Gaveston is back in England.'

'What! But he was exiled on pain of forfeit of life and limb!'

'Some life, some limb!' Smallbone scoffed. 'He's been seen in London and there's similar gossip from the port reeves but whether he's still here is not known.'

'Continue.'

'The King is deeply interested in the dead Fitzalan's physician. You know Lord Henry had, for some time, patronised an Italian, Pancius Cantrone. He hired him during his travels.'

'And why should the King be interested in him?'

'Because he once worked with Gilles Malvoisin.'

Corbett lowered his blackjack of ale.

'Malvoisin? He was formerly physician to the French court. In particular, Johanna of Navarre, Philip IV's dead wife. I thought Malvoisin died in a boating accident on the Seine?'

'He did,' Smallbone replied, gulping the venison, allowing the juices to dribble down his chin.

'And what else, Master Smallbone?'

'Well, the King is so interested, Simon Roulles has been despatched to Paris.'

'Roulles!' Corbett exclaimed.

'Who is he?' Ranulf asked.

'I trained with him,' Corbett replied. 'He's a merry rogue, Ranulf, a nimble dancer, a chanteur, a troubadour, a man who loves the ladies. I thought he had been killed in a street brawl in Rome.'

Smallbone shook his head. 'He's alive and kicking in Paris and, if the truth be known, paying assiduous court to Mistress Malvoisin. That's all I have to sell.'

'The dead physician's wife?'

'The same.'

'My, my, my,' Ranulf remarked.

'Do you know why, Master Smallbone?' Corbett asked.

The little clerk shook his head.

Corbett pushed away his trauncher of venison, gave his thanks and, followed by Ranulf, left the chamber. At the top of the stairs Corbett paused.

'Mark my words, Ranulf. When we reach Ashdown, you be on your guard: that place will prove to be a pit of treason and murder!' He paused. 'There's something very nasty, very secretive about all we've been told.'

Chapter 3

Robert Verlian, chief verderer of the deceased Lord Henry Fitzalan, would have agreed with Corbett. He had not bathed or changed, and his face and hands were stung by the nettles and brambles he had crawled through.

He had returned to Savernake Dell and seen Lord Henry's corpse, the yard-long arrow embedded deep in his chest. Verlian had crept back to the manor only to realise he was the prime suspect; tongues were soon wagging, fingers pointing. Verlian had killed his master! He was to be captured and tried! Verlian had fled, like the wolfs-head he had become, back into the forest. What justice could he expect at Sir William's hands? The manor lord had the power of axe and tumbril. Verlian could be hauled before the manor court and hanged before the day was out, his possessions confiscated, and what would happen to Alicia then?

Verlian crouched beside an oak, an ancient tree which, forest lore maintained, had once been used by the pagan priests for their sacrifices. Verlian hadn't eaten, apart from some bread and rotten meat he had filched from a charcoal-burner's cottage. Now he listened, like the many animals he had hunted, for any sound of pursuit on the morning breeze.

Verlian folded his arms across his chest. He had slept at night out near Radwell Brook, and his body now ached from head to toe, but what could he do? Ashdown Manor was a hostile place, the local sheriff was many miles away. His tired mind went back to the events of the last few weeks. Lord Henry's infatuation with his daughter Alicia had grown by the day. He would never leave her alone. There had been presents of sweet meats and wine, costly cloth, gifts, even a snow-white palfrey. Alicia had been obdurate.

'I am no man's whore!' she had snapped. 'And no lord's mistress!'

She had sent the gifts back. Lord Henry had only become more importunate, even forcing himself into the cottage they occupied on the Ashdown estate. Alicia, her temper knowing no bounds, had taken a bow and arrow from his war chest and threatened Lord Henry that, if he did not leave, she would kill him and claim it was self-defence. Fitzalan had turned nasty, mouthing threats and warnings. He had reminded them that Verlian and his daughter were his servants; he owned the roof under which they lived and the roads of Sussex were no place for a landless man and his daughter. Verlian had gone to Sir William for help but that secretive younger brother could provide no assistance.

Verlian heard the undergrowth crackling and scanned his surroundings, but it was only a badger coming out of his sett to sniff the morning air. Had Sir William killed his brother? Verlian wondered. To seize his wealth and put the blame on a poor verderer? Verlian was not sure of anything. He was weak from hunger, his mind fitful, his wits wandering. Hadn't he dreamed of killing Lord Henry? Or, even worse, Alicia, where had she been that morning? Could it have happened? He suddenly started. Was that his imagination? No, the sound of a hunting horn brayed through the forest. Verlian had heard the rumours: how Sir William, now lord of the manor, was determined to hunt down his brother's killer. Already rewards had been posted, a hundred pounds sterling for his murderer, dead or alive. Verlian, a soldier who had seen experience on the Scottish march, whimpered with fear. Perhaps he had it wrong? Again the blast of a horn, perceptibly nearer, followed by the bellowing of the Fitzalan hunting dogs, mastiffs trained in tracking a man down.

Verlian rose to his feet and ran at a half-crouch as

fast as he could from that terrible sound but, the further he went, the closer the hunt grew. Verlian tried to remember where he was. He recalled his own hunting days. If he could get to Radwell Brook, he could use the water to hide his scent, but where would that lead him?

He broke into a clearing and saw a cottage. The door was open, a plume of smoke rose from the middle of the thatched roof. He tried to recall where he was and squatted down for a while taking his bearings. Yes, yes, that was it: Jocasta the witch lived here, she and her fey-witted daughter. Surely they would help? He ran across to the open door. The women inside were seated at the table. Jocasta was a tall, swarthy-faced woman, with coal-black hair tumbling down her strong face. Her eyes never flinched. Her daughter, with mousey-coloured hair and vacant eyes, just lifted a hand and went back to crooning over the little wooden doll in her lap.

'I need food!' Verlian gasped.

'Then you'll find none here, Robert Verlian!'

'I am innocent.'

'No man is innocent.'

'For the love of God!' Verlian screamed as the sound of the hounds drew nearer.

Jocasta went to a basket near the door and thrust two apples into his hand.

'You are a dead man, Verlian. If Sir William doesn't kill you, his hounds will!'

'Please!'

'Use your noddle! Are your wits as wandering as my daughter's? You have appealed to God, then to God you should go!'

She slammed the door in his face. Verlian bit at the apples. They tasted sour; he found it hard to chew, his mouth was so dry. He was about to run on when he remembered what the witch-woman had said and gasped in relief. Of course, there was only one place which could house him. He fled across the clearing. Gasping and retching, Verlian forced his way through the brambles, desperate to seek the path he needed. The hunt grew closer, the howls of the mastiffs sounding like a death knell. On and on Verlian ran, ignoring the bile at the back of his throat, the tears which stung his eyes, the shooting pains at the back of his legs and the terrible cramp in his left side. He stumbled, falling flat on his face, the hard pebbled tracks scoring his hands, bruising his cheeks. He got up, ran on and, at last, he reached the clearing where before him stood the open doors of St Oswald's-in-the-Trees. Gasping and stumbling, Verlian threw himself inside, slammed the door shut, pulling the bar down and leaning against it. The little church was dark, with only a glow of light from beneath the crudely carved rood screen. He was aware of benches and stools in the darkening transepts.

'Who is there?'

A figure came through the rood screen. Verlian

recognised Brother Cosmas. He stumbled up the church. The Franciscan held a knife in one hand, a candle he had been tapering in the other. Verlian reached the rood screen, pushed by the priest and staggered up the narrow steps. The verderer touched the altar then crouched down beside it as the Franciscan towered over him, a ghostly figure in his brown garb, the lower half of his pale face hidden by the shaggy black beard which fell down below his chest.

'You are Robert Verlian!' he declared. 'Once chief verderer to Lord Henry. They say you are a murderer, an assassin!'

'I am no assassin!' Verlian spat back. 'I am innocent of any crime! I claim sanctuary!'

The Franciscan sniffed and crouched beside him. 'There's little I can do for you, man.' The hard eyes were kindly. 'Sir William is lord of the manor.'

'But not lord of this church!' Verlian retorted.

'No, no, he isn't.'

The Franciscan rose to his feet at the hammering which rained on the door.

'And, perhaps, it's time I reminded him of that!'

In the spacious, well-timbered house which stood on the corner of the Rue St Denis within earshot of the bells of Notre Dame, Simon Roulles, the perpetual student, the wandering scholar, the loyal servant of King Edward of England, had found his own sanctuary in the opulent bedchamber of

Madame Malvoisin. Simon, who now was known to his rather venerable lover as Bertrand, rolled over on the bed and stared down at his latest conquest.

'You are indeed,' she whispered, 'a veritable cock, a strutting stag!'

Simon laughed and threw himself back on the bolsters.

'Why me?'

The question had been asked many times over the last few days. Simon always tried to be honest. After all, what was he, just past his twenty-fourth or was it twenty-fifth summer? Well, the grey-haired lady who lay beside him was at least twice that age. In her youth Madame Malvoisin must have been comely: lustrous eyes, generous lips and the paint she had put on her face hid the seams and wrinkles of passing time. Her body was plump, warm, soft as silk and, if Simon was honest, a comfortable berth for a wandering soul such as himself.

He had met her in the marketplace, his hair crimped and prinked. He was wearing his best scholar gown, displaying the coloured silks of the student of the Quadrivium and Trivium at the Sorbonne. She had lost her maid and the bale of cloth she was carrying was heavy. Simon had helped. When they returned to the comfortable mansion with its wooden panelled chambers, Simon had agreed to a goblet of sweet wine and a plate of marchpane. Of course, he had been invited back and, of course, he accepted. He had taken Madame Malvoisin around the Latin Quarter, to those taverns full of devil-may-care, merry students, who drank, carolled and danced so expertly; then in the fields or a boat along the Seine, Simon had proved himself to be an assiduous suitor.

Madame Malvoisin had thrown discretion to the winds. This young student was the master of both her heart and her bedchamber. She really couldn't care about the whispers and giggles of her maids or the gossip of her sharp-eyed neighbours. After all, what were they but jealous? Envious of her good fortune? Didn't she deserve all this? She, the wife of a royal physician, until poor Gilles, too full of wine, had suffered that boating accident. He had been returning from a meeting of fellow physicians: according to the boatman, Gilles had insisted on standing up; the wherry had capsized, and only days later had poor Gilles' fish-pecked body been dragged from the Seine.

Madame Malvoisin contemplated the golden tester over the four-poster bed. She often wondered about her husband's death. Was it an accident or was it murder? Hadn't Gilles hinted at certain dark secrets about the court, things no man should ever know? In turn she had poured out her heart to this handsome young clerk whose hands, once again, were caressing her breasts, running down her stomach to her secret place. She rolled over on her side, knocking his hand away.

'You say you are going away?'

He kissed her on the lips. 'Soon, my dear, but I will be back. A little business. My cousin owns a farm on the Calais road. I've been promising him a visit since midsummer.'

'And when will you go?'

'Around Michaelmas. But I'll be back before October is halfway through.'

Simon tensed as he heard a creak in the gallery outside.

'I thought you told your maids not to come up here, at least not until you had risen.'

Madame Malvoisin giggled like the young girl she felt. Simon was such a lusty lover and she could not help her cries and moans. She'd banished the servants from this gallery, strictly forbidding them to come anywhere near her chamber until she had risen and dressed for the day.

'Why are you so nervous?' she accused playfully. 'That only intrigues the servants.'

'Which servants?' Simon's voice was sharp.

'My maid Isabeau. She's always asking questions.'

Simon sat up. He heard another creak. He always prided himself on his prudence and cunning. Hadn't he seen Isabeau talking to a stranger the afternoon before? He was sure he'd glimpsed coins being dropped into her hand. Again a sound. Ignoring the protests of Madame Malvoisin, Simon jumped from the bed. He hastily pulled on his woollen leggings and white cambric shirt. Madame Malvoisin was now sitting up, round-eyed. Simon looked at the door. The latch handle went down, and he was drawing both sword and dagger when the black-garbed assassins slipped into the chamber. Madame Malvoisin screamed, pulling the sheets up under her face. She gazed appalled at these horrors, hoods over their heads, masks across their faces. This could not be happening! This was some nightmare! Five, six figures she counted. They ignored her, intent on the young clerk. They could not be house-breakers. Where were her servants? She opened her mouth to scream but found the sound would not come. One of the black-garbed figures edged forward.

'Monsieur, you are to come with us.'

Simon darted forward, sword and dagger snaking out. His opponent met him in a clash of steel. Simon withdrew. He looked back towards the window but the casement was too narrow and he knew the drop was too far. He cursed his own stupidity. He had made a mistake, one he'd vowed he never would: to be in a room where there was no escape, no other door or window which he could jump through, as he had so many a time. Again he closed but this time his opponent moved faster, twisting and turning as his sword dug into Simon's shoulder. The English spy dropped his sword, doubling up at the fiery shaft of pain which raced across his chest. His opponents closed in, forcing him to the floor, twisting his arms behind him, before dragging him to his feet. The pain in his shoulder was intense.

'Monsieur, you are under arrest!'

'On what charge?' Roulles gasped. 'I object!'

'Murder!'

'Whose murder?'

The leader went across to Madame Malvoisin, still transfixed in terror. She struggled as he forced her back down the bed and, taking a bolster, clamped it over her face. Roulles stood horrified, watching his former lover struggle for her life, her body jerking, legs and arms lashing out. The assassin held firm until at last Madame Malvoisin lay still.

'There's your victim,' the assassin replied. 'Take him away!'

Corbett shaded his eyes to survey Savernake Dell and bent down to dig with the tip of his dagger at the dark patches still staining the dew-wet grass.

'Your brother was standing here?'

Sir William Fitzalan nodded. 'He'd notched an arrow to his bow; he was about to shoot when the assassin's shaft took him full in the heart.'

'And that assassin?' Ranulf asked.

Sir William's sweaty face twisted into a grimace.

'You know full well: our verderer Robert Verlian, who fled! He has now taken sanctuary in St Oswald's-in-the-Trees.'

'How do you know he's guilty? Because he's fled? Because he's taken sanctuary?'

'He was the only one that wasn't here when my brother died. Verlian knew this forest and he's a master bowman.'

Corbett looked back to where the dark-garbed Italian physician, Pancius Cantrone, stood beneath the outstretched branches of an oak tree. A further distance away stood Fitzalan's retainers holding the horses. A quiet, peaceful place, Corbett thought. The early morning mist was still lifting. Even the birds were quiet, not stirring until the sun fully rose. A ghostly place where tendrils of mist hovered and shifted. The early morning glow caught the dew on the leaves and grass, making the dell shimmer in the strengthening light. It reminded Corbett of Leighton, of his walks with Maeve down to the great meadow. They'd sit by the stream, cloaks wrapped around them, and watch the sun rise. A quiet part of the day and one Corbett loved, but this was different.

'Verlian wasn't the only one absent, was he?' Corbett asked.

Sir William looked askance.

'You weren't here.' Corbett smiled. 'I talked to your servants. I made careful enquiries.'

'You only arrived in Ashdown last night.'

'Yes, but a tavern like the Devil-in-the-Woods is full of gossip. Mine host has a nose for all the news but, if he was wrong, I can set the record straight.'

Sir William glanced away. He was a warrior, a hunter, who prided himself on being frightened of no one, but this dark-faced clerk with his royal commissions and warrants, his cat-eyed servant, unnerved him.

'I'd walked away,' he replied. 'I went into the trees to relieve myself.'

'An inappropriate time. I understand that at least two deer had raced into the dell. The huntsmen were close,' observed Ranulf.

'I couldn't care if the Holy Father galloped in!' Sir William snapped. 'A loose belly is a loose belly! I'll not soil myself for anyone!'

'Yet you have a physician on hand?'

'He was back at the manor,' Sir William snarled. 'Sir Hugh, you embarrass me. The night before the hunt Lord Henry and his guests stayed at Beauclerc hunting lodge.'

'Ah yes!' Corbett scratched his chin. 'You ate or drank something tainted?'

'Both I and my brother did. We were sick, running to the latrines.' He shrugged. 'But it passed.'

'No, no,' Corbett insisted. 'Tell us precisely what happened?'

'We ate and drank late. We roistered and then we retired for the night. I was hardly in my bedchamber when my stomach began to purge itself. I vomited like I never have done in my life. So intensely that my stomach and bowels ached.'

'And your brother?'

'The same. Yet by morning we felt well enough and did not want to disappoint our guests.'

'Were they ill?'

Sir William narrowed his eyes. 'No, now you ask it, I don't think they were. My brother and I were too embarrassed to ask but they showed no ill effects.'

Cantrone was still standing silently, almost like a statue, lost in his own thoughts.

'Have you discussed this with your household physician?' Corbett queried. 'I mean, you and your brother were violently ill but, apparently, no one else was?'

William licked his dry lips.

'And you know my next question?' Corbett insisted.

'And the answer is yes,' Sir William replied. 'My brother and I, we shared a special flask of wine.'

'Who brought it?'

'I – I don't know. It was unstoppered by one of the servants.'

'And you felt no ill effects before that?'

'None.'

'Who else was in the lodge?'

'Seigneur de Craon, members of his household, our retainers. Oh, and Verlian as well as Brother Cosmas the priest at St Oswald's. He came to deliver warnings.'

'What about?'

'My brother was a harsh lord, Sir Hugh. He enforced the forest law with great vigour.'

'Ah yes, I've heard of the steel traps laid out in

the forest. Poachers who've had their ears cut and noses slit for the first offence then been hanged out of hand for the second.'

'The lords of Savernake have the right of axe and tumbril.'

'Not while I'm here!' Corbett snapped. 'But I'll come to that in a moment. Do you realise what you are saying, Sir William? It would seem that someone tried to poison you and your brother. Everything becomes tangled,' Corbett continued. 'Some might even whisper that you were not ill though your brother was.'

Sir William's face suffused with rage.

'What are you saying?' His hand went to the dagger hanging from a ring on his belt.

'Don't touch it!' Corbett warned. 'Ranulf is of a quick disposition and may misunderstand you. Moreover, in these matters, Sir William, I must remind you that I represent the King. Look.' Corbett sighed. 'I merely point out what gossips might say. It would seem that someone did plot mischief against you at Beauclerc hunting lodge but facts can be twisted; people can jump to false conclusions.'

'And if false conclusions can be drawn by you, Sir William,' Ranulf intervened, 'they can about Robert Verlian. All of Ashdown knows you hunted him through the forest, intent on his life.'

Sir William swallowed hard. 'He killed my brother. He fled.'

'You have no proof,' Corbett countered. 'And while I am here, Sir William, such actions will cease forthwith. Anyway, we were talking about your whereabouts when your brother was killed.'

'I went in the trees,' Sir William blustered. 'Quite a distance away. I undid my points, I relieved myself. When I came back my brother was dead.'

'And you stayed and grieved?'

'You know what I did! My brother had an arrow through his heart. He was dead, there was nothing I could do.'

'So you took horse. You and your faithful retainers rode back to the manor leaving others to bring your brother's corpse back?'

'Lord Henry was dead,' Sir William repeated. 'It is well known, Sir Hugh, what happens when a manor lord dies suddenly. Servants turn to plundering and pilfering. Ashdown Manor houses many treasures. If you accept the courtesies of staying there you'd see that for yourself.'

Corbett crouched down again to examine the stain on the ground.

'I thank you for your courtesy, Sir William, but you know Seigneur de Craon resides with you. It would not be appropriate for us to share the same roof.' He got to his feet and looked at the holes along the ground. 'This is where the hunting palisade was erected?'

'Yes, I've had it taken down.'

But Corbett wasn't listening. He was already

striding across the dell. Ranulf looked and Sir William shrugged and they followed. On the far side Corbett was already pushing into the brambles. He drew his sword and hacked a path through. The forest stretched ahead of him. The great oaks, the bracken sprouting between. A place of shifting darkness. Shadows flittered and Corbett was sure that, if he were by himself, his mind would play tricks, these shapes become figures, soft and menacing. No wonder legends were rife about eerie forest creatures; the dell reminded him of the heavily wooded valleys in Wales and the dense forest of Sherwood. He repressed a shiver when he thought of the ambushes in which he had nearly died. The others came crashing behind him. Corbett gazed back across the clearing to where Lord Henry had stood.

'The assassin must have had a good view,' he observed.

Corbett walked up and down. Sometimes the other side of the dell was hidden by overhanging branches and high stems of bracken but there were also clear views where a master bowman could stand, hidden in the shadows, and loose a shaft.

'Ranulf,' he ordered. 'Go back to Lord Henry's retainers. One of them must have a bow and a quiver of arrows. Bring them across.'

Ranulf hastened off. Corbett tried to put himself into the mind of the assassin.

'This was no hunting accident,' he said confidently.

He walked up and down and, at last, chose his spot where he stood until Ranulf returned. Corbett took the bow, selected an arrow from the quiver and stared at the cruel, steel-pointed head.

'This is a war arrow?' he asked.

'Yes,' Sir William replied. 'If we were hunting, Sir Hugh, it would be sickle-shaped.'

Corbett held the cord grip round the middle of the yew bow and notched an arrow to the string. He took a deep breath and lifted the bow up. Once the shaft came level with his eye, he pulled back.

'Right, Ranulf!' he ordered. 'Start counting!'

Corbett lowered the bow again and looked across to where Lord Henry had been killed. Then he raised the bow and took careful aim. He was conscious of a slight breeze on his cheek; his eyes remained fixed on that spot as he steadied his breathing. He could feel the power of the bow, the two forefingers of his left hand grasped the shaft just behind the grey goose quill. He sighed and, as he did, loosed the arrow. In a blur the shaft hurtled across the glade and disappeared into the trees on the far side. Ranulf had reached the number nine as he lowered the bow.

'A very short time,' Corbett declared. 'A few seconds. The assassin has found his mark, now he must retreat. Across the glade all is chaos and consternation. What would the assassin do now, Ranulf?'

'If it was I, master, I'd have left a horse some way

off. I'd run as fast as I could, put as much distance between myself and here as possible.'

'Sir William?'

'I'd do the same.'

'But that's not the problem, is it?' Corbett mused, handing the bow to the manor lord. 'The assassin would have fled. The real danger wasn't in that.'

'It was beforehand, wasn't it?' Ranulf asked.

'Yes. It took me some time to find a spot, the best place to shoot. Now the assassin may have known that Lord Henry intended to organise a hunt in Savernake Dell but he wouldn't know where the manor lord would be standing. Nor would he know if he'd get a good view of him.'

'Of course,' Ranulf said. 'The assassin may have come here, only to find Lord Henry screened by his retainers and his guests.'

'Precisely. In which case our assassin may have tried to kill Lord Henry before or even waited for another day.' He smiled over his shoulder at Sir William. 'But there's a weakness in what I say?'

The manor lord stared stonily back.

'You know there's a weakness, Sir William. Your brother Lord Henry was a man of power. He would stand second to no one. He would have to be in the front. He was the host, the great huntsman.'

'But anyone would know that,' Sir William stammered.

'You mean not just his family?' Ranulf taunted.

'As Sir Hugh says,' Sir William replied defensively, 'Lord Henry was the first in all things. First born, first in the tournament, in the cavalcade and, yes, in the hunt.'

Corbett walked away, studying the great oak trees. He strode across to an ancient, hollowed one, probably struck by lightning. It was at least two yards in girth. Others, similar, stood nearby.

'What is this place?'

'We are on the edge of Savernake Dell,' Sir William replied. 'But they call this "Hollowman Place" after the oak trees. My father, when he was a boy, told of a great storm in which some of the trees were struck by lightning.'

'And?' Corbett asked.

'It's well known as a lovers' tryst or a place where children play.' William gave a lop-sided smile. 'My brother and I often came here to play "Catch and See".'

Corbett stepped into one of the hollowed oaks, where he smelt the strong odour of mildewed wood, fungi and forest bracken. It was like being in a small cell. He peered up at the sky. Such a place would be favoured by any child or outlaw, or an assassin waiting for his victim to appear.

'Ranulf! Search the other hollow trees!'

'What am I looking for?'

'When you find it, you'll know.'

Sir William stood nonplussed as Corbett and Ranulf moved from tree to tree in that dark-green glade. At each one Corbett crouched down, sifting among the soft moss and fern, dry twigs and rotting leaves. The hollowed trunks were dark but there was enough light to search carefully.

'Over here!' Ranulf called.

He was standing by one of the oaks further away. Corbett hurried across. Ranulf was sifting the dirt in the palms of his hands. Corbett glimpsed the small tassels of leather, the thin grey goose feather. He picked these up, scrutinised them and moved into the hollow trunk where Ranulf had found them but could discover no further traces. He put what they had found into his pouch.

'We know this was no accident,' he declared. 'And this is where the assassin hid. I think he came here early in the morning, even the day before, and hid a bow and quiver. The feather and tassel are from these. He then came back and hid in one of these hollowed trunks, making sure Lord Henry was in Savernake Dell and this side of the wood was deserted.'

Corbett walked to where he calculated the assassin must have taken aim, counting under his breath all the time.

'A very short while!' he shouted. 'The assassin would then hasten back, the bow and quiver are placed back in one of the hollow oaks and then he'd go looking for his horse.'

Ranulf had already anticipated this and was deep in the trees, kicking at the carpet of fallen leaves.

'Sir Hugh! Sir William! Over here!'

Ranulf pushed away the leaves with his dagger, revealing scattered horse dung.

'He tethered his horse to a tree,' Ranulf explained. 'Probably bridled, the hooves may have been covered in rags.' He cut a piece of the dung with his dagger. 'He even had time to cover this.'

'So we know how,' Corbett concluded. 'But who or why?'

Chapter 4

Corbett sat on a fallen tree trunk and gestured at Sir William to join him.

'How many people wanted your brother killed?' he asked.

'Lord Henry was a law unto himself, Sir Hugh. Our family own vast estates. We have an ancient name. He was much favoured by the King, a nobleman who travelled to Italy, Sicily, Northern Spain and France.'

'So have many people,' Corbett replied. 'But that doesn't make people want to murder them in a lonely dell on a lovely autumn afternoon. Sir William, I would be grateful if you would answer my questions as bluntly and honestly as possible. You know, I know, we all know there's more to this than meets the eye.'

'The physician and my retainers are waiting.' Sir William's voice was tinged with complaint.

'Ranulf,' Corbett ordered. 'Tell Sir William's men that they can either stay or go back to the manor.'

'Tell them to stay!' Sir William snapped.

'Good.' Corbett sighed. 'Now, Sir William, your brother?'

'He was hated by Robert Verlian, his chief verderer.'

'Why?'

'He lusted after Verlian's daughter, Alicia. A beautiful young woman, it's hard to imagine Verlian having a daughter like that. Lord Henry said she had a face like an angel. He was used to having his way with wenches.'

'And Alicia resisted?'

'She despised my brother.'

'And Verlian himself?'

'At first he was the loyal retainer but even a worm will turn. On one occasion, the Verlians threatened to kill Lord Henry if he didn't desist in his wanton lechery.'

'So, that's why you suspected your chief verderer?'

'Yes. Verlian's also a master bowman and he was not with the hunting party.'

'So, where could he have been?'

'It's possible,' Sir William looked shamefaced, 'that Verlian stayed behind the hunters as they drove the deer into Savernake Dell. After all, that was his responsibility.'

'But you think he may have gone ahead, seized his concealed bow, killed your brother and fled?'

Sir William picked up the corner of his cloak and dug with a dirty nail at the golden arrowhead stitching. He was about to answer when Ranulf came crashing back through the undergrowth.

'Your men wait, Sir William!' he called.

Corbett's manservant sat down with his back to a tree, stretching out his legs. With his dagger he began to whittle away at a branch, humming softly under his breath.

'You do think Verlian killed your brother?'

'Sir Hugh, he had good reason and he had the means.'

'But it isn't logical, is it?' Corbett demanded. 'Verlian is a Sussex man who holds profitable office. He has a daughter; he must have known that murder of his lord would bring summary execution.'

'A man can do anything, Sir Hugh, when his blood is heated and his wits disturbed.'

'But Verlian, and I know I can ask him, was no rash fool. A chief verderer is a man of patience, of cunning, of steady wit. I gather, at first, he showed no objection to Lord Henry's pursuit of his daughter?'

'He turned a blind eye,' Sir William agreed. 'But Alicia has a will like steel and a tongue as sharp as a razor.'

'And who else is there?' Corbett persisted.

'Brother Cosmas, the priest of St Oswald's-in-the-Trees. As I have said, my brother was harsh. Cosmas was also a soldier, until he found God. He fought in the retinue of Henry, Earl of Huntingdon.'

'And who else is there?'

'My brother had strange ways, Sir Hugh. He had little time for God and even less for God's servants.'

'He didn't like priests?'

'No, Sir Hugh, he didn't like priests. He didn't like what he called their mumbling, mouldering words. Henry had visited the universities at Salerno and Bologna, he was aware of the new knowledge coming out of the east. He claimed there was more to man than what the Church taught. He collected grimoires, books written by magicians and wizards. He often went into the forest. There's a witch-woman, Jocasta, and her fey-witted daughter Blanche. My brother gave them a cottage and a little plot of land.'

'Why?' Corbett asked. 'Was your brother a generous man?'

'No. Jocasta appeared about three or four years ago, her daughter trailing behind. She told some story about being cast out by the good burghers of Rye. My brother met her alone in the parlour of Ashdown Manor. They must have been closeted for hours. Afterwards I learned that he had given Jocasta a cottage and, about once a week when he was in residence, he'd visit her by himself.'

'Why?'

'The servants claimed he was interested in the black arts. Jocasta could weave spells.'

'Is that the truth?'

'No, I don't think it is. Once my brother entertained a wandering magician. The man claimed he could ask Lord Satan to come up from hell. My brother riposted, "Yes, but would he come?" and bellowed with laughter. No, to be honest, Sir Hugh, my brother probably went there for another reason. If the truth be known, I have seen no evidence that Jocasta or her daughter are witches.'

'And your half-sister?'

Sir William snorted with laughter. 'The Lady Madeleine, prioress of St Hawisia's? Madeleine has always been, and always will be, Lord Henry in petticoats. She is stubborn, arrogant and bows to no one.'

'Was she on good terms with your brother?'

'Like two cats, Sir Hugh. They would be welcoming but wary. They'd circle each other, hackles up, teeth bared, but they rarely fought.'

'A clash of wills, eh?'

'Sir Hugh, St Hawisia's is deep in the forest. You are welcome to ask my half-sister whenever you want. I am sure she will give you the benefit of her wit and wisdom.' He pulled a face. 'Lord Henry did recently refurbish the shrine, for Madeleine nagged him until he did.'

Corbett looked across to where Ranulf had now fashioned a sharpened stake, his knife slicing into the white wood.

'We do have one other person.'

'Myself?'

'Yes, Sir William, yourself. You are hardly the grieving brother. You were not present when Lord Henry was killed. You mentioned gossip. It's possible that you disappeared into the forest, followed a trackway round the palisade, took the concealed bow, loosed the killing shaft, hid the weapon and hurried back.'

'In which case, Sir Hugh, I wouldn't have needed a horse, would I?'

Corbett threw his head back and laughed.

'There's another possibility,' Ranulf intervened. He threw down the piece of wood and re-sheathed his dagger. 'Whoever killed Lord Henry was a master bowman. How do we know it was someone he knew? There are enough landless soldiers, archers from the King's wars, who could be hired, given a horse, a bow and arrow, and instructed whom to kill.'

'Are you saying that I did that?'

'No, Sir William, all I said was that it could be done.'

'Did you love your brother?' Corbett asked sharply.

Sir William put his face in his hands and rubbed his eyes.

'When I was a child, when Henry, Madeleine and I ran in these woods like imps from hell, there was no rancour, no jealousy, no bitterness.' He fought to keep his voice steady. 'Indeed, Madeleine and I, we worshipped the ground Henry trod on. We used to play in Savernake Dell. Henry was Arthur, Madeleine Guinevere and I was Sir Galahad. Summers which never seemed to end. Days which stretched like eternity. You see, Father married twice. Our mother, Henry's and mine, she died fairly young. Father married again; his second wife died in childbirth but Madeleine survived. Father became morose and withdrawn, more concerned about his estates and his revenue than he was about his three children who, in his opinion, had cost the lives of the two women he loved. We were allowed to run wild.'

'When did it change?'

'Henry was sent up to the Halls of Cambridge. When he came back it was as a stranger: tall and arrogant, quoting Greek and French. He mocked me for my childhood games and Madeleine for her piety. More and more he became closeted with Father, immersing himself in the running of the estate. He went to court. He became the King's friend, serving, as you know, with distinction on the Welsh and Scottish marches. Madeleine went into the priory. She would have nothing to do with the world of men. Father died. Everything was left to Henry.' His voice grew bitter. 'I am a knight, Sir Hugh. I have the right to carry a sword but I became a reeve, a steward. "Run here, William! Run there, William! Do this, William! Do that!" ' He stopped, breathing heavily. 'I asked my brother for a portion of the estate, the honour of Manningtree. He gave his word, promised solemnly that he would . . .'

'But then he reneged?'

'He told me I would have to wait.'

'But you could have left?' Corbett insisted. 'Many a younger brother has.'

'I did. For a while I served as a knight banneret in the retinue of the Prince of Wales. Prince Edward often came to Ashdown as a child.'

'Yes, yes, he did.' Corbett held Ranulf's gaze. So far he was secretly impressed by this manor lord's candour and honesty, but was Sir William only telling the truth as far as he could see it?

'Well, you can guess what happened.' Sir William got to his feet and stretched. 'The Prince of Wales is not a warrior, Sir Hugh. He prefers to dig a ditch, fight a mock tourney, be a Lord of Misrule. There was no profit in his service and so I came home. Oh, Henry was generous enough: silver, gold, horses, armour, but he was always the lord and I the constant petitioner. I had to beg, and sometimes I hated him.'

'Enough to kill him?' Corbett asked abruptly.

Sir William lowered his face, tears brimming in his eyes.

'God forgive me, clerk! We all carry the mark of Cain within us, but Lord Henry was no Abel.' He stood back. 'Now, Sir Hugh, I am the manor lord. I own Ashdown and its estates. I bend the knee to no one except the King. You've listed possible assassins, but you forget one: the Frenchman de Craon.'

Corbett shook his head. 'Sir William, on my oath, I may forget many things but I can never forget, will never forget, Seigneur de Craon! He is constantly in my thoughts.'

'Why should de Craon want Lord Henry dead?' Ranulf asked.

'I don't know. You are the royal emissary. De Craon is a mystery, an enigma, eager for my brother to lead the English envoys to Paris. But, Sir Hugh, why not ask him yourself? You may not stay under my roof but, tonight, I insist that you be my guest at Ashdown Manor. So, if you have no more questions, I'll rejoin my men.'

Corbett got to his feet.

'Why the hurry, Sir William? The day is good and it will be long.' He stopped and listened as a blackbird began to sing, so clearly, so sweetly, Corbett marvelled at its beauty. 'They say these forests are ancient, Sir William. And house all forms of creatures?'

'Good and bad, Corbett. There are outlaws, we even have a hermit who lives in Dragon Rocks beyond the priory.'

'Why Dragon?' Ranulf asked.

'If you visit there you'll see a cave-mouth shaped like the mouth of a snarling dragon. The hermit's harmless enough, slightly lame, his hands are mutilated. He lives off the goodwill of the forest people.'

'A young man?'

'Of mature years,' Sir William replied. 'I know little of him. He calls himself Odo Rievaulx.'

'And the Owlman?' Corbett asked. 'The tavern keeper talked of him.'

'A wolfs-head, an outlaw. He waged his own petty feud against my brother and, before you ask, Sir Hugh, I don't know why.'

'Yes, the taproom of the Devil-in-the-Woods is full of such gossip.'

'The Owlman,' Sir William said, 'is a vexatious flea my brother wanted to scratch.'

'In what way?'

'Cryptic, secret messages tied to the end of an arrow shaft and shot into a door, or a tree, or the path Lord Henry used. The messages were often one word, badly written, "Remember".'

'Remember what?'

'I don't really know. My brother would curse and then destroy them.' Sir William's hand went to his lips. 'One time I did see the message, because I found it.' He closed his eyes and then opened them. 'Yes, "Remember the Rose of Rye"!'

'What does that mean?'

'At first I thought it was a tavern so I made enquiries, but there's no such place. Look, Sir Hugh, this forest divides the south coast from London. It is rich in game, has secretive, dark places. Pilgrims travel to St Hawisia's. Wolfs-heads and outlaws hide well away from the sheriff's men.'

'And murder?' Corbett asked.

'It happens.'

'Including that young woman whose corpse was found?'

Sir William shrugged. 'Sir Hugh, I know nothing of that. However, if a young wench was stupid enough to travel on the forest paths by herself, well, she's like a chicken which runs into a fox's lair.'

'And you know nothing of her death?'

'Sir Hugh, if I did, I would tell you. The corpse was left outside St Hawisia's priory. My good half-sister gave it Christian burial, more than that I cannot say.' Sir William picked up the bow and quiver of arrows and slung them over his shoulder. 'You have reminded me that you are the King's envoy, so, please, be my guests tonight just after Vespers.'

And, not waiting for an answer, the manor lord turned and walked back across Savernake Dell.

'Now there goes a worried man,' Ranulf observed. 'Master, I'll collect the horses. Is it back to the tavern?'

'No, I think a visit to St Hawisia's would be opportune.' Corbett smiled. 'The more I know about Lord Henry's family, the more intrigued I become. Sir William's a worried man. Yet I don't think he's a murderer, though I could be wrong.'

Corbett studied his mud-stained boots. Blood-red, of high quality Moroccan leather, they had been made in Spain. Maeve had bought them at a fair held just outside the Tower. He looked at the silver spur attached to the heel and absent-mindedly brushed some moss from his leather leggings.

'The forest is a quiet place,' he mused. 'But a man intent on murder. Wouldn't he be noticed, Ranulf? The clinking of spurs, horse neighing, the crack and snap of twigs and fallen branches?'

'Not if there's a hunt going on,' Ranulf said.

He stared up at the tree, searching for the blackbird which was singing so lustily.

'Remember, Sir Hugh, Lord Henry was excited, as were his companions. The morning he was killed, the forest was full of noise, the shouts of huntsmen, the barking of dogs, the chatter of his guests.'

Corbett grinned. 'I'll make a countryman of you yet, Ranulf: fetch the horses!'

Ranulf, muttering under his breath at how he hated the countryside and loathed these dark-green places, walked back across the dell. One of Sir William's grooms was guarding the horses, a pasty-faced youth with corn-coloured hair and a cast in one eye. He was talking to Corbett's horse, gently stroking the muzzle, whispering into the cocked ear like any young swain to his sweetheart. He was short and thickset, podgy-fingered; one of the heels had fallen off his riding boot which made him limp as he moved.

'What's your name, boy?' Ranulf asked.

'Baldock. I used to be called Burdock but that didn't sound well so I changed it.'

'Strange name.' Ranulf swung himself into the saddle and took the reins of Corbett's horse. 'Why did your mother give it to you?'

The ostler looked up. Despite the cast in his eye, he had a merry, open face.

'Don't know my mother,' he replied. 'Don't know my father. I was a foundling left at the manor some years ago.'

'And Lord Henry took you in?'

'He was a kind enough man, a good lord. Oh, he was arrogant but they all are, aren't they? They walk the earth as if they own it and don't notice the worms they've trod on.'

'You are a philosopher,' Ranulf taunted, leaning down.

'I'm an ostler,' Baldock replied. 'And a good one! Nothing better for your belly than riding the back of a horse. God's gift to man they are. Horses love you. Never ask for anything except a bit of care.'

Ranulf recalled Maltote.

'And what else can you do, Baldock? Are you good in a fight? Or when you draw that dagger, do you cut yourself?'

Baldock pointed to a pole still left from where the palisade had stood.

'You see that, master?'

'As sure as I do the nose on your face.'

Baldock turned away and Ranulf glimpsed a quick movement of his arm. The ostler's hand came up in an arc; the knife, a thin-bladed stabbing dirk, flew through the air and hit the pole dead centre.

'I learned that,' Baldock boasted. 'A wandering mountebank taught me. I've won many a coin in the taverns.'

'And what else can you do?' Ranulf had now forgotten Corbett. 'Do you play dice, Baldock?' He fished in his pouch and took out two of his genuine dice.

The change in the ostler's face was wonderful to behold. Such a woebegone expression, anyone would have thought he had been threatened with a hanging.

'What's the matter?' Ranulf purred. He pointed down to the piece of level ground. 'Throw the dice!'

Baldock was about to refuse.

'I am a royal clerk,' Ranulf told him softly.

Baldock's lower lip jutted out stubbornly.

'Go on!' Ranulf urged. 'Look!' He fished out a penny and threw it at Baldock, who deftly caught it. 'For the love of God, man, throw the dice. I am paying you to!'

Baldock finally took the dice and crouched down. 'You'll see why,' he grumbled. 'You'll see why and leave me alone.'

He let the two white polished dice fall. Ranulf blinked.

'Two ones!' he exclaimed. 'Throw them again, Baldock!'

The young ostler heaved a sigh but obeyed.

'Two ones! I don't believe this! Again!'

This time it was a one and a two. Baldock picked up the dice and thrust them back into Ranulf's hands.

'I didn't tell you my full name,' he confessed. 'Unlucky Baldock!'

'No, no.' Ranulf, intrigued, dug into his purse and took out another die heavily weighted to fall on six. 'Go on, Unlucky Baldock, I'll prove you wrong!'

The young ostler blinked. 'Must I?'

Again another coin exchanged hands. Ranulf watched in fascination; he'd used these dice so many times to fleece an opponent. Baldock rolled the die along the ground until it turned over on the three.

'It must be the forest floor,' Ranulf whispered. 'That's never happened!'

'If you think that's bad,' Baldock said, 'have you ever heard me sing?' His pale face had become flushed, his eyes gleaming with anger. 'If you really want to make fun of me, I know you'll go back to the manor and tell people what you saw, then they'll all jeer and say, "Didn't you hear him sing?" '

Before Ranulf could answer, Baldock opened his mouth.

'A nut brown maid . . .'

The horses reared and whinnied. Ranulf cursed and dug his heels in, at the same time grasping more firmly the reins of Corbett's horse. But the more Baldock sang, the greater the horses' agitation grew. Ranulf had never heard such a terrible sound, whether in tavern brawls, street fights, or from men suffering from the most hideous wounds. Baldock's voice was indescribable, a harsh grating noise, like a man slowly choking.

'Stop it!' Ranulf bellowed. 'For the love of God, stop it!'

Baldock closed his mouth. Ranulf quietened the horses and the young ostler came over and whispered to both of them. The horses whinnied and relaxed. Baldock fished into his purse and brought out an apple which he cut and fed half to each.

'There! There!' he crooned. 'Unlucky Baldock is sorry. So, sir.' He held the bridle of Ranulf's horse, the cast in his right eye more pronounced. 'Now you know why they call me Unlucky Baldock. Cross-eyed, crossed in luck and crossed in love!'

'Ranulf!' Corbett was standing at the edge of the glade looking impatiently across at him.

His manservant threw Baldock another penny before he dismounted and led both horses across the dell.

'What is the matter?' Corbett demanded. 'What was that terrible noise?'

Ranulf hid a smirk. 'Master, I'll tell you later. We were discussing poor Maltote and I may have found a replacement.'

Corbett looked askance at him as he grasped the reins of his horse and walked into the trees.

'If I remember rightly, the priory must be this

way. So, if we get lost, Ranulf, it will be my fault.'

Ranulf quietly cursed and hung back. He hated the forest, the noises he couldn't identify, the shapes and shadowy forms which seemed to move between the trees. Corbett walked ahead of him, lost in his own thoughts. The previous evening, the tavern master of the Devil-in-the-Woods had drawn a crude map. Corbett believed he was going in the right direction, towards a path that would widen into a trackway which would take him up to the priory.

Ranulf, behind him, thought about Maltote and Baldock. Every so often he would stop and peer between the trees, recalling the warnings about the creatures who lurked here: the cutthroats who would take a man's life simply for the boots he wore. Ranulf's hand went to his dagger. As he was about to protest the treeline suddenly broke, the ground dipped and he saw the trackway winding through the forest. Corbett led his horse down and mounted. Ranulf followed suit and drew alongside his master.

'We are not wandering around, are we?' he demanded. 'Going from one place to another?'

Corbett glanced up at the fleecy white clouds. The sky was light blue and the sun strengthening. He breathed in the sweet smell of the forest, the damp ferns, that warm humid smell from trees soaked with rain.

'At first this will be easy,' he predicted. 'We will be allowed to go where we wish. However, this is a pretty mess of pottage and the deeper we dig our spoons, the more dangerous it will become. Lord Henry was murdered and, somehow or other, I think that unmarked corpse has something to do with this business. That young woman was killed, stripped and, if the reports are true, secretly buried before someone dug her up and placed her corpse outside the priory gates. Outlaws don't do that.' He paused, gathering the reins in his hands. 'We have the Fitzalans, two brothers and a half-sister. A great deal of antipathy, even hatred, swirled between them. We have this strange outlaw the Owlman with his secret threats. We also have, standing in the shadows, Jocasta and her daughter, Verlian, Brother Cosmas, even Odo the hermit: that's one game. Then we have the King and what he intends. Nor must we forget the Prince of Wales, God knows what mischief he's plotting! And last, but not least, our beloved brother in Christ, Seigneur Amaury de Craon. Now each group could be separate but, I suspect, the more we stir the pot, Ranulf, the more they'll mix together. So.' He smiled. 'In a while it might be very dangerous to ride around Ashdown Forest. I won't go to them. I'm the King's commissioner, I'll make them come to me.'

Ranulf was about to ask how when an arrow whirred in front of him and struck the ground, embedding itself deep in the trackway. Ranulf immediately dismounted, unhitching the small arbalest he carried on his saddle horn. Again came a whir and an arrow dug into the trackway behind him. Corbett, too, dismounted, using his horse as a shield.

'To the right!' Ranulf shouted.

And, as if in answer, two more shafts whistled above their heads, striking the trees behind them.

Chapter 5

Corbett and Ranulf hid behind their horses which whinnied and shook their heads as they caught their agitation.

'How many archers, Ranulf?'

'Just the one, master. I don't think he intends to kill us. He's loosed at least four shafts, one would have found its target.'

Corbett peered over the saddle, scrutinising the trees, but it was futile. The forest edge could have concealed an army and he would have been none the wiser. At last the horses became more placid.

'Do you know, master, I think he's gone.'

Ranulf tentatively stepped from behind his horse, one hand on its muzzle, talking quietly to it. He watched for any movement among the trees.

'You are safe!' a man's grating voice shouted. 'I

mean you no harm! Look at the arrow!'

Ranulf turned to the shaft, still embedded in the trackway before him, and noticed the piece of parchment tied with red twine just above the quill. He ran forward to pluck the arrow out. Sheltering behind his horse, he undid the red cord; the piece of parchment was yellow and greasy but its message was clear enough.

> The Owlman sends greetings to the King's emissary! Justice has already been done. The Owlman sees what he wishes and hears what he wishes! He goes where he wants. Farewell.

Corbett plucked the scrap of paper from Ranulf's fingers and read it.

'He's well named,' he commented. 'The Owlman, a bird of the night which swoops silently on its prey. I wonder if he's our assassin?'

'Why the message?'

'He's simply making his mark!' Corbett grinned. 'Or telling us, in his own way, he's not Lord Henry's murderer.'

He thrust the scrap of parchment into his wallet and remounted.

'He means us no harm.'

They moved on cautiously, studying the forest on either side, fearful of another attack, until they reached the crossroads where a decaying gibbet post hung lopsidedly, the piece of hemp in the rusty iron hook dancing in the morning breeze.

'We follow the path straight on,' Corbett said.

The trackway dipped, turned and then broadened. In a large clearing before them rose the honey-coloured stone walls of St Hawisia's priory. Despite the early hour, the place hummed with activity; lay brothers were going out into the fields, traders and chapmen were making their way up to the main gates. Peasants, their carts piled high with produce for the priory kitchens, were also assembled, waiting for the gates to be opened.

'The priory must own its own lands,' Corbett decided. 'From what I gather, it's a little kingdom in itself, so let's see its ruler.'

He gazed appreciatively at the buildings rising above the curtain wall: black and red slate roofs, a soaring church tower. Somewhere deep in the priory a bell tolled and the morning air wafted rich, savoury odours from the kitchens.

They asked directions from a peasant.

'Well, you can wait like us,' the pock-marked fellow replied, his nose and cheeks chapped by wind and sun. 'Wait, as we always do, in the snow, rain or sun for their ladyships to open the gates.' He pointed further down the wall. 'Or you can try the postern door. But God help you if it's not urgent business!'

Corbett thanked him and dismounted. He led Ranulf across and they rapped on the small, metal-studded gate. A grille high up the door was pushed back. Small, black, inquisitive eyes peered out.

'What do you want? Who are you?'

'I am Sir Hugh Corbett, King's emissary, and this is my clerk Ranulf. We demand entrance. We wish to see Lady Madeleine.'

'You are a liar!' the querulous voice objected. 'You are not dressed like a royal clerk!'

Corbett drew out his letter of commission and thrust the red wax seal up against the grille.

'Open up!' he ordered. 'Or I'll kick this door until it flies off its hinges!'

'You should have shown me the seal first,' came the aggrieved reply.

The bolts were pulled back, the gate swung open. The nun standing on the other side was small. She was dressed in a white woollen veil, a cream-coloured coif, and a white gown almost covered by a black apron.

'I am Sister Veronica!' she informed them. 'Cellarer, porter, you name it, I do it.' She peered up at Corbett, her thin lips tight, her white, wizened face full of hostility. 'You look like a clerk.' She glanced at Ranulf. 'But you don't. More like a gibbet bird!'

'Would you say this priory is noted for its charity and Christian welcome?' Ranulf asked.

The cellarer shook her head. 'Don't be impudent, Green Eyes! In my former life I had seven children. Two husbands long dead. Now I am a nun consecrated to God.'

'And he's welcome to you!' Ranulf murmured.

'What was that?' Sister Veronica's hand went to her ear. 'My hearing's not what it should be, but did you say something impertinent?'

'My clerk was simply exclaiming in amazement.' Corbett took the old woman's hand. 'We wish you well, Sister Veronica. However, we are on urgent business. We must see Lady Madeleine as well as the famous shrine.'

Sister Veronica's face softened. 'Well, you can see how busy we are going to be. I'd best take you across to the church. You can wait there while I tell the prioress.'

She led them along a pebble-dashed path, through gardens carefully laid out in the French fashion: raised flower beds, herb banks and turfed seats. The air was fragrant with a variety of perfumes. Corbett particularly appreciated the rose bushes planted on either side of the path, which gave off their own special scent. The garden occupied one side of the priory but, in the distance, he could see small orchards of apple, pear and plum trees. Sister Veronica pointed to another wall, its great wooden gates being opened.

'Beyond that are the stables, outhouses, store-rooms and bakery. On the far side are meadows. We raise good sheep and we even have our own windmill.'

Corbett nodded. St Hawisia's looked a wealthy establishment. The church before him was built of dressed stone, with a roof of iron-grey slate. The morning sun glistened in the stained glass windows and on either side of the church rose stately mansions of honey-coloured brick, every window sheeted in glass.

'Our dormitories and refectory are over there,' Sister Veronica pointed out. 'We have a guest house and infirmary. Lady Madeleine has her own chambers on the far side of the cloister path near the forest wall. We also own a library and a scriptorium,' she added proudly.

'So, your priory is well endowed?'

Sister Veronica stopped abruptly. 'We bring our own dowries here. The priory has fruitful estates and, of course, St Hawisia looks after us.' She marched on, her shoulders stooped. 'I can't take you into our enclosure. The priory is not yet ready for visitors and Lady Madeleine is very strict about men coming here, be they clerk or prince. That's why you have to wait in church.'

She waved them up the steps but, as Ranulf passed, she caught him by the sleeve.

'You be careful what you touch. This is God's house, not some stall in the marketplace!'

Ranulf seized her hand and, before she could protest, raised it to his lips.

'Sister, I wouldn't dream of it. I have had the deepest devotion to St Hawisia ever since I was a child. Do you know, when I was a boy I even had a vision of her?'

Sister Veronica's jaw sagged.

'Later, Ranulf!' Corbett warned.

Ranulf again kissed her hand and, before the good nun could think of a suitable reply, followed Corbett into the church.

They stood in the doorway marvelling at the beauty and elegance of this jewel of a chapel. The flagstone floor was scrubbed clean. The pillars, shielding off the transepts, were painted a dark blue with gold crowns. The walls beyond glowed with brilliantly coloured frescoes illustrating scenes from the Bible. At the far end a heavily carved rood screen sheltered the choir stalls and sanctuary. The air was perfumed by flowers in small copper pots at the base of each pillar. Faint clouds of incense still drifted through the air, catching the coloured sunlight shafting through the stained glass windows.

'Well endowed indeed,' Ranulf commented. 'Better than a royal chapel.'

'With one difference,' Corbett said. He pointed to the windows painted in shimmering reds, golds, greens and blues.

'You are a senior clerk in the Office of the Green Wax, Master Ranulf. You have to be keen of wit and sharp of eye. Have you noticed anything? The paintings and the windows?'

Ranulf walked along the church. He prided himself on his education. Hadn't he his own copy of the Bible and two Books of Hours? And, wherever he went, Ranulf always watched and listened. Some of the scenes he couldn't recognise but others he could. Judith, from the Old Testament, cutting off her enemy's head. Ruth the Moabite. One scene caught his eye and he smiled: it showed the serpent tempting Adam. But this time Adam's body was concealed, only his head stuck out from a thick wall of privet. Eve, however, was shown in all her glory, hand raised as if warning Adam not to succumb. On the wall beneath the window a dramatic scene showed Christ harrowing Hell after the crucifixion where he divided the good from the bad. Ranulf laughed.

'It's women,' he said. 'Every scene depicts women! There are hardly any men, apart from Adam's head and Christ. And look, master, even the Saviour, with his long hair and delicate face, has a girlish cast about him.'

'And have you noticed the damned?' Corbett asked. He pointed to the dark shadowy forms, each of whom was dressed in battered armour. 'Look, Ranulf, all those cursed by God are male but the saved are . . .'

'They are all women!' Ranulf exclaimed. 'Even the angels!'

They walked along the church. On the one hand the paintings were lavish, brilliant in their colours and expertly depicted but their message was the same. In Heaven as on earth, the woman was good, the male worthy of condemnation.

Corbett looked up the nave. He saw the Lady Chapel to the left and, to the right, a gleaming oak wood sarcophagus, the glass case at its head shimmering in the light of dozens of beeswax candles.

'St Hawisia's last resting place,' he explained.

He was about to go up and investigate when from the choir stalls in the sanctuary came a young woman's voice intoning the *Salve Regina*: *'Salve Regina, Mater Misericordia, Vita Dulcedo et Spes Nostra, Salve!'*

Corbett raised his finger to his lips and, followed by Ranulf, entered the gorgeously decorated sanctuary with its polished wooden choir stalls on either side. At the far end stood a marble altar on a raised dais which was carpeted in thick blue and gold wool. Silver candlesticks stood on the altar and, above them, a jewel-encrusted pyx which held the Blessed Sacrament hung by a filigree chain. The nun standing in the stalls was facing the altar, hands by her sides. Corbett expected her to continue singing but she faltered and began again.

'Salve Regina, Mater Misericordia, Vita Dulcedo et Spes Nostra, Salve.'

'Hail Holy Queen, Mother of Mercy, Hail Our Life, our Sweetness and Our Hope.'

'Ad te clamanus . . .' But then her voice faltered off.

'Ad te clamanus, exules filii Evae,' Corbett sang in a rich baritone voice. *'Ad te suspiramus, gementes et flentes.'*

'To you, we cry, poor banished children of Eve. To

you we send up our sighs, mourning and weeping in this Vale of Tears.'

The young nun turned. Her pretty face, framed by its coif, was white with shock.

'I . . . What are you doing here?'

'Waiting for Lady Madeleine.' Corbett walked forward. 'You seem to be having trouble with the hymn. Do you not have a Book of Hours?'

The young nun, more composed, grinned impishly at Ranulf.

'I'm Sister Fidelis,' she said in a rush. 'I'm only a novice. I just cannot remember the words. So Lady Johanna, the choir mistress, not to mention the Lady Marcellina the novice mistress, have told me to stand here and sing it until I've learned it correctly.'

Corbett bowed. 'I am Sir Hugh Corbett, Keeper of the Secret Seal, special emissary from His Grace the King.'

Sister Fidelis' eyes rounded in amazement.

'We are not as important as we sound.' Corbett smiled. 'Indeed, we have just met your Sister Veronica, who regarded us as two marauders.'

'She would! I asked her for help but she says she's too busy.'

'Then we'll help,' Corbett replied. 'Won't we, Ranulf?'

'Men aren't supposed to sing here,' Sister Fidelis simpered.

'I don't think the good Lord will object,' Corbett

replied. 'And you must learn the words.'

'It's something I will talk about for days,' Sister Fidelis laughed. 'You begin, I'll repeat each line.'

Ranulf, too surprised to join in, watched his master stand next to the young nun and, in a deep, rich voice, begin the *Salve Regina*. At the end of each line he paused and the young sister repeated it; at the very end Sister Fidelis triumphantly joined in the last line.

'*O Dulcis! O Pia! Virgo Maria!*'

'I sang it!' she exclaimed. 'I know it now. You won't tell them, will you?'

Corbett turned to Ranulf. 'Our lips are sealed, aren't they?'

Ranulf just gaped and wondered, not for the first time, if the arrow which had struck his master in Oxford had damaged more than his chest bone.

'Thank you.' Sister Fidelis smiled. 'I never can remember the words in choir, Lady Johanna is so hard. She beats my knuckles with a ferrule.'

She held up a white, delicate hand; nasty red bruises marred the knuckles. Corbett kissed her fingertips.

'Such harshness is ill fitting,' he murmured.

Sister Fidelis blushed and withdrew her hand.

'So, you are awaiting Lady Madeleine. I tell you this, you'll tarry a long while! Lady Madeleine loves to keep people waiting. Even Lord Henry, when he came here, had to kick his heels in the guest house.' She paused. 'And he paid generously to refurbish the shrine!'

'Does the priory have many such noble visitors?' Corbett queried.

'Oh yes. The Prince of Wales came here.'

'I didn't know Prince Edward had a devotion to the St Hawisia?' Corbett asked innocently.

'Well, he has, he came in here. But I'm only a novice, sir,' she trilled on. 'Such comings and goings do not concern me.'

'What comings and goings?' Corbett quietly prayed that Lady Madeleine would indeed tarry a while, since this fresh-faced young novice seemed eager to chatter.

'Lady Johanna shouldn't hit me with a ferrule.' Sister Fidelis sucked on her knuckles.

Corbett studied her intently. He wondered if the young lady had been placed here, not for any vocation but because she was slightly fey.

'What were you saying?' she asked.

'You were going to tell me about strange comings and goings.'

'Well, I am! Oh, sir, what is your name?'

'Sir Hugh Corbett, I'm the King's emissary.'

'Well, you see, Sir Hugh, I often daydream, particularly in the refectory; I never finish my food! So, I'm given tasks, little punishments. I hate leaves!'

'I beg your pardon?' Ranulf asked.

'Leaves,' Sister Fidelis repeated. 'Because I don't eat my food quickly enough, when the other novices go to recreation, I have to sweep the yard. I'm given a thick, heavy apron which scores my neck and a broom that's far too heavy. I'm told to sweep the cobbled yard which divides our refectory from Lady Madeleine's house.'

'I don't like leaves either,' Corbett told her. 'And, I promise you, I'll have a word with Lady Madeleine not to punish you so rigorously.'

'Oh, would you, sir, and would you also mention Lady Johanna's ferrule?'

'For the love of God!' Ranulf whispered.

'The leaves?' Corbett asked.

'Well, one night, I think it was on the eve of St Matthew.' Her fingers flew to her lips. 'Or was it the feast of St Cornelius?'

'You were sweeping leaves in the yard?'

'Yes. I went into a corner when it was growing dark and no one would see me. I'd stolen a piece of marchpane from the refectory and my fingers were cold. Anyway, I ate the marchpane. I was very cross because the novices were in their house and all the other sisters were enjoying themselves. Suddenly.' Her head came forward and Corbett nearly jumped. 'Suddenly,' she whispered hoarsely, 'I saw a man, cowled and cloaked, cross the yard.'

'You are sure it wasn't one of the sisters?' Corbett asked.

'They don't wear spurs which clink nor do they carry swords! They certainly don't walk with a swagger. Anyway, he enters Lady Madeleine's house. Oh, I say to myself, what goes on here? In he goes, just opens the door. Now downstairs is her own refectory and chambers; upstairs is her own bedchamber. No one ever goes up there! I put the broom down and stole across the yard. I looked through the window but saw no one there.'

'So, the man must have gone upstairs?' Corbett asked.

'He must have done. Do you know, sir, I swept that yard time and again but he never came out. A week later, it was the end of the month because we had celebrated the feast of St Jerome, he was the man who . . .'

'Yes,' Corbett intervened. 'I know who St Jerome was. And you were sweeping the yard again?'

'No, sir, I was sweeping the refectory floor all by myself, another punishment. I am sure,' Sister Fidelis confided, 'that I saw the same man cross the yard.'

'But surely, the prioress would not entertain male friends?'

'But that's it, sir, she has no male friends! Lady Madeleine believes men are no better than devils.'

'Has she said as much?'

'No, it's just in her warnings to us. How we should act when male guests arrive.'

'Like me?'

'Oh, you're the King's emissary and you have helped my singing. You are also going to tell Lady Johanna not to use that ferrule!'

'And do you know who this stranger was?' Corbett asked.

The young novice shook her head. 'Perhaps I've said wrong,' she mused. 'The stranger could have left the other way?'

'What way?'

'Lady Madeleine's house is a little palace. It has its own kitchen and stables beyond, with a yard and a small postern door in the forest wall.'

'And this stranger could have left by that?'

'It's possible!'

'Have you seen anything else suspicious?' Ranulf insisted.

Sister Fidelis gazed round fearfully.

'Oh no! I haven't told anyone else. I daren't! Lady Madeleine's rages are terrible to behold.'

'Does she ever leave the convent?' Ranulf asked.

'Yes, the priory owns properties in the town of Rye. She sometimes goes there with the almoner or one of her brothers to collect the rents and inspect the steward's accounts. She's gone four or five days, it's always a relief. However, in many ways Lady Madeleine is kind and very proud of her shrine.'

'Yes, I was going to ask about that.' Corbett looked over his shoulder at the door. Lady Madeleine was sure to arrive soon and he didn't want to get this young, very naive novice into trouble. 'I know little about St Hawisia.'

'Oh, then let me tell you. I've learned everything.'

Sister Fidelis took them out of the sanctuary and around to the side chapel. Corbett stared appreciatively at the long oaken tomb.

'How old is that?'

'Lady Johanna says at least two hundred years. The oak was brought specially from the West Country.'

Corbett looked round the side chapel. On the marble altar built into the far wall stood a statue of what must be St Hawisia, a young woman, hair falling down to her shoulders, dressed in royal robes of purple and white. In her outstretched hands lay a sword. On the walls huge frescoes depicted scenes from the saint's life in a gorgeous array of colours. These showed a young woman in flight, pursued by knights armed with clubs, swords and maces. Another scene showed a wood where the young saint knelt beside a pool, a lily in her hands.

'Who was St Hawisia?' Corbett tapped the glass case at the head of the coffin into which Ranulf was peering.

'It's hair!' his manservant exclaimed. 'Look, Sir Hugh, beautiful golden tresses!'

Corbett removed the purple, gold-edged cloth covering half of the glass and saw the locks coiled in a circle, lustrous and golden as full-grown wheat.

'What is this?' he asked.

'It's the relic,' Sister Fidelis explained. 'It's St Hawisia's hair.'

Corbett stared at the fresco behind him. He

noticed the date, painted in silver gilt at the bottom of the picture: A.D. 667.

'St Hawisia lived centuries ago!' he exclaimed. 'Almost seven hundred years ago but this hair . . .!'

'That's because it's a miracle,' Sister Fidelis said. 'You see, sir, Hawisia was a Saxon princess. Her father was king of these parts.' She closed her eyes as if memorising a lesson. 'Now her father wanted her to marry a powerful thane.' She opened her eyes. 'What's a thane?'

'A nobleman,' Corbett replied.

'Hawisia said that she was dedicated to God and would not marry this prince. Her father became very angry. Hawisia was beautiful. She was particularly famous for her golden hair. Now.' Fidelis pointed to the fresco. 'Hawisia fled her father's palace but he pursued her with soldiers. Hawisia fled into a wood and reached the well, this very place. She cut off her golden hair and laid it beside a pool as an offering to God. Well.' The young novice closed her eyes. 'Ah, yes, that's right. When her father reached her, he was so angry at what she had done, he drew his dagger and drove it deep into her heart.' Sister Fidelis mimicked the action of a soldier striking; Corbett pressed on Ranulf's toe as a warning not to laugh. 'When his rage cooled, yes, that's right.' She opened her eyes. 'He deeply regretted what he had done. He converted to Christianity, gave his daughter honourable burial and founded a house of prayer which later became St Hawisia's priory.'

'And this is her tomb?'

'Yes, St Hawisia lies beneath the flagstones. This tomb was built by Lady Madeleine's ancestor. The Fitzalans have always had a great devotion to her.'

'But surely this isn't Princess Hawisia's hair?' Ranulf exclaimed.

'Yes it is,' Sister Fidelis insisted defensively. 'You see, that's why Hawisia's father converted. The hair remained as it had on the day his daughter died: over the centuries it has never rotted or decayed. If you put your hand on the glass case and say a prayer to St Hawisia, she always answers.'

Corbett studied the golden tresses. The hair was undoubtedly genuine yet it looked as fresh and lustrous as if it had been shorn off the previous day. In his travels he'd seen many a relic. Enough nails from the True Cross to use in the building of a shop. At least three heads of St John the Baptist, five legs of St Sebastian, feathers from Archangel Gabriel's wing and, on one famous occasion, even the stone Jesus was supposed to have stood on before He ascended into Heaven. Similar relics were found throughout Europe: holy blood which liquefied, statues which wept tears. They ranged from the sublime to the ridiculous, even including a sweat cloth which St Joseph supposedly used in his workshop.

Corbett tapped the glass case: the work of a

craftsman, it was cleverly riveted to the top of the tomb. Was there a logical explanation for this relic? Had it been sealed so as to protect it from the putrefying air? It was undoubtedly a phenomenon. No wonder St Hawisia's attracted so many pilgrims.

'It's all very beautiful.'

'Oh, Lord Henry recently refurbished it.'

'When?'

'About three months ago. The shrine was sealed and closed for a while so the walls and ceilings could be painted.'

'Has this reliquary ever been opened?'

'No, it hasn't.'

Corbett suddenly felt he was being watched and turned to see that two nuns stood at the entrance to the side chapel. The foremost was tall, severe-looking, dressed in a snowy-white habit. A gold medal hung from a filigree chain around her neck. Behind her the other nun was similarly dressed, though smaller, more anxious. If looks could kill, the young novice would have dropped dead on the spot.

'Lady Madeleine Fitzalan?' Corbett asked, coming forward.

Lady Madeleine didn't even shift her gaze from the petrified novice.

'What are you doing here, Sister Fidelis?'

'I was practising the *Salve Regina*.'

'And she sang beautifully,' Corbett declared. 'Even though her knuckles were very sore.'

'She's a clumsy girl,' Lady Madeleine replied, her eyes shifting to Corbett.

'But when I return,' Corbett went on, 'the bruises will have healed, will they not?'

Lady Madeleine snapped her fingers.

'Go to the novice house, Sister Fidelis!' She surveyed Corbett from head to toe. 'I am Lady Madeleine Fitzalan. This is Sister Agnes, my sub-prioress.'

The other nun forced a smile.

'And I am Sir Hugh Corbett, Keeper of the King's Secret Seal, his special emissary to these parts. I carry his warrant and authority. This is Ranulf-atte-Newgate, my manservant, senior clerk in the Chancery of the Green Wax.'

'You have no authority on church lands!'

'I can get it.'

Lady Madeleine's thin face broke into a smile.

'Could you really, Sir Hugh?' She brushed by him, walked towards the shrine and gave Ranulf the same critical look. 'You have a bold stare, man!'

'I was examining your habit, my lady, its snowy whiteness. Is that a symbol of holiness or just humility?'

Corbett closed his eyes at the hiss of indrawn breath.

'Lady Madeleine.' He came and stood beside her. 'Your half-brother has been murdered.'

'God assoil him!'

'And a young woman's corpse was left outside the

postern of your priory. I understand she, too, had been murdered, by an arrow to the neck.'

'Who told you that?'

'His Majesty the King. Not to mention the gossips at the Devil-in-the-Woods tavern.'

'It's well named.' Lady Madeleine's icy gaze never faltered. 'But, yes, the poor woman's corpse was found and we gave it Christian burial.'

'Why?'

'It's one of the Corporal Acts of Mercy.'

'Did you know the woman?'

'No, I did not!'

'Had she ever visited this priory or shrine?'

'No, she did not and you can ask that question of any of the community.'

'And where is she buried?'

'In our graveyard.'

Corbett produced his warrant bearing the royal seal.

'Then, my lady, by the authority invested in me, I wish the corpse exhumed so I can examine it.'

'You cannot do that.'

Corbett walked away. 'Ranulf, find a mattock, hoe and spade. Use your authority to find out where this poor corpse lies buried. My lady prioress, I will explain my actions to the King and to the Archbishop, and you can then account for your refusal to co-operate with me.'

'Sir Hugh.'

He turned. Lady Madeleine's face had softened.

'I did not mean to quarrel. First, let me answer your questions. The case containing the relic is never opened. Secondly, I will answer your questions in my parlour. Thirdly, since I am prioress here, I will have the body exhumed!'

Chapter 6

One of the priory lay brothers dug the edge of his spade under the coffin lid, pushed it up and hastily walked away. The casket itself was nothing more than a long narrow chest tightly nailed down. Corbett told Ranulf to stand aside and, putting a cloth soaked in wine, vinegar and herbs to his mouth and nose, drew his dagger and walked closer. The lay brothers had hastily withdrawn. Lady Madeleine and the community did not wish to be present. Ranulf stood some distance away under the spreading branches of a gnarled yew tree. Corbett pushed the lid away. Despite the wine-soaked cloth, the stench was offensive; the corpse beneath its gauze veil was now in mortal decay. Yet, at the same time, Corbett felt a deep sadness. The body, dressed in a simple white gown, looked young, pathetic and forlorn. He pulled back the makeshift coif and noticed the close-cropped hair. He rubbed a few strands between his fingers. For some reason he felt certain the hair was dyed. The wound in the throat was a repellent blue-black.

'God have mercy on you!' Corbett whispered. 'But it's true, there's no beauty in death.'

Suddenly he was back in Oxford, that wild-eyed assassin running towards him, crossbow coming up, its quarrel speeding towards him. Corbett pushed the thought away.

'Remember man, that thou art dust and into dust thou shalt return.'

'*Sic transit gloria mundi . . .*'

Corbett glanced round. A man stood, cowled and hooded. He seemed a Franciscan by his brown habit. In addition he wore simple sandals on his feet, and carried a thick ash cane clutched in his hand. Ranulf was walking towards them.

'Tell your manservant, Sir Hugh, that I am no threat.'

A vein-streaked hand pushed back the cowl. Corbett saw a black, bushy moustache and beard, a balding head, a harsh face but one with merry eyes crinkled in amusement. Corbett found the stench of putrefaction from the coffin unbearable. He got to his feet.

'I am Brother Cosmas, parish priest of St Oswald's-in-the-Trees. Lady Madeleine told me who you were.' The Franciscan's smile widened, revealing yellow, jagged teeth. 'Well, not her precisely, but the blessed Sister Veronica who, in a former life, must have been a town herald.'

Corbett grinned. He had always liked Franciscans: their devotion to the poor, their rough and ready ways and their blunt, straightforward speech.

'I come here for provisions,' the friar continued. 'Anything I can beg and Lady Madeleine loves acting the lady of the manor. In Paradise I am sure she will be given a position of rank, organising the angels!' He nodded at the corpse. 'The smell's terrible.'

Corbett pulled down the bandage round his nose and mouth and nodded in agreement.

'You seem unperturbed, Brother.'

'What's the body but a bag of blood?' the Franciscan replied. 'The soul it housed has gone.' His eyes softened. 'Poor bairn. And, to answer your question bluntly, Sir Hugh, I have been a soldier, a barber surgeon in the King's wars. I've seen more corpses than I'd like to count. We humans love killing, don't we?' He crouched down beside the coffin, muttered words from the Requiem and sketched a cross in the air. 'An arrow wound.' He pointed to the throat. 'A good marksman.'

'You know about archery, Brother?'

'I was a master bowman in the King's armies. Always aim for the neck I was told. The head, the chest, the belly, they are protected. But there's no cure for a piece of steel in the windpipe. She must have died instantly. Do you want any help, King's clerk?'

Corbett pulled the bandage back up. He felt slightly nauseous and wished to be away from this paltry grave and its grisly cadaver. Assisted by the Franciscan, he turned the body over. From under the yew tree he heard Ranulf cough and curse as the smell wafted across but he grimly pressed on. He pulled the rope up to examine the back and front of the corpse.

No marks except a brand on the shoulder, in the form of a lily. The mark was old and peeled. The corpse was placed back and the gauze veil pulled down. Corbett had to walk away to take the air while the Franciscan, grasping a piece of stone, hammered the lid back on.

Corbett reached the yew tree, took off the cloth and watched a bird skim over the herbal plots. A thrush, he wondered? He tried to concentrate on something pleasant. Ranulf went to speak but Corbett just shook his head. The Franciscan finished and strode across.

'It won't be left there, will it?'

'No, the lay brothers will put it back.'

Corbett squinted up at him. 'Do you know anything of her death, Brother?'

The Franciscan shook his head. 'Nothing! I don't even recognise her and I know most faces in these parts. A strange death,' he continued. 'Rumour has it that her body was buried but then dug up and left at the priory gates.' He studied Corbett carefully. 'I saw you once, you know? Years ago on the Welsh march. They said you were a moody bugger but the King's trusted clerk.'

Ranulf stifled a laugh.

'And this must be your manservant? The one who has got devil's eyes and hair to match. Two of the King's bully-boys, eh?'

'I'm a royal clerk,' Corbett replied. 'And I am still a moody bugger. However, I dispense the King's justice and that remains the same, constant.'

'Does it now? Does it now? In which case I must introduce you to one of my parishioners: Robert Verlian, chief verderer to Lord Henry Fitzalan, now deceased. He's taken sanctuary in my church. It was either that or Sir William would have strung him up from the nearest tree.'

'Is he innocent?' Corbett asked.

'He says he is.'

'And what do you think, Brother? I mean, you've set yourself up as a judge of other people.'

The Franciscan laughed and clapped Corbett on the back.

'Well said, royal clerk.' He beat his breast. '*Mea culpa, mea culpa*, I have sinned. If you are the royal judge in these parts, Verlian has some chance. Yes, he says he's innocent and, yes, I think he is. Will you come and visit him?'

'I'll do better than that,' Corbett replied. 'I carry the royal warrant of Oyer and Terminer. I have the right to set up a court and hear any cases.'

'And so you want to use my church?'

'Yes, it would save a lot of time. And I will name you as a royal witness. I'd prefer St Oswald's than anywhere else. Now. I'll wash my hands and face and see if Lady Madeleine will have words with me.'

'In which case I'll say goodbye.' The Franciscan clasped Corbett's hand. 'You are for my lady's parlour and I'm for the kitchen to beg some scraps.'

'Oh, Brother!'

Cosmas turned.

'You went to Beauclerc hunting lodge the night before Lord Henry was killed?'

'Yes, just for a short while. I warned him against his harsh enforcement of the forest laws.'

'And on the morning he was killed?'

'I was praying, clerk, as I always do!' And the Franciscan walked away.

A short while later Corbett, his hands and face scrubbed clean, a half-cup of red wine settling his stomach, was ushered across the cobbled yard and into the comfortable parlour of the prioress's house. The room was wood-panelled, carved in the linen fashion. This stretched three quarters of the way up the wall; above it the plaster was a washed pink. Small pictures in ornate gold frames were placed along the walls above the panelling. Each contained scenes from the life of the Virgin Mary. Carpets of pure wool were laid across the scrubbed paving stones. Coffers, cupboards, chairs and benches were arranged round the room. The prioress's desk stood before the main bay window which looked out over her own private garden. Lady Madeleine was seated behind it, dictating to another sister who sat at a high desk to her right. When Corbett and Ranulf came in, Lady Madeleine dismissed the sister; she did not rise to greet them but waved Corbett to a rather high stool on the other side of the desk. Ranulf she ignored.

'You've seen what you had to?' she asked.

Corbett ignored the stool but stood, arms folded, looking down at her while Ranulf leaned against the door and whistled softly under his breath. He intended to annoy and it had the desired effect. Lady Madeleine, looking daggers at him, pushed back her chair so she was forced to look up at Corbett.

'You have questions for me, master clerk?'

'No, my lady, the King has questions for you. Your brother's death?'

'He was killed while hunting,' Lady Madeleine replied tartly. 'He loved blood, did Henry. Blood and destruction! Showing off, as he always did, to his French visitors.'

'You are not the grieving sister?'

'Half-sister, master clerk!'

'But still not grieving?'

'Grief is a private thing. Lord Henry lived in his world and I in mine.'

'And you have no knowledge of his death?'

'I beg your pardon?'

Corbett stared coolly back. 'Why should someone want your brother dead?'

Lady Madeleine threw her head back and laughed.

'Master clerk, you have seen our church, yes? I could fill the nave with people who wanted him dead. His cruelty, his lechery. Oh, I grieve for him, for the boy he once was as well as his immortal soul.'

'You were informed of his death immediately?'

'I was here in my own chamber when Sir William sent a messenger.' Her face softened. 'I am sorry, Sir Hugh.' She gripped the edge of the desk. 'Look.' She pointed to a chair in the far corner. 'Would you like to sit? Some wine?'

Corbett went across and pulled the chair over.

'Your sisters in the kitchen were most kind,' he replied, settling himself. 'But my stomach is still queasy after what I have seen. So, you cannot help me with your brother's death or that of the young woman whose corpse I have viewed?'

Lady Madeleine shook her head.

'Did you meet Lord Henry often?'

'Sometimes I would visit Ashdown Manor. When I travelled to Rye, he or Sir William would accompany me. We have property there managed by a steward.'

'The priory is wealthy,' Corbett confirmed.

'On certain afternoons we open the gates to pilgrims. Their offerings are generous,' she replied, glaring at Ranulf, who was still whistling softly.

Corbett glanced across, winked and the whistling stopped.

'Did Sir Henry believe in St Hawisia, I mean her relic?'

'Henry believed in nothing!'

'But he refurbished the shrine?'

'The Fitzalans have always maintained it!'

'But it was generous of him to do it?'

Lady Madeleine yawned. 'I nagged him.' She put her hand to her mouth, stifling another yawn. 'Henry always had to be nagged to do his duty.'

'And this Owlman?' Corbett asked.

'Yes, I know about him. I suspect he is the killer rather than poor Verlian.'

'What makes you think that?'

'I believe the Owlman is someone from Lord Henry's past,' she continued. 'Both Henry and William were feckless young men. They seduced and they lechered to their hearts' content. No man's sister, wife, daughter, even mother, was safe from them.'

'You know of this?'

'I heard stories. Rumours of a young wife who hanged herself somewhere on the outskirts of Rye.'

'Do you know what the Rose of Rye is?' Corbett asked.

'Ah yes.' Her fingers flew to her lips. 'Lord Henry

mentioned that. The Owlman left messages, asking if he remembered such a name.'

'And did Lord Henry?'

'Yes, I think he did. What's more, I think William does as well.' She paused. 'I heard a vague rumour about a tavern or alehouse called the Red Rose. It's supposed to have stood on the road leading out of Rye. It was owned by a married couple, a taverner and his pretty young wife. According to the gossip, Henry and William stayed there years ago. Henry is said to have seduced her, made the young wife his mistress, but then abandoned her.'

'And?' Corbett asked.

He started as a black shape jumped on Lady Madeleine's lap. The cat was black as night; it nestled, purring deep in its throat.

'Now, now, Lucifer.' Lady Madeleine stroked it gently. 'My constant companion.' She smiled. 'The scourge of our mice and other vermin.'

'The young wife?'

'According to the gossip, she committed suicide, hanged herself from a beam in the taproom. I had entered the priory when that occurred. Father, then in his last years, hastily covered the story up.'

'How long ago was this?'

'Oh, it must be some twenty or twenty-five years. They say that the ghost of the young woman haunted that tavern, so the name was changed.'

'And this Owlman could be the dead woman's husband?'

'It's possible.'

'And the corpse which lies buried in your churchyard?' Corbett asked. 'You know nothing of her?'

'Nothing. Nothing.'

'She never visited here?'

'I've told you, Sir Hugh, I know nothing.'

Corbett chewed the corner of his lip. 'She had a lily, like a brand mark, on her shoulder.'

Lady Madeleine shook her head. 'Sir Hugh, I cannot help you.'

'And His Highness the Prince of Wales visits here?'

'The shrine of St Hawisia is visited by many nobles. The King himself has been here.'

'And the King comes with a retinue?'

'One or two of his household.'

'But no man comes here unannounced?'

Lady Madeleine coloured. 'Sir Hugh, you go too far! But why do you ask that?'

'I am sorry,' Corbett apologised. 'But the King demands answers to the mysteries here, my lady, and I have to deliver them.' He got to his feet and bowed. 'I thank you for your time and courtesy. If there are further questions, I shall, of course, return.'

Lady Madeleine didn't answer. She picked up a quill from the ink pot and pulled across a piece of vellum as if returning to her duties.

'Then I bid you farewell, Sir Hugh. One of the sisters will show you to the stables.'

A short while later Corbett and Ranulf left the priory. They took directions from one of the lay brothers and found the forest path which would lead them back to the Devil-in-the-Woods tavern.

'A high born lady,' Ranulf commented. 'Full of arrogance and a liar to boot!'

'What do you mean?' Corbett reined back his horse.

'Master, with all due respect, Edward of Carnarvon may be many things, but a pilgrim?' Ranulf snorted with laughter. 'If he came here, he's up to devilry and we both know that. But,' he continued, 'at least we know who the Owlman is.'

'I wonder?' Corbett mused. 'This is a murky pool, Ranulf. The Fitzalans had their secrets and they won't be dragged to the top of the mire without a great deal of struggle and hard work.'

They arrived back at the tavern just after midday. Labourers, peasants from the fields, verderers and charcoal-burners had all flocked in. They sat around the cobbled yard, backs to the wall, sunning themselves. A group were laying wagers on a dog baiting a badger. A huckster selling pilgrims' badges, gewgaws, ribbons and laces, wandered about the yard, trundling his little cart before him. A pickpocket who had been expelled from the town of Rye was sitting by the well bathing the tips of his ears where the town bailiffs had clipped them. Grooms and ostlers brought horses and pack ponies in and out of the stables. At the far end, the small dovecote was being cleaned and the pungent smell of dung filled the yard, raising protests from those eating their midday bread and cheese.

Corbett and Ranulf handed their horses over to a groom and walked into the spacious taproom. The ceiling was of timbered rafters, the stone floor covered in thick green rushes. At the far end shutters and doors had been opened allowing in the fragrance from the tavern's herb gardens. Flitches of ham, hunks of bacon, and even cheeses in white linen cloths hung from the rafters to be cured. Despite the fair day, a roaring fire burned in the hearth and a sweating tapboy slowly turned the spit on which a huge side of pork had been fixed. Beside him a little girl, braving the heat, ladled a thick herb sauce over the crackling meat. The sweet smell filled the taproom and even Corbett found his mouth watering at the delicious aroma. The taverner, a fat-bellied, balding, deep-eyed man, came striding across. He recognised good custom when he saw it and was eager to please these envoys from the court.

'The pork will be done in a trice,' he told them. 'I recommend it, sirs! A jug of our ale, some port and the best bread you'll find this side of Rye.'

Corbett agreed and the taverner ushered them over to a more private table, as he put it, near the window. Corbett and Ranulf took off their sword belts and sat on the benches. Corbett ordered the taverner to bring three ales, one for himself. Then he gestured at a stool beside him.

'Do you have any important visitors here? I mean, of good quality?'

'They come and go,' the taverner replied cautiously.

'Anyone mysterious?' Corbett asked.

'Well, sir, this is Ashdown Forest. The roads are often used by those travelling between the coast and London, if they decide not to travel by Canterbury. We have scholars, sailors, the usual beggars, pilgrims and merchants.'

'You know what I am asking!' Corbett demanded. 'Anyone of note? Cloaking themselves in mystery, paying good gold and silver to be left alone.'

'We have outlaws,' the taverner said. 'Wolfs-heads.'

Corbett sighed in exasperation. 'Anyone else?'

The taverner glanced away.

'And the Prince of Wales has been here?'

'Yes, he took the best chamber on the first gallery, the one which has a four-poster bed and woollen rugs on the floor.'

'I'm not interested in your furnishings!' Corbett said. 'Was there anyone else here when the Prince arrived?'

'There was one,' the fellow replied quickly. 'Tall, blondish hair, soft hands. He walked with a swagger. A knight, I think. He spoke in a cultured way but rarely showed his face down here.'

'I wager he didn't,' Corbett replied drily. 'He would also take a chamber on the first gallery and pay you well for food to be brought to his room.'

The taverner gaped in astonishment at this dark-eyed clerk.

'How did you know?'

'Did this knight show any insignia?' Corbett asked. He tapped the man on his bulbous nose. 'I wager a silver coin to a gold one that he did. A red eagle with two heads?' He pressed the toe of his boot on Ranulf's foot as he stirred in surprise.

'Yes, yes, he did.' The taverner was now frightened. 'He kept himself well hidden, dressed like a monk in dark cloak and cowl. But, on his chamber table, I saw a ring which bore the escutcheon you describe.'

Corbett slipped a silver coin across the table.

'You've nothing to fear,' he told the nervous man. 'I assure you, you've done no wrong. This stranger was here while the Prince of Wales visited the tavern?' Mine host nodded, fingers now covering the silver piece.

'And he left shortly after the Prince did?'

'Yes, he was on pilgrimage to St Hawisia's.'

Corbett picked up the tankard and sipped from it, licking the white foam from his lips. He recalled the cadaver he'd studied so carefully earlier that day.

'And you've heard about the corpse?' he asked. 'The young woman?'

'Ah yes, the one left outside St Hawisia's priory. I wager it fair gave those nuns a shock!'

'She was a stranger round here, wasn't she?'

'Oh yes. If any young wench from the forest villages had gone missing, the hue and cry would be raised. It would be "Harrow! Harrow!" throughout the forest.'

'So, if she was a traveller or a pilgrim,' Corbett continued, 'she must have stopped here?'

'Not necessarily.'

'Oh, come, come, master taverner. Young women just don't walk along forest trackways, naked as the day they were born. I have seen this woman's flesh, it's soft, that of a lady of quality.'

'She may well have been,' the taverner replied. 'But, sir, she didn't stop here. Describe her to me!'

Corbett gave the best description he could; the taverner shook his head and held up his right hand.

'You can put me on oath before the local coroner, sir. I've never seen or heard of such a person.'

Another silver piece appeared between Corbett's fingers. He played with it, moving it along the back of his hand, a trick much envied by Ranulf.

'You are very generous, sir. But, give me all the silver in the kingdom's exchequer, I still can't say I met someone I didn't.'

'No, Master . . . ?'

'Taybois. Edmund Taybois.'

'It's something else I want to ask you. Well, a number of things to be exact. The Owlman?'

The taverner laughed, a deep growl in his throat,

his eyes never leaving the silver coin on the back of Corbett's hand.

'He's like the flies in summer, sir. He's a nuisance but he doesn't trouble us.'

'Does he come here for sustenance?'

'Never. I mean, sir, he'd be a fool to come into this taproom, say, I'm the Owlman and can I have some venison to eat?'

Corbett flicked the coin and caught it.

'No, sir, I was thinking more of the dead of night, when prying eyes and ears are closed.'

'We are named the Devil-in-the-Woods tavern, sir, but we don't give sustenance to outlaws.' The taverner scraped back his stool and made to rise.

Ranulf leaned over and squeezed him gently on the shoulder.

'You rise when my master tells you.'

The taverner sighed. 'I meant no offence.'

'None taken,' Corbett replied. 'Now, sir, the Fitzalans, your taproom last night was fair full of gossip about them.'

'The Fitzalans come from the devil and, as far as I am concerned, they can return to him.' The taverner sipped from his blackjack of ale.

'What do you mean?'

'Lords of the soil, sir, they don't bother the likes of us.'

'Are you a free man, Master Edmund?'

'I am a yeoman, sir. I own this tavern and the fields beyond. I pay my taxes. I'm an upright man.

I'm an honest taverner and I show charity to those who need it.'

Corbett studied the taverner's fat, thickset features.

'But you were an archer once. I can tell from the calluses on your fingers. You've pulled back a bow many a time?'

'Aye, sir, and I buy my venison from those who sell it. I don't go hunting in the greenwood.'

Corbett tapped his blackjack against the taverner's.

'Then God bless you, sir. How long have you been a taverner?'

'Like my father before me.'

'You are a member of a guild?'

'Aye. We meet at Christmas and Easter, usually at one of the ports, Winchelsea or Rye.'

'Have you ever heard of the Red Rose?' Corbett asked. 'A tavern which stood on the outskirts of Rye?'

'No, sir, but I think I know someone who has.' The taverner finished off his blackjack and got to his feet. 'And that silver coin will be mine?'

Corbett tossed it over. 'It's yours already.'

The taverner led them out through the back door and across the garden. In the far corner was an orchard of apple and pear trees. One of the pot boys was there, picking up the fallen fruit and placing it gently into baskets. Beyond the orchard, surrounded by a small garden, stood a thatched cottage. An old man sat sunning himself on the stool outside its door, carefully munching on one of the pears.

'My father,' the taverner said. 'We call him the Ancient One.'

Corbett could see why. The old man looked as old as Methuselah with his lined, seamed face, milky-blue eyes, scrawny beard and moustache. He peered up as they approached.

'Is that you, son?'

'It is, oh Ancient One of days,' the taverner replied jokingly. 'I've brought visitors.'

'I'm ninety-five years of age,' the old man cackled. 'Do you realise that? I remember the King's grandfather, John Lackland. He came through Ashdown when he was on his way to Runnymede. I've seen them all. They call me the Ancient One but my memory's still good.' His smile widened in a display of half-munched pear. 'But I always says, it's not what's between your ears, but between your legs, which counts.' He peered at the ring on Corbett's right hand. 'You are a King's clerk, aren't you?'

Corbett crouched down.

'Father.' He touched the old man's hand. 'It is good to see you.'

'Plums,' the Ancient One replied. 'It's autumn now and there'll be damsons ripe and full like a young maid's tits.'

Corbett marvelled at this old man, who must have been a lad when King John led his armies against his barons.

'What is it you want?' The old man's head came forward like a bird.

'Father, did you know a tavern called the Red Rose outside the town of Rye?'

'I knew a wench we called Red Rose. She lived in Rye. We called her Red because that's the colour she painted her tits.'

'A tavern, Father?' Corbett insisted. 'Owned by a young man and his wife. She killed herself.'

'Ah, I remember that.' The old man tapped the side of his nose. 'People tell me everything. There was such a tavern, but it's now called the Golden Cresset. It was a brothel once you know, in the King's father's time, often visited by the soldiers, then it changed hands. The sheriff cleaned it up. A young man owned it, yes, that's right, Alwayn, Alwayn Rothmere and his wife, I think she was called Katherine. Well, the Fitzalan boys used to visit it. One thing led to another.'

'This was about twenty or twenty-five years ago,' Corbett interrupted.

'They were just lads at the time. All mouth and cock,' the Ancient One declared. 'Henry was the bad one. Not a bodice he didn't rip or a petticoat he wouldn't lift. He acted the young lord, nimble on his feet, quick of wit and sharp of eye. He seduced her. Alwayn found out, so the poor girl killed herself, stepped on a table she did then hanged herself.'

'And Alwayn, he disappeared?' Corbett asked.

'No, he didn't disappear. You've only been told

half the story.' The old man cackled and peered at his son. 'I don't think I've told you this, have I? Alwayn found the corpse and took her down.' The old man sniffed. 'Then he hanged himself in the same place.' He must have glimpsed the astonishment on Corbett's face. 'Both gone,' he murmured sadly. 'Into the dark! I am sure they were there to greet Lord Henry.'

Chapter 7

Corbett and Ranulf left the Ancient One and walked back into the tavern. Mine host hurried off to cut slices of pork.

'My, my, my,' Ranulf exclaimed as they took their seats. 'If the King knew of this, he would have one of his royal rages.'

'The King will know of this,' Corbett replied. 'It would appear that Gaveston, who is supposed to be exiled, has now returned to England and is hiding in these parts.'

'That's why the Prince of Wales wanted to see us, wasn't it?'

'Yes, I think it was. Sir William Fitzalan is one of the Prince of Wales' coterie. I suspect, at the Prince's insistence, Sir William brought Gaveston up into Ashdown. He stayed here where he was arrogant enough to wear his insignia. I also believe he was Lady Madeleine's secret visitor. The Prince of Wales, full of false piety, came to Ashdown, ostensibly to hunt or pray at the famous shrine; but secretly, he was meeting his lover.'

Ranulf stared back alarmed.

'If the King heard that,' he replied, 'your friendship, Sir Hugh, would not save you.'

'The King knows the truth,' Corbett replied drily. 'The Prince of Wales is a man who likes the best of both worlds. Oh, he'll marry whatever princess is trotted out.' Corbett's voice dropped to a whisper. 'I suspect the true love of his life is, and always will be, the Gascon Piers Gaveston.'

'And he sheltered here?' Ranulf asked.

'Here and in the priory.'

'And the other matter?'

'I am disappointed,' Corbett said. 'I really did think the Owlman was the husband of the young woman who killed herself at the Red Rose, but both are dead, so I have to think again.'

'Lady Madeleine has to answer a few questions.'

'She has more to answer than she thinks. You saw that hair, Ranulf? Do you think it's a genuine relic?'

'The world is full of trickery, master. Aren't there oils, potions, herbal concoctions which could keep it supple and fresh?'

They paused as the tavern keeper brought back traunchers with strips of crackling pork, freshly cut bread and some leeks and onions, diced and sprinkled with marjoram.

'You made the Ancient One's day,' he told them. 'But the other matter?' He glanced nervously at Corbett and the clerk wondered if mine host had known the identity of his secret visitor all the time.

'Act the innocent,' Corbett advised. 'And innocent you'll stay.'

The tavern keeper smiled and walked away. Corbett drew his knife, took a horn spoon from his wallet and began to cut up the pork.

'Are you the King's emissary?'

Corbett stared and turned. The young woman appeared as if out of nowhere. She was dressed in a sea-green cloak, fringed at the hem with red stitching. It covered her from neck to toe though Corbett glimpsed muddy-toed boots peeping out beneath. Yet it was her face which fascinated him. With the hair piled back beneath a dark-grey veil, it was so composed, so perfect she reminded him of a life-like statue of the Virgin Mary he had once seen in a church outside Paris. She was olive-skinned, blue-eyed, with a perfect nose and red lips slightly parted displaying white and even teeth. She held Corbett's stare.

'Am I wasting your time, sir? I understand you are Sir Hugh Corbett, the King's emissary.'

Corbett rose and pulled across a stool. He took the young woman's gloved hand and gestured that she sit.

'You are Alicia Verlian?'

The beautiful face broke into a smile.

'How did you know?'

Corbett pointed to the cloak. 'I suppose that hides a multitude of sins. You've left your house rather urgently. You've ridden along a muddy trackway so I wonder which woman would want to seek me out so urgently. I tell a lie. I've heard of your beauty.'

Corbett smiled at Ranulf, only to be shocked at the change in his manservant. Ranulf was never lost for words but now he sat like a man stricken: eyes staring, mouth gaping, a piece of meat, poised on his knife, half-raised to his mouth.

'Ranulf!'

Ranulf closed his mouth and lowered his knife but his eyes never left Alicia's face.

'My servant is tired,' Corbett explained.

Alicia smiled at Ranulf. 'You've certainly been upsetting people,' she said softly. 'It's common gossip both here and among the forest folk. Sir William came storming back to the manor and his servants were all agog.'

'You want some wine?' Corbett asked.

'No, sir, I want justice.' The young woman's head came up, eyes bright and hard. 'Lord Henry was a lecher, God rest him.'

Other customers turned. Corbett gave them a warning look and they went back to their meals.

'Lower your voice, madam.'

'Lord Henry was a lecher!' This time her voice was louder. 'A cruel and vicious man who received due punishment. God's justice has been done.'

'But not for your father,' Corbett replied evenly.

'My father is innocent of any crime.'

'But he was not with the hunt!'

'Neither was Sir William.'

'Your father fled?'

'Any man of wit would have done!' she replied. 'He was not with Lord Henry when he was killed. It was well known we had justifiable grievances against Lord Henry. If Sir William had caught my father, he would have hanged him out of hand.'

'And now your father shelters in St Oswald's?'

'He shelters, sir, because that is the only place which will protect him, until royal justice is done.'

'You can continue to shout at me,' Corbett told her. He put his fingers on her leather-gloved hand; she did not withdraw it. 'While I am here,' he went on, studying those beautiful eyes, 'no man will be hanged, no sentence carried out till the truth is known.'

'Pilate asked what was truth. He was a judge.'

'My name is not Pilate. It's Sir Hugh Corbett. The truth will be discovered by careful questioning.'

'Such as?'

'Where was your father when the hunt was taking place?'

Alicia swallowed hard. 'My father was with the others, the verderers.'

'No, he wasn't. He was with you, wasn't he?'

Alicia blinked and nodded. 'My father was terrified that Lord Henry would use the hunt, and his absence, to slip back and . . .'

'Meet you?'

'No, Sir Hugh, accost me! Kick down the door, force himself upon me. As he tried to do on numerous occasions. I was frightened. My father was agitated. He came back to our house on the estate. I told him all would be well, then he left, hurrying back before he was missed.'

'And during that time Lord Henry was killed?'

'My father arrived at Savernake Dell shortly after the assassin struck. He took one look at what had happened and ran back to me. He wanted to flee, reach one of the ports, Rye, Winchelsea, go abroad.' The young woman paused. 'I refused. I said it was unjust to flee from a crime of which we were both innocent.'

'Why didn't you flee before?' Corbett asked.

'Sir Hugh, where could we go? My father is a verderer. The roads are full of landless families while Lord Henry's arm was both strong and very long. Why should we give up our lives because of his lust?'

'Are you glad he's dead?'

'He can burn in Hell for what he did to me and my father.'

'And now?' Corbett asked.

'Sir William is one of the same stock. But, deep in

his heart, I think he's shamed by what his brother did.'

'And so, why have you come to me?'

'My father's in sanctuary.'

'You can still visit him.'

'For how long?'

'Tomorrow,' Corbett replied quickly. 'Tomorrow I will hold court in St Oswald's church. I will summon all those involved in this matter and search out the truth. Is that not correct, Ranulf?'

Corbett was now alarmed by his manservant: he hadn't touched his food or uttered one syllable but stared fixedly at Alicia. Usually, in the presence of a pretty young woman, Ranulf was all merry-eyed and quick-witted, ever ready to flirt. Now he sat like a moonstruck calf, though Alicia seemed not to notice.

'I must return.' She moved back the stool and rose.

'I . . . I will see you to your horse.'

Ranulf pushed his trauncher away and rose like a sleepwalker. He took the young woman's arm and gently escorted her across the taproom and out to the stable yard. A groom led across a sorry-looking cob, the saddle across its back battered and worn. Ranulf made an angry gesture with his hand and grabbed the reins himself. He then helped Alicia up into the saddle.

'You ride like a man?' He found the question stilted and clumsy. He just wished this young woman would notice him and not ride away. She glanced down.

'You must be Ranulf-atte-Newgate?'

'Yes,' he answered in a rush. 'Senior clerk in the Chancery of the Green Wax.'

She smiled. 'Do you always stare at women?'

Ranulf rubbed sweat-soaked hands on his jerkin. 'I've never seen anyone like you before.'

Alicia laughed. 'With two heads!'

'No, you've only got one,' Ranulf replied seriously. He grabbed the reins again and stared fiercely up at her. 'Your father's innocent,' he said hoarsely. 'He must be innocent.' He caught the look of disquiet in her eyes. 'No, no, you wait and see. Old Master Long Face in there, I mean Sir Hugh, he will discover the truth.'

'Are you looking for a bribe?' she asked sweetly. 'Is that why you are here, Ranulf-atte-Newgate? Are you like the rest, your brains in your hose?'

Ranulf blushed. 'You misunderstand me, madam.'

'Do I now? I have never misunderstood a man in my life! All sweetness and light, ready to play Cat's-Cradle?'

'That is not the case!' Ranulf snapped, spots of anger high on his cheeks. He was mystified, baffled by what was happening, but the young woman's face, her mannerisms, the shifting moods in those eyes, entranced him. Ranulf quietly cursed. He was tongue-tied. Strange, the woman reminded him of

Lady Maeve, Corbett's wife: she had the same effect. If he was honest, Ranulf felt overawed, even frightened, and this made him angry. He, Ranulf-atte-Newgate, clerk, bully-boy, fighting man! Alicia was still studying him.

'You are telling the truth, aren't you?' she said quietly. 'You really don't mean any offence? I've never seen a man blush before.' She gathered the reins up. 'I am sorry if I was brusque.'

She stretched out a hand. Ranulf seized it and kissed the back of the leather glove. He glanced up. Alicia glimpsed the passion in his eyes and withdrew her hand.

'They said your master was a strange one. But he keeps even stranger company.' She raised a hand. 'I bid you adieu, Master Ranulf-atte-Newgate.'

And, turning her horse, she cantered out of the yard. Ranulf watched her go. He felt like running after her, explaining exactly how he felt. Had he done the right thing? Shouldn't he have offered to escort her? He heard a snigger and looked across. Two stable boys were watching him. Ranulf's hand brushed the hilt of the dagger and both boys suddenly remembered they had tasks to do. He walked back into the taproom, where Corbett had finished his meal.

'Ranulf, are you well?' He gestured at the half-full trauncher. 'Won't you finish your meal?'

'I don't feel hungry.'

Corbett got to his feet. 'Ranulf, in God's name,

what is the matter? Do you know that young woman?'

'I wish to God I did!'

'Ah, that's it!' Corbett put a hand gently on his shoulder. 'Ranulf-atte-Newgate, the terror of the ladies, the man who even thought of becoming a priest!'

'Don't taunt me!'

'I'm not taunting you.' Corbett's hand fell away. 'It happens, Ranulf, it always happens as a terrible shock, and like death, we never know when.'

He studied Ranulf's face, which looked paler than usual. Two red spots burned high in his cheeks, a rare sign when Ranulf was disturbed or agitated; his green cat-eyes gleamed as if he had been drinking.

'There's a time and a place,' Corbett said. He took Ranulf by the arm and led him out through the taproom into the garden. 'Always remember, Ranulf, the garden is the best place to plot.' He grinned. 'As well as to pay court. No listening ears, no watching eyes.'

They sat on a turfed seat. Corbett took his chancery ring and moved it so the sun glinted in the reflection.

'What do we have here, Ranulf? Sunbeams or substance? Shadows or something more tangible? It's the old dance, isn't it? Whenever a murder takes place, people tell you what they want you to hear, make you see what they want you to see.' He nudged his companion sharply. 'Less of the lovelorn squire. Where is the keen-witted clerk of the Green Wax? Item.' Corbett used his fingers to emphasise the points he made. 'Lord Henry Fitzalan is very rich, powerful, disliked by all and sundry and he is killed during a hunt.' He glanced at Ranulf but his manservant's mind was elsewhere. 'Item,' Corbett continued. 'Lord Henry was disliked by his younger brother over whose purse strings he kept strict control. Sir William was not present when Lord Henry was killed. Item – we have Robert Verlian, chief verderer. He hated Lord Henry for his lecherous intentions to his daughter. He, too, was not present when his lord was killed and inexplicably flees. Item – Sir William seems intent on placing the blame fairly on Verlian's shoulders. Item – St Hawisia is now standing in that carp pond over there. Don't you agree, Ranulf?'

'Yes, yes, of course!'

'Ranulf!' Corbett exclaimed. 'You are not listening to a word I am saying.'

The woebegone clerk mumbled an apology. Corbett secretly wondered if this was the first time the notorious Ranulf-atte-Newgate had been so smitten.

'Item – we know that Sir William has been assisting his lord, the Prince of Wales. He probably brought Gaveston into Ashdown. He was helped in this by his sister, the indomitable Lady Madeleine. I suspect the man Sister Fidelis observed slipping into Lady Madeleine's house was no less a person than the Gascon favourite. He probably sheltered in the priory waiting for the Prince of Wales to arrive. And?'

'Item – ' Ranulf spoke up. 'We have an outlaw, a wolfs-head. He seems to do little damage but he has waged a vexatious war against Lord Henry, despatching cryptic messages, making reference to the "Rose of Rye". We now know the owners of that tavern killed themselves, the result of Lord Henry's lechery.'

'Good,' Corbett mused. 'Item – we have the corpse of the young woman killed by an arrow to the throat. Her naked body is buried in the forest; it is later dug up and placed outside the priory gates. Item – we have a number of local notables whom we would like to interrogate more closely. The Franciscan, Brother Cosmas, had no love for his dead manor lord and we know he was an archer.'

'So is our taverner,' Ranulf interrupted. 'We also have this hermit. He may have known, seen or heard something.'

'True,' Corbett agreed. 'But there's one person missing, isn't there? Or rather two. This mysterious physician Pancius Cantrone. What was his relationship to Lord Henry?'

'And who else?' Ranulf asked.

'Why, most learned of clerks, the lady we have just met.'

Ranulf started.

'Don't jump like a hare in March.' Corbett patted

him on the knee. 'And don't let your wits be fuddled. Alicia Verlian is a redoubtable young woman. I would wager that she can draw a bow and hit the mark.'

'But she was at home the morning Lord Henry was killed!'

'No, Ranulf, her father said he left her there. How do we know she didn't follow, take a bow and quiver of arrows with her? We do know that someone left such weapons in one of the hollow oaks. She also has a horse. She could murder as quickly and expertly as anyone else.'

'I don't think so.' Ranulf set his mouth in a stubborn challenge.

'Fine, fine,' Corbett replied softly. 'But let's keep up the hunt, Ranulf. What else do we know?'

'That the King is not being truthful with us.'

'Yes.'

'And why did the French want Lord Henry to lead the English envoys to France? In the main,' Ranulf concluded, 'that's the challenge which faces us.'

Corbett got to his feet. 'So, I will leave you to think sweet thoughts and compose a poem. Tonight we journey to Ashdown Manor. It harbours all our opponents.' Corbett rubbed his hands. 'And, of course, there's one name I must not forget, my arch-enemy, that Lucifer in the flesh, Seigneur Amaury de Craon.'

Corbett strode back into the tavern. Ranulf watched him go and then put his face in his hands.

He couldn't understand what was happening. One minute he was eating his food, the next he was looking on a face which made his heart skip, his blood race. 'Lecherous and hot as a sparrow' Maltote had once called him. But not now! He felt no spurt of lust! Ranulf just wanted to be with the woman, to sit on a chair and watch the different expressions on that lovely face. Engrossed in this way, Ranulf was hardly aware of the shadow which slipped into the garden and stood beside him until the unexpected guest shuffled his feet and coughed loudly. Ranulf glanced up.

'Ah, Master Baldock. What do you seek?'

'This morning,' the groom replied, 'there was no one to look after your horses. I am a free man . . .'

'You seek employment, Master Baldock?' Ranulf smiled. 'It's possible. But, come, sit down next to me. Tell me all you know about Alicia Verlian.'

The Louvre Palace was the private preserve of Philip IV of France. The gardens around it, with their flower beds and herb plots, orchards, fountains, carp and stew ponds, were the delight of his life. Only he and his close confidants were allowed to walk and rest there. Indeed, members of his household, particularly those who felt the lash of his cutting tongue, were reluctant to accept an invitation to what Philip called his 'Garden of delights'. At the far end of this garden, in its own enclosure, stood what Philip called his 'orchard of the hanged'. Its ancient pears and apple trees carried a different fruit, besides those the good Lord allowed to grow in glorious profusion. Here, Philip's executioners and torturers hanged those guilty of crimes against their royal master: a cook suspected of poisoning; a door-keeper found guilty of selling secrets to foreign merchants; clerks who had been too garrulous in their cups and, above all, English spies whom Amaury de Craon's agents tracked down and captured. The place stank of death. The corpses were gibbeted until the smell became too offensive, at which point Philip would order them to be cut down and buried in the derelict cemetery his torturers called 'Haceldema', a Jewish term for the 'field of blood'. Sometimes Philip would summon suspects there. He would take them by the arm and walk round the trees, pointing to the rotten fruit, describing the crimes and felonies of each miscreant. Such a walk always jogged the memory and loosened the tongue, but this time it had failed.

Philip now sat in his garden bower and looked across at the bloodied, bruised face of Simon Roulles, that perpetual English scholar who had, at last, been caught. Philip, his face impassive, his corn-coloured hair falling down to his shoulders, smoothed his moustache and well-trimmed beard and scrutinised the English spy.

'You are in deep pain?'

Philip's eyes moved to the black-clad torturers

standing behind their victim.

'Monsieur Roulles has been on the wheel?'

The red-masked executioner nodded.

Philip wetted his lips. Roulles was barely conscious. He was lashed by cords to the chair. Philip picked up a napkin and gently dabbed at the streak of blood trickling out of the corner of the Englishman's mouth.

'Do you know, Simon?' he murmured. 'I always wanted to meet you.'

Roulles' lips moved but no sound came out.

'No, no, it's useless.' Philip scratched his head in annoyance. 'It is futile. You do understand my English?' Philip didn't wait for an answer. 'It is futile,' he repeated, 'to claim that you are an English scholar, to demand to be expelled from France on some ship leaving Calais or Boulogne. You carry letters claiming to be a Frenchman. You have a fictitious cousin in the countryside. But it's all lies, it's all shadows. Your master, Sir Hugh Corbett . . .'

'He is not my master!' The words were spat out.

'Of course, he isn't. I do apologise. Edward of England never lets his left hand know what his right hand is doing. Still, you are an English spy. You ferret out secrets and send them back to your Prince.' Philip leaned across and again gently wiped the Englishman's mouth. 'Would you like some wine?'

One of the torturers picked up a jewel-encrusted cup and held it to his victim's lips. Roulles lapped like a dog, allowing the wine to swill round his mouth. He knew it would be the last he ever tasted. His whole body was a sheet of flame. He'd been placed on the wheel and spun round and round while the torturer had struck at his arms and legs, pinching his flesh with burning tongs. The same questions, time and time again. What had he learned? What had Mistress Malvoisin told him? Simon had not broken, confident that the messenger he had despatched to England would already have handed the secret to his royal master.

'I ask you again,' Philip said. 'Or it's back to the wheel. I do not wish that, Monsieur Roulles, I want you to tell us the secret.'

'But, if you know what it is,' Roulles gasped as his lips bubbled blood, 'it is no longer a secret. You do know it, Philip of France.'

The king leaned across the table and smacked him with the back of his hand. The amethyst ring he wore gouged the prisoner's cheek.

'The secret?' he repeated. 'And, if you tell me it, I'll tell you one.'

Roulles attempted to smile. Like a dreamer he kept going in and out of consciousness. Sometimes he was back in Oxford. At others he was in a tavern singing a carol with friends and the snow was falling outside. Or King Edward was walking arm-in-arm with him through the rose gardens of Westminster.

'Do you know Pancius Cantrone?' Philip asked.

Roulles jerked.

'You must know him,' Philip insisted. 'And the scandalous tittle-tattle he depicts as the truth.'

'I know of no such man.'

'Come, come, Master Roulles. Let me refresh your memory. Monsieur Malvoisin, before he died in a most unfortunate boating accident, believed he had learned certain secrets.'

'It's the truth!' the prisoner blurted, fighting a wave of nausea. He must not collapse; if he could only ignore the pain!

'No, no, Monsieur Malvoisin shared this gossip with Signor Cantrone. Somehow or other you discovered it.'

Roulles kept his head down.

'You are going to die,' Philip continued remorselessly. 'Either quickly or at the end of a rope in my orchard.'

Roulles refused to reply.

'What was the secret?' Philip insisted. 'Is that why your master sent you to Paris?' Philip nodded to one of the torturers, who yanked back Roulles' head. 'Lord Henry Fitzalan is dead,' he declared. 'Killed by an arrow to the heart. And as for Signor Cantrone. Well, Seigneur Amaury de Craon is now within breathing distance of him. Or perhaps you'll take comfort that the secrets you discovered have been despatched to England. That pedlar, the chapman, the tinker, the trader, what's his name? Ah yes, Malsherdes. You think Malsherdes reached

Boulogne and took ship to England?'

Roulles tried to concentrate. Despite the agony in mind and body, he thought of little Malsherdes and his pack pony going along the cobbled streets of Paris and out into the countryside.

'You drank with him, didn't you?' Philip continued. 'At an auberge on the Fontainebleau road. Two of you there in the corner, whispering away like children. Malsherdes left.' Philip paused. 'You can have some more wine. Take as much as you wish.' He waited until the prisoner's mouth was full. 'Malsherdes is dead. My men caught him out in the countryside, a quiet place.'

Roulles coughed and spluttered the wine he had drunk. Philip, as gentle as a mother, patted his lips with the blood-soaked napkin.

'However, Malsherdes was faster than we thought. He'd lit a fire for himself. Before we could stop him, your letters were burned, so my men burned him!'

Roulles forced a grin. 'Then you know as much as I do, Philip of France.'

The king leaned back in his throne-like chair and, cocking his head, he half-listened to the songbird imprisoned in a silver cage hanging from the branches of a cherry tree. From another part of the palace he heard the bray of trumpets and realised it must be time for the midday prayer. He was wasting his time here. He nodded to the torturers.

'Take him out! Hang him!'

Roulles was dragged to his feet and bundled out. Philip fastidiously wiped the blood from the goblet's brim and sipped at it. He was glad Fitzalan was dead. There would be no more letters, no hints of blackmail. But Cantrone? Would de Craon kill him? Philip couldn't care less. What was one man's death in the great design? However, he must not give offence to Edward of England! Would Cantrone, whom he would have loved to hang alongside Roulles, bargain with his secret? Or flee? If he bargained, how much trouble would he cause? What scandal would Edward's agents here in Paris or in Avignon fan with their tongues? Philip looked towards the door. Did de Craon have a hand in Fitzalan's death? Had he taken his orders too literally? Philip rubbed the side of his face. He must go and pray, must petition his sainted ancestor Louis that Cantrone's path, and that of the meddlesome clerk Corbett, never crossed.

Chapter 8

Philip would have been pleased at the agitation which now troubled Pancius Cantrone. Indeed, the French king would have prostrated himself in thanksgiving for, on that sunlit autumn afternoon, Pancius Cantrone had only a very short time to live. The Italian, of course, did not know his death was so close. He was just determined to flee England, to escape the French and not to allow the English Crown to use him as a pawn, a bargaining counter with Philip of France.

The Italian physician had visited St Hawisia's priory. He had ostentatiously attended the young novice Sister Fidelis, whose knuckles had swollen up so her fingers looked as if they had been stung by bees. Cantrone had acted the role of professional physician. He'd examined the skin, felt the bone and, even though the young novice was embarrassed, carefully scrutinised her urine lest the swelling had been caused by a malignant disturbance in her body humours. Of course, Lady Madeleine had welcomed him and they had chatted quietly in her chamber, both before and after he had attended the young novice. Pancius Cantrone had then taken a little wine and some sweetmeats in the refectory before collecting his horse. Now he was riding back through the forest paths to Ashdown Manor.

The Italian physician kept his thick woollen cloak tightly around him. He even wore wool-lined gauntlets because, although the English said it was not yet winter, Cantrone felt cold. He hated these gloomy, wet forests and yearned for the lush valleys of Tuscany. Cantrone was determined to flee. He had come to England because Lord Henry had offered him protection. In return Cantrone had whispered the secrets he had learned from Monsieur Malvoisin. Now those secrets came back to haunt him as his horse found its way along the lonely forest paths. Sombre images plagued his mind: black-cowled monks, tapers in their hands, winding their way up a cathedral church; behind them a velvet-draped coffin resting on the shoulders of pall-bearers. The solemn chorus rising and falling like a distant wave with a sequence from the funeral mass. Outside the cathedral mailed horsemen milled about, controlling the crowds.

Cantrone had been in that procession. He'd stood next to Malvoisin. They had watched the royal mourners bend over the wax effigy placed on top of the coffin. Roses had been placed there along with pure white lilies. Malvoisin could apparently stand it no longer. Standing by themselves, he'd turned and whispered, 'Not an infection of the lung.'

'What?' Cantrone had asked.

'Not an infection of the lung,' Malvoisin had repeated, keeping his voice low, speaking out of the corner of his mouth, eyes glittering, rubicund face flushed with wine. 'She was poisoned.'

Cantrone had gone cold but Malvoisin, cunning as ever, had chosen his moment.

'You know that I speak the truth.'

His watery eyes had held those of Cantrone and the Italian physician had given way to the doubts seething within him. Afterwards, when the church was empty and the incense hung like a forgotten prayer, curling up towards the stone ceiling, Cantrone had taken Malvoisin aside.

'If you repeat what you said,' he whispered, 'it's the scaffold for both of us!'

Malvoisin, now sobering up, had glanced nervously around.

'My duties are finished now,' he'd declared. 'I have had enough. It's time for peace, a little quiet.'

Malvoisin had resigned his post in the household. The general expectation was that Cantrone would seek the vacant preferment, but the Italian had studied intrigue as well as physic. He had noticed the men who had followed him to a tavern or stood outside his house when darkness fell. Cantrone knew the signs like a good physician should. He'd packed his coffers and fled in the dead of night. First to Italy and then, by sea, to the English-held city of Bordeaux. Even there he had felt hunted; he was looking further afield when he had met Lord Henry Fitzalan. The English milord needed a physician and, impressed by Cantrone's skill, had offered him a place in his household. Cantrone had quickly accepted. Weeks turned into months. Cantrone discovered Fitzalan was high in the English court, a trusted envoy to France. So, to make his own position more secure, Cantrone had revealed his own dark secrets. Lord Henry Fitzalan seemed delighted. Cantrone had come to trust him, the only person he had ever done in his long, suspicion-laden life. Fitzalan had used those secrets against the French, hinting at what he knew both at meetings and in letters.

Cantrone reined in his horse and raised his eyes to the interlacing branches above.

'I was a fool,' he muttered, 'to put my trust in him!'

Lord Henry had sworn that Cantrone would never have to accompany him to France. However, in the confusion following Fitzalan's death, Cantrone had discovered that, although Lord Henry had given his solemn word, when he reached Rye, Cantrone would not have received sweet kisses and embraces of farewell. Instead he would have been bundled aboard some ship and handed over to the French. In return for what? More influence? More power? A bag of gold? Cantrone dug his heels in and the gentle cob ambled on. How could Lord Henry betray him when he had done so much?

Now Lord Henry was gone and Sir William? A blunt, naive young man, it was he who had unwittingly revealed that when they reached Rye, Cantrone would not have returned to Ashdown Manor. Did Sir William know the dark secret? Would he offer him protection? Cantrone shook his head. He doubted it. Sir William was more interested in clearing every vestige of his brother from his manor. Household retainers, servants, even grooms were being told to seek employment elsewhere.

Cantrone had kept well away from Seigneur Amaury de Craon but, on one occasion, he had caught the French envoy studying him; those cunning eyes had smiled and Cantrone had glimpsed more danger there than in a chamber full of horrors.

Cantrone breathed in then wrinkled his nose at the smell of rotting vegetation. He had been unable to find Lord Henry's Book of Hours, which was the place where he kept all his secrets, but Cantrone had turned, like the snake he was, striking hard and fast, using the information he himself had discovered to earn more gold. He would return to

Ashdown, collect his valuables and be away before nightfall, hide in one of the Channel ports and perhaps go north to Flanders, Hainault or even to the Baltic and German states.

Cantrone could have hugged himself. A simple sentence and he had provoked such suspicion and laughter in Lord Henry's soul, one thing had followed another. Now he had the means to leave!

A sound just to his right made him rein in his horse. He peered among the trees. He was in no danger here. The Owlman, the outlaw, his quarrel was with the Fitzalans, not some Italian physician, while as for the French, Cantrone doubted if they'd strike now. Not here, where they could be detected and cause great scandal.

Cantrone took the small arbalest which hung over the horn of his saddle. Fumbling beneath his cloak, he took out a cruel barbed bolt and placed it in the groove, slowly winching back the cord. He laughed to himself, he was becoming as nervous as a maid!

The afternoon sun streamed through the trees. Birdsong broke the silence. Again a sound came as a rabbit raced across the trackway. Cantrone relaxed. He pulled the bolt out but still gripped the arbalest as he rode on. On the branches above him the leaves were turning a golden brown, a sure sign of autumn, but when the mists came he'd be gone with all this behind him. He pulled down the collar of his white cambric shirt, undoing the clasp at the neck. Little did he know that by this action he presented a clearer target for the archer hidden in the trees. The yew bow bent, the cord pulled back; there was a twang, soft, musical, and the grey-feathered shaft took Cantrone full in the throat. The physician dropped the reins and toppled gently on to the trackway. His horse, a little startled, moved on but then stopped and began to crop at the grass. The archer, garbed in a black cloak, hood and cowl, slipped out of the trees. For a while the figure just crouched, looking carefully up and down the trackway, and then it hurried across to the corpse. Pockets and pouches were emptied. Cantrone's horse was brought back. The corpse was lifted over it and both killer and victim disappeared into the trees.

Sir William's dinner at Ashdown Manor proved to be a magnificent occasion. Corbett and Ranulf had been met by grooms bearing torches on the great broad pathway which wound from the manor gates up to the main door of the beautiful stone and timbered manor house. Retainers wearing the Fitzalan livery had taken their cloaks and war belts then ushered them into the great hall. The walls of this magnificent chamber were half-covered in wooden panelling, the whitewashed plaster above decorated with flags, pennants, shields, pieces of shining armour and costly gold-tasselled drapes. Banners bearing the arms of

France and England, as well as those of Flanders, hung from the rafters. The wooden floor had been swept, polished and covered with the freshest herbs. Silver pots of flowers stood in window embrasures and corners. Whippers-in and grooms kept the dogs well away from the great dais where a large table had been set out covered in green and white samite cloth bearing the costliest cups, goblets, traunchers, plates and ewers all stamped with the Fitzalan crest. Torches and beeswax candles provided light and a pleasing fragrance.

Sir William, seeming decidedly nervous, had met them there, loudly declaring that they should have come sooner while explaining that, though his brother's body had not yet been buried, he would follow the Fitzalan tradition of magnificent generosity. Sir William's hair, moustache and beard had been neatly clipped and oiled. He was dressed in a gold linen gown with a jewel-encrusted belt and wore soft red buskins on his feet. He told them that he was worried that Signor Cantrone had not returned and kept looking over his shoulder to where de Craon and his principal clerk already sat in their places on the dais.

'I understand you know the French envoy,' Sir William said.

'Like my own cousin,' Corbett replied with a smile.

Followed by Ranulf, he swept up on to the dais. De Craon, face wreathed in smiles, rose and came forward to meet him. They clasped hands, embraced, exchanging the kiss of peace.

'Hugh, God save you, we thought you had been killed!'

'God only knows, Amaury, how you must have mourned at such news!'

De Craon stood back.

'You have not aged at all, Sir Hugh. Lady Maeve must take great care of you.'

Corbett studied de Craon's red, thinning hair, yellowing face, straggly beard and moustache. De Craon would have been ugly if it hadn't been for those eyes full of life and cunning. A charming courtier or a cold, ruthless killer? Corbett sometimes felt a slight affection for this most deadly of adversaries; he wondered if de Craon ever felt the same. The Frenchman's face became a mask of concern.

'And yet these are sad times! Lord Henry is dead! Most of my retinue are still lodged outside Rye. We want to return.'

'The King will send someone else,' Corbett replied. 'Sir William here or my lord of Surrey.'

'Would you not come to Paris?' de Craon asked, taking his seat. He smirked at his grey-faced clerk. 'We have so much to show you, Hugh, especially my master's gardens behind the Louvre.'

Sir William came between them and sat down in his great throne-like chair. Corbett decided not to reply. The steward standing nervously behind Sir

William raised his hands. Trumpeters in the gallery at the far end of the hall blew a fanfare and the meal began. Brawn soup; fish in cream sauce; beef; venison; a whole roast swan. One dish followed another, the wine jugs circulating. Sir William strove to be a genial host. The conversation ebbed and flowed like water, ignoring the deeper undercurrents. Most of the chatter was about different courts and chanceries, the funeral arrangements for Lord Henry and the prospects of a lasting peace between England and France once the marriage of Princess Isabella and Prince Edward was consummated.

Ranulf sat picking at his food, his silver-chased goblets of red and white wine already emptied. De Craon noticed this and narrowed his eyes. He asked about the attack in Oxford. This was followed by a general discussion on maintaining the King's peace. Only once did the tensions surface.

'Where is the Italian doctor Cantrone?' de Craon asked. 'I would, so much, like to have words with him.'

Sir William, who had drunk deeply and rather quickly, shrugged. He belched and, picking up scraps of meat, flung them down the hall at the waiting mastiffs.

'If I knew,' he slurred, 'I'd tell you.'

De Craon was about to press him further when the festivities were ended by an arrow which shattered one of the hall windows and buried itself deep in the wooden panelling. Dogs barked and yelped. Retainers hurried in. Sir William sat, mouth open, cup half-raised to his lips.

'We are under attack!' the old steward shouted. 'Man the battlements!'

Corbett wondered if the fellow had drunk too deeply of the wine he had been serving.

'Nonsense!' De Craon leaned back in his chair, laughing with his clerk.

Corbett hurried down the hall. He noticed the scroll of parchment tied with a piece of twine to the arrow shaft.

> The Owlman goes wherever he wishes!
> He does whatever he chooses!
> Remember the Rose of Rye!

Corbett studied the arrow, which was like any other, without distinguishing marks. Sir William had now joined him, slightly unsteady on his feet.

'I need to have words with you, sir,' Corbett said in a low voice. 'About this.' He held the manor lord's gaze. 'About the Owlman and, more importantly, this Italian physician and Piers Gaveston.'

The colour drained from Sir William's face.

'I, I don't know what you mean!' Sir William gasped.

'I want the truth!' Corbett urged. 'My lord, we could play cat and mouse all night.'

He glanced back at the dais where de Craon slouched in his chair. Of Ranulf there was no sign.

'Sir William,' Corbett went on, face close to the manor lord's. 'De Craon is one of the King's greatest enemies and a man who plots my destruction. Forget all the flowery language, the kiss of peace. If de Craon had me alone in an alleyway, it would be a rope round my neck or a dagger in my belly.'

Sir William's face was now damp with perspiration.

'Now, sir, what's it going to be? I cannot blunder round here, in the presence of my enemies, chasing will-o-the-wisps! Will I hear the truth or shall I go out and hire one of your minstrels and listen to his stories?'

Sir William turned round. 'Seigneur de Craon,' he called out. 'This is a petty nuisance.'

De Craon waved a hand and shrugged.

'I must have urgent words with Sir Hugh,' Sir William continued.

'As we all shall, sometime or other!' the Frenchman sang out.

But Sir William, followed by Corbett, was already walking down the hall. They went out along a cloistered walk, then through a door into a clean, paved porchway and up black oaken stairs.

'Your brother's chamber?' Corbett enquired.

Sir William looked as if he was about to refuse. Corbett glanced over his shoulder and quietly cursed Ranulf. He suspected where he had gone, in pursuit of the lovely Alicia Verlian. Sir William went further along the gallery until he stopped at one door, fumbled with some keys and opened it to reveal a lavishly furnished but untidy chamber. Corbett was aware of a large four-poster bed with curtains of dark murrey fringed with gold and silver tassels. Two large aumbries stood on either side of the windowseat, and there were chests and coffers, their lids thrown back. Armour lay piled on a stool. A sword rested in the centre of the broad oaken table. Sir William waved at Corbett to sit on a chair at the far side of this table. He brought across a tray bearing a wine jug and goblets. Corbett refused.

'I have drunk enough, Sir William.'

'But I haven't and, as the scholars say, "*In vino veritas*".' He splashed a cup full to the brim, sat down opposite Corbett and toasted him silently.

'Did you kill your brother?' Corbett began.

'I was emptying my bowels,' Sir William replied. 'I had no hand in his death. My name's William, not Cain!'

'And this woman's corpse found in the forest?'

'Nothing.'

'Why would the woman have a lily stamped on her shoulder?'

Sir William's head went down.

'Come on!' Corbett snapped. 'You've visited the fleshpots like your brother. I half suspect what it is. It's a brand sign for a whore.'

'But not a common bawd. It's usually a brothel keeper or a high-class courtesan.'

'But why the lily?'

Sir William snorted with laughter. 'Sir Hugh,

ride down to Rye and then cross the Narrow Seas to France. The woman must have been French. If what you say is correct, she must have come from Abbeville or Boulogne. The French are more tender with their whores than we English. If a woman is convicted of keeping a disorderly house that's the brand they use. She is king's property, liable to be fined.'

'So, what was she doing in England?' Corbett asked.

'I don't know, Sir Hugh, but, naked, we are all the same, aren't we? The English like whores, the French like whores, the Germans like whores. Even the priests like whores. It's a currency common in every country.' Sir William slammed his wine cup down. 'For God's sake, man! English whores work in France and the French come across to England. Oh, they pose as ladies in distress. For a farmer visiting Rye, Dover or Winchelsea, a French whore is regarded as a delicacy. However, I didn't know this one! I don't know why she was in Ashdown or why someone should loose an arrow at her throat!'

'Did you discover her corpse and leave it outside Hawisia's priory?'

'No, I did not.'

'Or your brother?'

'Henry would never have soiled his hands.'

Corbett leaned back in the chair. He noticed, for the first time, shelves full of calfskin tomes. Some of the bindings, threaded with silver and gold, glowed in the candlelight.

'These were alight when we came in here.' Corbett gestured to one of the candles. 'Aren't you frightened of fire?'

'Sniff the air,' Sir William replied. 'They are pure beeswax. They do not splutter. The holder is bronze, the cap is of copper. A fanciful notion of my brother's.' Sir William gestured around. 'Ashdown is made of stone, the best the Fitzalans could purchase. Fire is not one of our fears.'

'But mysterious bowmen are,' Corbett observed. 'And I know about the "Rose of Rye".'

'I had nothing to do with that.'

'I didn't say you did, but you lied to me. You do know what it means.'

'Henry was a mad fool,' Sir William explained, half-turning in his chair. 'He whored and he lechered to his heart's content. The wife of the taverner at the Red Rose was much taken by him. Henry deserted her so she hanged herself; her husband did likewise. The tavern was sold and changed its name. Father did his best to keep the scandal secret.'

'So, who is this Owlman?'

'Henry made careful search. The taverner and his wife died but they did have a boy, a son, five years old.'

'Ah!' Corbett breathed.

'Lord save us,' William continued. 'I was only ten years old at the time.'

'And this son could now be the Owlman?'

'It's possible. But it's strange, Sir Hugh, he's a master bowman yet he never poaches the venison, attacks our retainers, or offered violence to me or my brother.'

'Do you think it could be a priest?' Corbett asked. 'Someone like Brother Cosmas?'

'God's bully-boy?' Sir William replied. 'He really did hate my brother. We had the church watched, but it's not him.'

'And de Craon?' Corbett asked.

Sir William pulled a face, for the wine was making him morose and sulky. Corbett stretched forward, picked up the sword and let it drop back with a crash on to the table, where it skittered about on the polished surface.

'De Craon? You also mentioned Gaveston!' Sir William lifted his head, a half-smile on his drunken face.

'Ah, I see how this game goes,' Corbett said, leaning his elbows on the table. 'You will answer my questions if I protect you from the King.'

'Sir Hugh, I did nothing wrong. The Prince of Wales came down here. It's well known that Piers Gaveston is in England hiding. Now the Prince would never have anything to do with Lord Henry but he approached me. Gaveston has been hiding in manor houses and villages along the south coast. Would I bring him here to Ashdown? I told the Prince my brother would be furious. He became petulant; he reminded me that one day he would be king, that I was of his retinue and that he would remember younger brothers who had not helped him, so I agreed. Gaveston travelled to Ashdown disguised as a pilgrim. He hired a chamber at the Devil-in-the-Woods tavern and visited St Hawisia's priory. The Prince met him in the tavern, and in the forest as well as the priory.'

'And where is Gaveston now?'

Sir William splashed more wine into his cup. 'He left as soon as he knew a royal clerk was visiting here.' He snapped his fingers. 'Like a morning mist.'

'And Lady Madeleine? She knew all this?'

'Oh, Madeleine knew. The Prince of Wales visited her, all sweetness and light, talking about that damnable shrine of hers.'

'Damnable?'

'It's the only thing she cares for. The Prince sang the same song as he did to me. How, when he was king, he would frequent St Hawisia's as often as he did Becket's tomb at Canterbury. Madeleine rose, like the sour fish she is, to the golden bait. Gaveston was allowed into the priory and the Prince met him there.'

'If the King knew of this?' Corbett straightened in his chair. 'You'd be summoned to Westminster and, how can I put it, while waiting for an audience, be lodged in chambers in the Tower.'

Sir William sucked in his lips. 'I have committed no crime. Gaveston's a popinjay. He's no threat to the King or kingdom. You should remember, Sir Hugh,' he said hoarsely. 'One day, God forbid, the King will die and the crown will rest on another brow.'

'You speak the truth. But don't you forget, Sir William, that it's that crown I serve, not its wearer!'

'Ever the lawyer, eh, master clerk?'

'No sir, ever the truth. And the truth is that you have done no real harm but de Craon, now he's a different dish. Why did the French king demand that Lord Henry lead the English envoys to Paris?'

'Henry travelled a great deal,' Sir William said. 'He was a scholar, a collector of artefacts. He was well known at foreign courts.'

'So am I,' Corbett retorted. 'The French were quite particular. They asked for Lord Henry Fitzalan. Now, sir, why?'

Sir William looked up at the rafters. 'The truth, Sir Hugh, is that I don't really know.' He held up a hand. 'I will take an oath on it. My brother was certainly on pleasant terms with the French king.'

'Did they correspond?'

'Just gifts and brief letters.'

'May I see these?'

'If you wish.'

'But come, Sir William, you can offer more than this.' Corbett spread his hands. 'You want my protection at court, then buy it.'

Sir William clumsily got to his feet. He went to

pull back one of the shutters and stared through the latticed window.

'The key to all that, Sir Hugh, is Pancius Cantrone. But God knows where he is! It's dark and I am feared for his safety.'

Corbett sat back. Aye, he thought, and where is Master Ranulf?

Ranulf-atte-Newgate, who'd drunk a little more than he'd wished, slipped out of the hallway, as planned, to meet Master Baldock. He found this new friend and ally sitting on the steps outside the main hall.

'You are ready, Master Ranulf? You will mention my name to Sir Hugh?'

Ranulf clapped him on the shoulder. 'I'll take you in to the King himself, Baldock. But the house of Mistress Alicia?'

Baldock beckoned him on. The ostler led him along a warren of passageways, through the kitchens, still thick with the odours of the cooking and baking which had preceded Sir William's feast. The scullions, kitchen boys and slatterns were now feasting on the remains, picking at the bones, dipping their hands into the blancmange, oblivious to the two silent figures who slipped out by a postern door across the yard.

It was a warm, soft night with a full harvest moon. Baldock found the cresset torch he had hidden, lit it and led Ranulf over a small footbridge past the stables, across the orchards to where the chief verderer's house stood. A two-storied building, its base was built of red brick, while the rest was plaster and black beams. Its thatched roof had long been replaced with tiles and a chimney had been neatly built on one end. At the back was an outside staircase. Ranulf would have stopped there but Baldock urged him on. They climbed a fence into a herb garden. Eventually Baldock stopped beneath a pear tree.

'I leave you here,' he whispered. 'You'll not hurt the girl?'

'Oh shut up!' Ranulf hissed. 'Go back and wait for me by the bridge. Keep the torch hidden. When you hear me come, lift it.'

Baldock scurried off. Ranulf pulled down the collar of his stiff white cambric shirt and looked up at the window where a night-light glowed. He prided himself on his reading and self-education and knew all about the troubadours of France: the chanteurs, the minstrel men who recited poetry beneath their lady's window and then left their poem pinned to the door. Ranulf had spent all afternoon preparing for this. A night of mystery! Of outpoured passion! He would not disturb this young woman who had smitten his heart so deeply, but would be the perfect, gentil knight, the chevalier of love. Alicia was no tavern wench but his lady in the tower to be courted, praised, flattered. Ranulf closed his eyes. The sweet smell of blossom on a cool breeze wafted across his hot face. He was alone under the stars. All thoughts of priesthood, of preferment at court or in the Chancery had now disappeared.

He loosened his pouch and took out the love poem. It was too dark to read but he knew the lines by heart. He moved one foot forward like he had seen the minstrel men do.

Eyes on the window, one hand on his heart, Ranulf began his poem:

'Alicia my love,
The love of my heart,
My morning star!
My tower of ivory!
My castle of delight,
Light of my life,
Flame of my heart,
All beauteous . . .'

He felt a touch on his arm.

'Good evening, Master Ranulf.'

He whirled round.

Alicia Verlian, wrapped in a dark cloak, looking as lovely as the night, stood looking up at him.

Chapter 9

'Love by moonlight, eh Ranulf?'

His manservant sat on the edge of the cot bed and gazed dreamily back. Corbett undid his sword belt and threw it on the floor.

'You shouldn't have done that,' he warned. 'You shouldn't have left! I need you at my back and you shouldn't be alone when de Craon's around.'

'I had Baldock.'

'Ah yes, the ubiquitous, if not inquisitive, Baldock.'

Corbett sat on the bed resting against the wall. He had met the ostler just before they had left Ashdown Hall and was secretly impressed by the young man. Indeed, he bore an uncanny resemblance to Maltote, not so much in looks but in manner and attitude. Already he revered Ranulf, was his willing accomplice in mischief, while, by the way he handled their horses, he was an accomplished rider and groom.

'Will you take him, master? Fitzalan intends to pension off most retainers by Yuletide. I think he'll remove every sign of his brother from that manor!'

'Is Baldock honest?'

'As I am, master.'

Corbett laughed. 'And the love of your life?'

Corbett was secretly alarmed by the faraway look in Ranulf's eyes. He wondered whether it was the wine or the secret amour in the dead of night. Corbett had seen many a man smitten, had felt the pangs of love himself, but always thought Ranulf was different. Now he mentally beat his breast and said, *'Mea culpa, mea culpa.'* He was arrogant to consider he knew his manservant so well.

'And you, master?'

Ranulf realised attack was the best form of defence. Corbett had left Ashdown looking like a cat who had stolen both the cream and the cheese, even humming a tune under his breath as they took the forest paths back to the Devil-in-the-Woods tavern.

'Sir William is in trouble,' Corbett said. 'He confessed little but he has given aid and sustenance to Piers Gaveston, supposedly exiled by royal decree from this kingdom. He and his sister have a great deal to answer for.'

Ranulf rubbed his hands. There was nothing like

Old Long Face teaching a lesson of humility to arrogant nobles and proud prioresses.

'But that's only a flea above our dish,' Corbett continued. 'Sir William told me that the corpse of the young woman found in the forest was probably a French whore, an expensive one.'

'What on earth . . . ?'

'I don't know. I don't know what she was doing in Ashdown. Sir William also told me that both de Craon and Philip of France were not so much friendly towards Lord Henry as frightened of him. The key to this fear is that sallow-faced physician, Pancius Cantrone, but he has disappeared. Lord Henry and his precious physician! It's my belief, as well as Sir William's, that his brother discovered a secret scandal, something which could grievously harm Philip of France. Now, Lord Henry and Philip exchanged letters; England and France are at peace, so there's no crime in that, but Philip also sent Lord Henry expensive gifts. Sir William showed me some of these: gold crowns, precious goblets, little gewgaws, but, assayed and weighed by some clerk of the Exchequer, it would amount to a small fortune. Now.' Corbett bit his lower lip. 'I believe Philip asked for Lord Henry to be sent to France, not only to conduct the negotiations regarding his daughter's marriage but to buy back, once and for all, this secret.'

'In exchange for what?' Ranulf asked.

'A small fortune.'

'But wouldn't that be dangerous? I mean, if Lord Henry visited Paris an accident could happen.'

'I asked the same of Sir William. He said that Lord Henry, when he travelled abroad, always left Pancius Cantrone in England.'

'Ah, and he would control the secret?'

'Yes, but then Sir William confided in me how Lord Henry, in his cups, had intimated that when they reached Rye, he would entrust certain secrets to his brother while Cantrone would be bundled aboard ship and be taken to France.'

Ranulf rubbed his brow. He tried to remove the lovely face of Alicia from his mind as he concentrated on the conundrum his master now posed.

'It would seem, Ranulf,' Corbett continued, 'that Philip of France asked for Lord Henry Fitzalan who wished to finish his private business with Philip once and for all. He would surrender the secret and betray the man who had handed it to him, probably for lands, castles or moveable treasures.'

'And if anything happened to Lord Henry while he was abroad?' Ranulf now warmed to the task in hand.

'Sir William would pass on Lord Henry's secret instructions to the King.'

'I suspect so.'

'But why didn't Fitzalan tell these secrets to Edward of England?'

Corbett laughed. 'Our King would demand them to be freely given as a vassal should to his liege lord.'

Corbett looked up at the ceiling beams. He sniffed and caught the different odours from the kitchen below. The tavern was falling silent, save for the odd creak of a stair. Somewhere from the kennel a dog growled softly and, on the night air outside, some drunk bellowed a hymn. A busy yet lonely place, Corbett reflected, ideal for Prince Edward meeting his blood-brother Gaveston.

'So, why has Cantrone disappeared?' Ranulf asked.

'Sir William thinks he may have fled. You see, Sir William was used to being his brother's principal retainer, travelling here and there which, of course, provided a suitable pretext for escorting Gaveston up and down from the south coast. Now, Sir William's mind is all a jumble with his brother's funeral as well as the finger of suspicion being pointed at him. He unwittingly let slip to Cantrone what his brother intended to do at Rye. Apparently Cantrone paled, became very agitated and confused, then withdrew to his chamber. The next day he left for St Hawisia's priory. Sir William sent a messenger there. The Italian physician apparently treated Sister Fidelis' swollen knuckles, collected his horse and left but neither hide nor hair has been found of him. He could have fled. He could have been waylaid by outlaws, the Owlman or the assassin.'

'Or one of de Craon's lovely boys?' Ranulf interjected.

'De Craon may be involved,' Corbett agreed.

'He must also be pleased.'

'Yes and no. Lord Henry is dead. Cantrone may have joined him. However, Lord Henry and Cantrone were the sort of men who would leave this secret somewhere in writing, a surety, a bond for their own safety.'

Corbett pulled across the bulging saddlebags he had taken from the manor, undid the buckles and pulled back the straps. He shook the contents, a roll of vellum and two Books of Hours, out on the bed.

'Now, because Sir William was eager to please, he handed over a copy of the letters between Lord Henry and King Philip.'

Corbett picked up the roll. Ranulf could see the letters had been stitched together by some clerk.

'So I quickly went through these. There is very little: greetings, salutations. Nothing that you wouldn't find in the chancery of every great nobleman of England. I am sure the Earl of Surrey has similar letters between himself and different rulers in Europe.' He sighed. 'But I will go through them again.'

'And the pouches?' Ranulf asked.

Corbett undid the neck of one. 'I found little in Cantrone's chamber. Books of herbals, lists of spices, a few tracts on medicines, potions, philtres. I suspect our good physician kept his secrets upon his person.' Corbett picked up a Book of Hours. 'Lord Henry bought this recently.'

He handed it to Ranulf who opened the gold-edged prayer book. The pages were of the costliest parchment, clean and supple, the calligraphy exquisite. Each prayer began with a small miniature painting done in breathtaking colours. At the back Lord Henry had written down private notes. Nothing unusual: observations, lists of jewels in his caskets, monies owing to a certain church, nothing that couldn't be found at the back of any such personal Book of Hours, Corbett's included.

'This second one.' Corbett held up the small, calfskin tome. The cover was frayed, blackened with age, some of the small precious stones clustered in the shape of a cross were chipped, others were missing. 'Now, Sir William told me that Lord Henry always took this with him.' Corbett opened the pages, which crackled as he turned them. 'Again nothing untoward, prayers, alms, readings from the scriptures, the lives of saints, even Saint Hawisia's mentioned.'

Corbett reached the end, where the blank pages of the folio were covered in black handwriting. Ranulf also noticed what looked like a loose page sticking out, which he tapped with his finger.

'What is that?'

Corbett leafed back. 'Ah yes, it's a devotional painting. Look!'

He handed it over. The painting was small, done on stiffened parchment. A scene from the Old Testament, it showed Susannah being accused of adultery by the elders: a painting often seen on the walls of churches or in Books of Hours such as this. Except here, the eyes of each of the figures had been cut out leaving a small gap.

'Why should Lord Henry do that?' Ranulf asked. 'Deliberately injure a picture, then keep it in this Book of Hours he takes everywhere?'

He stifled a yawn and Corbett looked up. Ranulf's eyes were now red-rimmed.

'You'd best go to sleep,' Corbett told him. 'Tomorrow's a busy day. At noon tomorrow I intend to set up my court of enquiry in the nave of St Oswald's-in-the-Trees. I have asked Sir William. And he's eager to please, to provide a small guard and to ensure that certain people are brought to us for questioning.'

'Not Lady Madeleine?' Ranulf scoffed.

'No, she's too grand for such an occasion and might refuse to come. But the hermit Odo, Brother Cosmas, Robert Verlian.' Corbett glanced up. 'And his daughter Alicia. Oh yes, and that strange woman Jocasta, the one they call the witch. It's best if I examine them there.'

'Sir William has been most co-operative.'

'Sir William is terrified,' Corbett replied. 'Lest I send you back to Westminster with the story of his doings with Gaveston. But the King's rage would be futile and I want Sir William where I can see him. He has also given me his word that he will keep a close eye on our good brother in Christ, Seigneur de Craon.'

Ranulf got up and undid his cloak. Corbett turned back to the old Book of Hours. At the front a blank page was filled with childish drawings, short prayers; Corbett recognised that Lord Henry had learned a clerkly hand. Some of the entries were years old, the ink fading to a dull grey. Others, in dark green or red, were of more recent origin. Corbett looked carefully at these. One was a short diary of a journey to France giving the dates when and the places where Lord Henry had stopped. Another, a drawing of a leopard Fitzalan had seen in the Tower of London. There was a list of provisions for the Feast of Fools and the costume Lord Henry designed for the Lord of Misrule. One full page, and Corbett noticed that here the ink was clearer, the writing done in a most clerkly way, told the story of a devout and holy woman called Johanna Capillana. Corbett read this but it was only a list of the woman's pious deeds, her devotion to the poor, her tending of the sick, her knowledge of herbs.

'Have you ever heard of a saint called Johanna Capillana?' Corbett asked.

Ranulf was already lying on the bed, his blanket wrapped round him, his face towards the wall. Corbett smiled and put the book down. He undressed, placed his clothes over a stool, blew out the candles and stared out of the window. The tavern was now silent. He glanced down at Ranulf. Usually the clerk would be snoring his head off.

'Love is a terrible thing,' Corbett remarked. 'A two-edged sword! It turns, it cuts and there is no cure.'

Ranulf, lying on his bed, just smiled but didn't answer. He heard his master settle for the night but his mind was back in that moon-washed garden and his heart fair skipped for joy. He had expected Alicia to laugh at him but she had not! She had explained how her own maid was in the room above and would have been very flattered to hear the poem.

'I always go out at night,' she had said, then pointed into the darkness. 'There's a brook. My father and I always visit it when the evenings are warm. I listen to the sounds of the night. I'm glad I went there.' She drew closer and gripped his wrist. 'I'm used to lust, Ranulf-atte-Newgate, to bold stares and saucy quips. But a poem! Read quietly in the moonlight! You are indeed a strange one. I had you wrong.' And, standing on tiptoe, she had kissed him gently on the cheek, plucked the poem from his hand and walked quietly away.

'As you are, so once were we! As we are, so shall ye be.'

Corbett read the inscriptions around the Doom above the dark wooden church of St Oswald's-in-the-Trees.

'In the end,' he commented to Ranulf, pushing open the door, 'all of us will be as God wants us.'

He paused inside the porch. The little church was

built entirely of wood: the builder had ingeniously used a row of oaks as pillars for the roof and on either side of the nave were darkened transepts with small, square windows providing light. The roof itself looked like that of a barn, great timbers running across. The rood screen at the top looked ancient; some of the carvings, St John and other saints clustered around the crucified Christ, were battered and worn. Corbett went through the rood-screen door and into the sanctuary. A man sat there dressed in a Franciscan robe. In the alcove behind was a small, thin mattress, blankets neatly piled on top of the bolster; the remains of a meal on a trauncher lay on the floor.

'Robert Verlian?' Corbett asked.

He studied the thin-haired chief verderer. Verlian nodded and got to his feet, wincing at the pain and rubbing his right knee.

'In my flight,' he explained, 'I must have injured it.'

He hobbled forward, hand outstretched. Corbett grasped it. The verderer was of medium height, his face, roughened by the wind and sun, was lined and seamed, the eyes bloodshot with fatigue and worry. He was clean-shaven but had cut himself a number of times.

'I apologise for my appearance,' he explained. 'But I am now prisoner of this place, dependent on the generosity of Brother Cosmas.'

'We met your daughter Alicia.' Ranulf, smiling

from ear to ear, stepped forward.

'Yes, I know. You must be Sir Hugh Corbett, King's emissary, and his clerk Ranulf-atte-Newgate. My daughter visits me but Brother Cosmas urged her not to bring a change of clothing or food and wine.' He glimpsed the puzzlement in Ranulf's face.

'The law of sanctuary,' Corbett explained. 'If it is to be maintained no one is to bring clothing, food or drink or provide any other sustenance.'

'But you are safe now,' Ranulf insisted. 'We hold the King's writ. There is no proof of murder and you are not guilty of any other crime.'

Verlian shrugged. 'I dare not leave this church, not now. Sir William's hand is turned against me. I'd best stay here until this matter is settled once and for all.'

'I would agree with that.'

Corbett turned round. Brother Cosmas had come out of the side door leading to the sacristy. He sketched a blessing in their direction.

'I received Sir William's assurances, but I heard what you said, Robert, and I agree. Stay here until this matter is finished.'

'What do you mean?' Corbett asked.

'Ashdown can be a lonely place.'

The priest came across the sanctuary, his sandals slapping the floor. He took a tinder and lit the two candles on the altar.

'Robert Verlian is an innocent man. I don't want some accident happening to him. He's claimed sanctuary. Let him stay. He's safer here than elsewhere. Don't you agree, Robert?'

The verderer rubbed his chin.

'You have the sanctuary,' the priest continued reassuringly. 'And at night you may use my house. What more could you ask?'

'But, if you are innocent,' Ranulf asked, 'why not go out and face your accusers?'

Verlian sat down on a bench and cupped his face in his hands. For a while he just sat then he looked up.

'The morning Lord Henry died I went back to my house to make sure that Alicia was safe. I came back to join the hunt. I saw nothing untoward. However, when I reached Savernake Dell, Lord Henry was dead, an arrow deep in his heart.'

'How did you come?' Corbett asked.

'I was hurrying from my house,' Verlian explained. 'Ahead of me I could hear the hunters and their hounds, the crashing of deer as they bolted through the thicket towards the dell.'

'Which side did you approach? The side on which Lord Henry was standing or the other?'

Verlian closed his eyes. 'I came from behind,' he said. 'Following the same path as the huntsmen.'

'So, you were at the entrance to the dell?'

'Yes, I stopped there. I could see something had happened. Figures clustered around a fallen man. Someone shouted Lord Henry had been killed.'

'But why didn't you hurry across?'

'I don't know!' Verlian glanced up, eyes blinking. 'I really don't know. I was frightened. One thought occurred to me. Everybody is where they are supposed to be, except me.'

'Sir William wasn't,' Corbett said. 'He had gone into the woods to ease his bowels.'

'I didn't know that.' Verlian shook his head. 'You must remember, Sir Hugh, I was all agitated. I was Lord Henry's chief verderer. I was also father of the young woman who was the object of his lust and lechery. I am not a man skilled in law. Even as I turned to run, I could think of what my accusers would say. When Lord Henry was killed, Verlian wasn't where he was supposed to be! Verlian is a master bowman! Verlian knows the forests like the palm of his hand and, above all, Verlian had the motive, good enough reason to slay his lord!'

Corbett took a stool from just inside the rood screen and sat down next to the verderer.

'Master Verlian, I came here early this morning because I wanted to question you before others arrived who might eavesdrop, take what you say and do mischief with it.' He saw the wary look in Verlian's eyes.

'What . . . what do you mean?' he stammered.

'I can understand your panic and fear.' Corbett tried to sound reassuring. 'But there are gaps in your story, aren't there? You see, Master Robert, I don't know the times, who was where when the hunt began. Your task was to lead the huntsmen and drive the deer into Savernake Dell, yes?'

Verlian nodded.

'But you didn't do that. We know from Alicia that you went home to ensure Lord Henry hadn't left the hunt and visited her. You left Beauclerc hunting lodge early, went to the stables and ensured the verderers, huntsmen and whippers-in had all the preparations in hand. You probably visited the deer trap in Savernake Dell, built for the quarry to be driven in. After all, Lord Henry would not wish to disappoint his guests. Now we know,' Corbett continued, 'the hunt went wrong. You were not present. The huntsmen drove the quarry too fast and, by the time they reached Savernake Dell, two deer were running like the wind! So fast the archers missed them and the deer jumped the fence cunningly built to trap them.'

'What are you implying?' Verlian nervously touched one of the cuts on his cheek.

'Oh, I'll come to that in a moment. I believe you are innocent, Master Verlian. What I am trying to say is that you were gone from the hunt far too long. You planned to leave it for a short while then come hurrying back. But something delayed you.' Corbett paused.

He glanced up at Brother Cosmas standing beside him. The friar was looking sternly at the chief verderer.

'Have you lied to me, Robert?' he demanded. 'Is there something you haven't told me?'

'Tell me.' Corbett tapped the verderer on the knee. 'When you fled did you go back home?'

'Well, no I wouldn't.' Verlian forced a smile. 'I . . . I mean . . .'

'You were frightened of Lord Henry's retainers capturing you?'

'Yes, yes, that was it.'

'No, it wasn't,' Corbett retorted. 'It would take some time for the news of their lord's death to reach the manor. You didn't go back home to Alicia because Alicia wasn't there, was she?' Corbett ignored Ranulf's quick intake of breath. 'You left the hunting lodge early that morning,' Corbett continued, 'and hurried back to your house. You expected to find Alicia there but she wasn't. You cast about, anxious, wondering where she had gone. After all, that was the day of the hunt. The last place Alicia should be was wandering the forest.

'By the time you returned, the hunters and verderers were too far ahead of you and, because they lacked your skill, your discipline, the deer were driven too fast into Savernake Dell. When you reached the dell you realised something terrible had happened. You knew you could be accused, as indeed, Sir William did, so you fled.' Corbett paused. 'Not home, because you knew Alicia wasn't there and what was the use of putting yourself in danger? So you fled into the forest, didn't you?'

'You are in God's house,' Brother Cosmas' harsh voice commanded. 'And in his sanctuary.' He pointed to the silver pyx. 'Beneath the appearance of bread, the Lord Jesus dwells among us. I have given you sanctuary, taken you as a guest.' His voice became softer. 'Not because of the law of the church, Robert, but because I believe you. Where was Alicia?'

Ranulf was now walking up and down like a man taken by shock.

'Where was your daughter? Had she taken a horse?'

Verlian just blinked. He was now staring at Ranulf.

'Had she taken a bow and arrow?' Corbett added. 'Alicia is the daughter of the verderer. She can draw and loose. Hadn't she once threatened Lord Henry with that?'

Verlian opened his mouth to reply.

'Don't lie,' Corbett warned him. 'If you lie, Robert, I cannot help you or your daughter. So, don't say you didn't know where she was. Alicia has visited you here. You must have asked her and she must have told you.'

'Tell them, Father!'

Alicia, shrouded in a brown cloak, stood at the entrance in the rood screen; in her hand she carried a linen bundle tied with a piece of string. She pulled back her hood and glanced quickly at Ranulf, who blushed and looked away.

'I've brought you some oatmeal cakes, Father.' She thrust these into the Franciscan's hand. 'You can share them with whoever you wish.' She went and crouched beside her father, put a protective arm round his shoulders and stared defiantly at Corbett. 'You are a dangerous man, Sir Hugh. You know they are talking about you at the Devil-in-the-Woods. How you sit and brood like a cat.'

Corbett smiled. 'In which case, mistress, you have nothing to fear from me. I am the King's cat. I only hunt those who disturb his barns.'

'My father is frightened. He's a verderer, Sir Hugh, and a good one.' She gently stroked her father's hair. 'He's used to the forest. The people who live there; the animals, their tracks, their secret pathways. And then, in what must have been the twinkling of an eye, his lord turns to lechery and that lord is killed.'

Verlian raised his head, his cheeks soaked in tears.

'What could I do?' he pleaded. 'If I was turned out where could I go? I was born in these parts, sir! Ashdown is my world, my life.'

'And you know that, master clerk, don't you?' Alicia demanded. 'You are a cat, you sit and you think.'

'So, you've visited the Devil-in-the-Woods tavern again?' Corbett asked.

'I did this morning.' Alicia didn't look at Ranulf. 'I wanted to see someone but he'd already left. One of the pot boys, however, said that he woke long before dawn. It's his job to kindle the fire. You, Sir

Hugh, were already in the taproom, wrapped in a cloak, contemplating the white ash in the grate as if you had been there all night.'

'I need little sleep.' Corbett held her gaze. 'I came down and read some letters. I studied a Book of Hours but I could make little sense of it. I sat and brooded about Lord Henry's death and your father, whom I now wish to question. I wondered why the hunt had gone wrong? Why he took so long to return? Why he didn't flee back to your house?'

'And what else did you think?'

'I will tell you that, mistress, when you tell me where you were.'

'There's a cemetery behind this church. My mother lies buried there. It's the one place in this forest I felt safe from Lord Henry and his henchmen. I took a horse, a small palfrey, and I rode there. I collected some wild flowers, left the horse at the lych-gate and put the flowers on my mother's grave. I sat and talked to her for a while.' Alicia ignored her father's muted sobs.

'And afterwards?'

'I left the cemetery and rode back to our house but I did so slowly. I wondered what Father and I should do for the future. By the time I reached Ashdown, isn't it strange, master clerk, the future had been decided for me. Lord Henry was dead and my father was in flight.'

'And do you often take a bow and a quiver of arrows to your mother's grave?'

Alicia's face suffused with rage.

'Yes!' she hissed through clenched teeth. 'And I tell you this, clerk, if I had met Lord Henry on the way, I would have put an arrow in his heart!' Her eyes glittered with hatred. 'But God disposes and someone else did that!'

Chapter 10

Corbett rose from his stool. 'Brother Cosmas, I thank you for your help. Sir William's soldiers will be arriving soon . . .'

'Master!'

Corbett felt Ranulf touch his sleeve. If Alicia's face was red with anger, Ranulf's was white. He was gnawing the corner of his lips, his fingers tapping the dagger in his belt.

'Master, a word with you?'

Corbett bowed coolly to the rest and followed Ranulf out of the sanctuary to a small side chapel dominated by a large statue of the Virgin and Child. Ranulf thrust his face close to Corbett.

'Why didn't you tell me about this?' He tapped the side of his head. 'Your brain clatters and turns like a wheel of a busy mill. I may be your servant but I am also a Clerk of the Green Wax: the King's commission bears my name.'

Corbett went round him and, taking a taper, lit one of the small night-lights on the iron rail which ran beneath the statue of the Virgin.

'One for Maeve,' he murmured. He took another. 'One for baby Eleanor! One for my unborn child.' He took a fourth and put a coin in the box which, he noticed with some amusement, was cemented into the floor near the statue. 'And one for my lovelorn Ranulf!'

'I do not think it's amusing, Sir Hugh!'

'Murder never is, Ranulf. I didn't tell you because I knew.' He came back to his clerk. 'I knew,' he continued, lowering his voice, 'what you would do. But, yes, I sat in the taproom this morning. I thought about Verlian, the hunt, his later flight. It's a matter of logic, Ranulf. Sometimes, God forgive me, love and logic clash. I am no threat to you or to Alicia. But murder is murder. The King's law is the King's law. Justice must be done: that's why you are a Clerk of the Green Wax, to enforce that. Otherwise we are no better than the animals in the forest where only the swiftest and most powerful survive.'

'Lord Henry was powerful.'

'And, Ranulf, Lord Henry was vulnerable. Think about it. If a great lord can be cut down with impunity, no matter what he was, or what he did, then no one is safe. You know that, be he a lord in his manor or a clerk on the streets of Oxford.'

Ranulf smiled ruefully.

'But you do not think Alicia is the assassin?'

'I'll be honest, Ranulf, I don't know.' Corbett ticked the points off on his fingers. 'She hated the Lord Henry. She was in the forest when he died. She was riding a horse. She carried a bow and quiver in the use of which she is skilled. Finally, there are no witnesses to where she was or what she did. So, like it or not, at this stage of the hunt, Mistress Alice is much suspected but nothing is proved.'

He looked over his shoulder; Brother Cosmas was now standing over the verderer and his daughter. Corbett gently pushed Ranulf deeper into the shadows of the side chapel.

'There's more to this forest and its people than meets the eye.'

'Such as?' Ranulf asked.

'Use your logic, Ranulf. You've been through Ashdown Forest and what did you see? I know,' Corbett held a hand up. 'Miles and miles of trees and dark lanes, swamps and marshes. You could hide an army there and no one would know. Really the forest is like a deserted street, long and dark, houses on either side. Despite the dark tunnel which runs between them, the inhabitants of those houses know when someone goes along that street, particularly if it's time and again.'

'And?' Ranulf asked.

'The same is true of the forest. There may be

trees as far as the eye can see but remember, Ranulf, what it was like? The dark, tangled undergrowth; those light green patches which may be marshes or swamp. Now, when you walk through a forest you are forced, whether you like it or not, to stumble through the undergrowth, crashing about like a wounded boar and blundering into God knows what danger, as well as being seen and heard by anyone who may be passing.'

'Or,' Ranulf intervened quickly, 'you will seek certain paths and trackways where, again, you are likely to be seen or heard.'

'Now there speaks a good and studious observer. So, let's return to the questioning and, if you can, my noble Galahad, my knight of the moonlight, curb your passion and use your mind.'

Corbett left the side chapel and walked back into the sanctuary. Ranulf sighed, fished a coin from his purse which he put in the box, and lit a candle.

'And that's for Master Long Face,' he muttered. 'And his damnable logic!'

He followed Corbett into the sanctuary, where the clerk had already taken his stool.

'Master Verlian?'

'I did not like the way you questioned my daughter, Sir Hugh, or what you implied.'

'If your daughter is innocent she has nothing to fear. And neither have you. True, my questions may bite.' He half-smiled at Alicia who was now sitting on the floor, her back resting against a pillar. 'But your answers are logical and you do not have the eyes of a murderer.'

Now Ranulf smiled to hide his anxiety. If they had been alone, he would have asked his master what the eyes of an assassin looked like, bearing in mind some of the sweet-faced villains they had crossed swords with over the years. When he caught the pleading look in the young woman's eyes he glanced away. Did she have anything to hide?

Corbett, however, was now rubbing the side of his face, a sure sign that his sharp brain was hunting an idea.

'You have questions for me, clerk?' Verlian asked.

'Yes, it's not about Lord Henry's murder. It's about the forest. You know it well?'

'As well as my child's face.'

'You are a skilled huntsman?'

Verlian shrugged. 'Lord Henry said as much.'

'You can track a deer?'

'I can track anything which walks the face of God's earth,' Verlian replied proudly. 'Be it man or beast.'

'And your companions, the huntsmen and verderers, are people who live in and use the forest?'

'Some are very good. Others have got a great deal to learn.'

'So, what about the outlaws?' Corbett asked abruptly.

Verlian looked guardedly at him.

'The wolfs-heads, the outlaws?' Corbett insisted.

'Many of them don't survive. They flee from the towns and villages. They do not last long in the forest. I have discovered many a corpse frozen in a snowdrift or the edge of some swamp. I've even found those who've hanged themselves, their wits disturbed. If they have any sense they do not stay long but travel on to another town.'

'And the rest? Those who do stay? The peasants who kill the deer? Or who've fled a cruel lord?'

'We leave them alone and they leave us. And we turn a blind eye to the little things they take.'

'So, you do see them?'

Verlian nodded. 'If they don't interfere with us, as I have said, we don't interfere with them.'

'I can say the same,' Brother Cosmas interrupted.

'Ah yes, I was going to ask you that.' Corbett smiled at the Franciscan. 'You live here, Brother. You describe Ashdown as your parish. You must know all the forest people, as well as those poor unfortunates who have to flee?'

'That's true,' the Franciscan replied proudly. 'I am a friar, not one of the King's officers. If a man snares a hare to put in his family pot, why should I object?'

'And Mistress Alicia here? You who ride through the forest armed with bow and arrow?'

'My father has answered for me. What are you implying, clerk?'

'My name is Sir Hugh Corbett.'

Alicia shrugged her shoulders prettily.

'I'd call you all lords of the forest,' Corbett said

humorously. 'You probably know its pathways and trackways better than Lord Henry ever did. Nevertheless, that puzzles me because, in the forest, we have the Owlman, an outlaw different from the rest. Indeed, he intrigues me. When I was sitting in the taproom this morning I thought about him. He is an outlaw who does not prey on travellers, at least, there's no proof that he does. He does not hunt the King's venison. Indeed, his only quarrel seems with the Fitzalan family. He sends them threatening messages tied to a yard shaft but no one ever sees him! No one ever hears him! No one even knows what he looks like.'

He glimpsed the puzzlement in Verlian's eyes, glanced quickly at Alicia then swiftly up at the friar. Brother Cosmas had turned away as if distracted by the candle spluttering on the altar. Corbett got to his feet.

'Now this is truly a conundrum.'

'I hadn't thought of it,' Verlian declared. 'It's now autumn and the Owlman has been in this forest since spring. I have never seen anything suspicious nor have any of my verderers or huntsmen.'

'Are you saying that he's someone else?' Alicia asked.

'That's one possibility,' Corbett agreed. 'He might even be one of you three. But, I tell you this . . .'

'Sir Hugh! Sir Hugh Corbett!'

Ranulf went to the mouth of the rood screen. The door of the church was flung open and archers wearing the Fitzalan livery stood in the entrance, a woman behind them. She had her arm round someone's shoulder. Ranulf couldn't see clearly because the figure was cloaked and cowled.

'Ah, our guests have arrived.' Corbett smiled. 'Brother Cosmas, if you could help us?'

'And you will reach your conclusions, clerk?'

'In time, but, if I could use that as my desk?' Corbett pointed to the offertory table.

Brother Cosmas helped Corbett and Ranulf move the table and place it at the top of the nave. He then brought benches from the transepts and a stool for himself. Corbett made himself comfortable. Ranulf opened his writing bag and laid out his sheaf of parchments, an ink pot carefully sealed and a velvet pouch of ready-sharpened quills.

'Who have you there?' Corbett called.

The archers shuffled their feet.

'The woman Jocasta, her daughter and the hermit who calls himself Odo.'

'I would be grateful if you would bring Jocasta forward. No, no!' Corbett got to his feet and leaned over the table. 'You stay in the porch, Brother Cosmas. Bring another bench for the lady to sit on.'

Ranulf was already writing down the woman's name and that of her daughter Blanche according to Chancery regulations.

Jocasta took her seat on the bench opposite him, one arm round her slack-jawed, wary-eyed daughter.

Corbett quietly cursed the poor light. Jocasta's face was hidden in the shadow yet there was strength in those high cheekbones, the sharp, slightly slanted eyes, the strong mouth and firm chin. Her black hair was unveiled and slightly tinged with grey. Corbett noticed the strong fingers and clean nails. The woman wore a dark-brown smock; a silver chain with a small gold crescent moon hung round her thick brown neck.

'You are the woman Jocasta?'

'And who are you?' The voice was low and throaty.

'You know who I am, mistress: Sir Hugh Corbett, King's clerk, and Ranulf-atte-Newgate . . .'

'By what authority am I brought here?' she interrupted. 'Am I on trial?'

Corbett took the King's commission from his pouch and spread it out on the table.

'You are not on trial, mistress, but I have the right to question you as my commission attests.'

'I cannot read, clerk, but I know letters bearing seals are important.' She glanced at Brother Cosmas. 'Good morrow, priest.'

'Good morrow, Jocasta. It is good to see you here at last.'

Ranulf's pen was moving across the page; when its tip broke, he quietly cursed, took another one out and dipped it in the ink pot.

'You are not one of Brother Cosmas' parishioners?'

'She is most welcome here,' the Franciscan interrupted.

'I do not come to St Oswald's,' Jocasta replied sharply, her arm protectively round her daughter. 'They say,' she closed her eyes, 'this is the House of God and the Gate of Heaven: a terrible place.'

'Why do you not come?'

'I am unworthy and my daughter becomes frightened.'

'Is that the truth?'

'Do you know any different, clerk?'

'They say you are a witch.'

'Who do?'

'So, you don't deny it?'

'Don't play words with me, clerk!'

Corbett raised his head. 'I am sorry, mistress. I tease rather than question. Let me begin again. Why do you not come to church?'

'I have led an unworthy life. My daughter is witless so I keep her away from others who might point the finger.'

'And these gossips who say you are a witch?'

'They are liars, as Brother Cosmas will attest. I know cures, I can distil potions, fashion a poultice, but I am no witch. I don't dig up the mandrake root or pay bloody sacrifice to the midnight moon.'

'So, why do you live in Ashdown?'

'It's the place I call home.' The woman sighed; she whispered softly into her daughter's ear and withdrew her arm. 'You've kind eyes, clerk, no malice in them. You are here because of Lord Henry's death, yes? Well, I shall tell you about Lord Henry. He is the father of this child.' She ignored the Franciscan's gasp of astonishment. 'Oh yes, Lord Henry in his youth was known the length and breadth of the Cinque Ports, not a brothel or house of whores was left untouched by his presence. In my youth I played the role of a Magdalene.' She half-smiled. 'Before that great saint's conversion. I have Spanish blood in me. I was married to a sailor, who got himself killed in a tavern brawl. The captain would not let me back on board, not even after I had favoured him with my body. So I became a streetwalker, a whore in the town of Rye. In my youth, clerk, I was considered beautiful.'

'I would say the same now,' Corbett commented. He caught the glint of amusement in Jocasta's eyes.

'Golden-tongued, eh clerk?' She lowered her head, placing her hands in her lap. 'Lord Henry Fitzalan was that. Oh, in many ways he had a soul of steel, locked and closed, with a heart of stone. But, when the fancy took him, he was generous with his praise and lavish with his purse. He came tripping into Rye. And bought my favours.' She nodded at her daughter. 'I was still unskilled. I became pregnant. Some kindly sisters took me in, not like the high-stepping ladies at St Hawisia's!'

'You've been to the priory?' Corbett broke in.

'Just once to ask for help. I swore never again.'

'What help?'

'Clothing and food for my daughter.'

'Lady Madeleine,' Cosmas said quietly, 'is not known for her charity.'

'And eventually you settled in Ashdown?' Corbett asked.

'I brought the child with me. At first, Lord Henry wouldn't believe me but I took a great oath. Blanche.' She stroked her daughter's silvery-white hair.

Corbett looked pityingly at the child: the vacant eyes, the drooling mouth, the look of a frightened rabbit as she crouched next to her mother.

'Blanche was born witless. God's judgement against me. But, Lord Henry studied her; he believed me. He provided a cottage and a small pension.'

'And he came to visit you?'

'Sometimes.' Jocasta's gaze shifted. 'Lord Henry was a man of fleshly desires. He did not lie with me but, how can I put it, clerk?' She lifted her hands. 'Sometimes I acted the whore for him.'

'Did you hate him?'

Jocasta glanced behind Corbett, studying the crude, wooden cross on the altar. Her gaze moved to where Verlian and his daughter still sat, heads together, at the far side of the sanctuary.

'Did you hate Lord Henry?' Corbett repeated.

'I felt nothing for him, clerk. Nothing but a terrible coldness. Age had not bettered him. A ruthless man, deeply in love with himself. There was no room in his heart or soul for anyone else, be it brother, sister, former lover or misbegotten bastard daughter.' She put an arm round Blanche's shoulders. 'Never once did he touch his own flesh like a father would. Oh, I heard what they said about the Fitzalans, they come from the devil and to the devil they can go!'

'Did you send him there?' Ranulf asked.

Jocasta studied him intently. 'Now, there's a bold-eyed bully-boy,' she said with a small smile. 'Are you Corbett's sword?'

'I am a clerk like him.'

'And an ambitious one too,' Jocasta noted. 'I did not kill Lord Henry.'

'How did you learn of his death?' Ranulf asked.

'The same gossips, who say I am a witch, chatter constantly. I met a packman coming from the Devil-in-the-Woods tavern. He had hurt his shin and came for a poultice. It must have been a few hours after Lord Henry's corpse had been removed from Savernake Dell.'

'Do you have a bow and arrow, mistress?'

'Why, yes I do. An old one and two quivers full of shafts, a gift from Lord Henry. Yes, clerk, I can use them with good effect. I have hunted when Lord Henry permitted it. Moreover, not everyone who passes through Ashdown is a courtly clerk or charming courtier.'

'Do you have a horse?' Ranulf asked.

'No, I do not.'

'And you know most people in the forest?' Corbett insisted.

'I know them and they know me. Verlian the verderer who now shelters here. He fled to my house. I told him to come here. Brother Cosmas, however, is the only man in the forest who would stand up to the power of the Fitzalans.'

'Have you ever seen the Owlman?' Corbett asked. 'This outlaw who wages such a strange war upon the Fitzalans?'

'I think so, once.'

'You've actually seen him?'

'I think so.' Her gaze shifted to Brother Cosmas. 'His face was masked, a sheet of leather with gaps cut for the eyes and mouth.'

'Was he on horseback?' Corbett asked.

Jocasta shook her head. 'He wore a grey cloak, fastened at the back. I remember the texture was stained and dirty, but it looked of good quality. I was near Ferndown Brook. It's a small rivulet, deep in the forest. I was collecting herbs. Blanche was sitting on a tree trunk some yards behind. I was by the brook, washing the plants I'd dug up, when suddenly this figure came out of the undergrowth and crouched by the brook. He was singing to himself, filling the waterskin he carried. I froze. He didn't know I was there and then Blanche called out. He glanced up and left as quietly as he came.'

'And he never saw you?'

Jocasta shook her head and demonstrated with her hand.

'He was here on one side of the brook, I was crouching down on the other side beside some bushes. He wouldn't have seen me.' She plucked at her own threadbare green cloak. 'In a way I was like some animal in the forest: I wore no bright clothes.'

'What makes you think he was the Owlman?'

She laughed. 'I've told you, clerk. Everyone in Ashdown knows everybody else. The other outlaws? Well, they blunder about dressed in rags. He was different. He moved with a purpose.'

'Describe him,' Corbett demanded.

'I've told you. A deerskin mask, a hood, a grey cloak. I glimpsed a quiver of arrows and a long yew bow slung across his back.'

'Was he old or young?'

'Sir, I'm no witch.'

Corbett smiled. 'But if you were on oath?'

'I would say he was about your age. He moved with ease, quietly.'

'What was he humming?' Corbett asked.

'Sir, I'm no witch nor am I skilled in music but it was no tavern tune. More a hymn you'd sing in church. I wouldn't swear to it but some of the words were Latin.'

'A dangerous thing to do,' Ranulf said.

'He thought he was alone,' Jocasta reminded him. 'Ferndown Brook is well off the beaten track. It was late in the afternoon. I wager he thought he was safe.'

'And the morning Lord Henry died?' Corbett asked. 'Did you see anything in the forest? Anything untoward?'

Jocasta shook her head. 'I knew, when I was brought here by Sir William's soldiers, that I would have to answer questions. I am not on oath, clerk, but you can put me on it. I have told you what I know. There is nothing else to say but I tell you this.' She rose to her feet. 'You are sharp-eyed, keen-witted men. You'll dig deep in Ashdown's dirt. Remember this: whoever killed Lord Henry knew these forests well. Someone who knows its secret ways and hidden paths.'

'And have you any suspicions?' Corbett asked.

'I am unlettered, clerk, but, at the end of the day, who profited most from Lord Henry's death? Are you finished?'

Corbett opened his purse and brought out two silver coins. Jocasta looked as if she was about to refuse.

'I take no favours, clerk.'

Corbett got to his feet. He took off his tunic, and undid the buttons of his shirt, revealing the dark purple scar high on his chest where the crossbow bolt had struck. Jocasta came and peered closely, her fingers pressing the healed scar.

'The skin is clean,' she said. 'But does it hurt?'

'Sometimes.'

'An arrow wound.'

Corbett looked into her beautiful eyes, dark with a quiet sense of humour. She smelt fragrantly of lavender and something sharper but not unpleasant. She pressed the scar with her fingers again. Corbett winced.

'You will feel sore,' Jocasta declared. 'This part of your body,' she tapped his chest, 'is protected by muscle and bone. The wound to the flesh soon heals, but the bone beneath . . .' She stepped back and took the silver coins from Corbett's outstretched hand. 'They will take months to heal properly. Even then, clerk, till the day you die, there'll be twinges, small stabs of pain; these, like the other blows of life, you will have to accept.'

Corbett smiled his thanks, buttoned up his shirt and put his tunic back on.

'Master,' Ranulf said as Jocasta led Blanche back down towards the door of the church. 'There are as good physicians in Sussex as there are in London.'

Corbett fastened the top button of his shirt.

'It wasn't my wound,' he replied. 'It was the final proof.'

'Of what?' Brother Cosmas asked.

'That she speaks the truth. The best physicians in London have examined my wounds. Isn't it strange, Brother, she said no differently to them? Now, she could have flattered, or offered some ointment or potion, but she told the truth. I suspect the same applies to everything she has told us.' He picked up the quill Ranulf had discarded. 'What she said will have to be sifted,' he added. 'Then I will reflect on her words.'

'She accused Sir William!' Brother Cosmas added eagerly. 'Or in so many words.'

'I'm not sure. But I was interested in her description of the Owlman. Well, let's see this hermit!'

Ranulf got up from his bench and was halfway down the nave when the door was flung open and Sir William strode in.

'Sir Hugh Corbett!' he called out. 'Come, man! And you, Brother!'

Corbett and Brother Cosmas hurried down the nave. Outside, the small churchyard was full of armed men. Jocasta and Blanche had stopped at the lych-gate and were looking back. Corbett glanced at the waiting soldiers, a ragged, dirty-faced figure, who must be the hermit, between them, but his attention was caught by the corpse which had been laid out on the ground, a threadbare cloak thrown over it. It had been unslung from a sumpter pony whose saddle was covered in slime and mud. Sir William pushed his way through his men, crouched by the body and pulled back the cloak.

'Pancius Cantrone,' he explained. 'Former physician to my brother.'

The cadaver was covered from head to toe in a muddy slime which only worsened the terrible rictus of death, the half-open mouth stained with mud and blood. The eyes stared, the sallow skin was damp and criss-crossed with streaks of dirt; the hair was soaking wet and in the neck gaped a ragged hole full of congealing blood.

'An arrow wound,' Ranulf said. He took his dagger out and scraped away the mud.

'Where was he found?' Corbett asked.

'On the edge of a marsh, deep in the forest.'

'And the arrow?'

'Plucked out.'

'By the killer?'

'It must have been,' Sir William replied. 'My huntsman only found it because the body had resurfaced, one boot sticking out of the water.'

Corbett turned the corpse over. Cantrone was still wearing his cloak, his dagger was still in its sheath, but the large wallet and small purse which hung from the belt were unbuckled and empty.

'And his horse?'

Sir William, crouching on the other side of the corpse, pulled a face.

'He was riding when he left St Hawisia's but, of that, there's no trace.'

'I suspect the horse was unsaddled,' Corbett said. 'The harness was thrown into a marsh and the horse left to graze. It wouldn't take long for such a valuable animal to be found and hidden away.'

'It's the same as the corpse we saw at St Hawisia's,' Ranulf remarked. 'An arrow wound to the throat. His purse and wallet have been rifled.'

'Amaury de Craon will be pleased,' Corbett

observed, wiping his hands and getting to his feet. 'Sir William, the good physician, he was your house guest. You will see to honourable burial?'

Sir William nodded.

'But who can this killer be, Sir Hugh?'

'I don't know. This mystery, Sir William, is becoming untangled. However, I have yet to pull a loose thread free. I would be grateful, sir, if you could keep your men out of the church.' He glanced across to where Jocasta and Blanche were now walking away. 'Did you know that the poor girl is your brother's child?' He glimpsed the astonishment in Sir William's eyes. 'We are all sinners, Sir William. As a kindness, I beg you, take good care of them.'

And Corbett walked back into the church, gesturing at Ranulf to bring the hermit in with him.

Chapter 11

Corbett settled himself on the bench and looked quickly at the memorandum Ranulf had been writing. Sometimes he found it unnerving, how his companion's style of writing so closely imitated his own. He idly wondered what dangers this might pose for the future.

Brother Cosmas, who had stayed to bless the corpse, came striding up the church. Corbett noted wryly how agitated the Franciscan had become. He went into the sanctuary and relayed what had happened to Verlian, who still sat with his daughter Alicia.

'My father wasn't there when he died,' Alicia declared in a loud voice.

Corbett turned on the bench. 'Hush now, mistress!' he said soothingly. 'There is no evidence against your father.'

The church door opened and closed. Ranulf walked up the aisle, the hermit Odo striding purposefully beside him. Odo sat on a bench before the table. A youngish man, his hair, black as a crow's feather, tumbled down to his shoulders. The ragged beard and moustache were slightly streaked with grey. He had large eyes, a hooked nose; his face was sallow and lined. Corbett studied the eyes: worried, anxious? He looked at the man's hands wrapped in blood-soaked bandages. The bare feet in the rather tattered sandals were dirty and chapped. His robe had once been bottle-green but now it was cut and sweat-stained. A piece of hempen cord bound his waist.

'You know why you are here?' Corbett began.

He was aware of Brother Cosmas coming back and sitting on the stool. Ranulf had eased himself down, taken a new quill and was busy writing the hermit's name.

'Master Ranulf has told me who you are,' the hermit replied. His voice was soft and cultured, in stark contrast to his rough appearance. 'He has also told me why you are here. But he gave no reason why you should question me.'

'We are not questioning you. Rather asking what you know, if anything, about the circumstances leading to Fitzalan's murder.'

'I am the hermit. I live out at Dragon's Mouth cave. I spend my life in prayer and penance. For your sins and mine.'

'Thank you,' Corbett said. He spread his hands on the table. 'I know my sins, Master Odo. What are yours?'

The hermit stared back in surprise.

'You are not a man of the church,' Corbett continued. 'You are not protected by its laws. I can ask for your assistance and you must give it. You, by your own confession, live in the forest of Ashdown. You must see, hear things that may be of interest.'

'I was at prayer when Lord Henry was killed. I rarely leave my cave.' He held up his bandaged hands. 'I was born with a rottenness of the skin. I cannot use my hands for work so I pray for God's faithful.'

'And how do you eat?' Corbett asked curiously.

'The goodness and generosity of the forest people is well known.'

'They bring you food and drink?'

'I would like to say that, like the prophet Elijah, I am fed by the ravens. But men like Verlian and Brother Cosmas,' he looked quickly at the Franciscan, 'are kind and generous.'

'Do you know anyone called the Owlman?' Corbett asked.

'I do not. I have neither seen nor heard anything which could be of help, master clerk. I beg you to let me go. I will remember you in my prayers.'

'Not so. Not so.' Corbett beat on the table-top. 'Shall I tell you what you are, sir? You are a liar. You are no more a hermit than I am.'

'How can you say that?' Brother Cosmas broke in. 'Odo has been . . .'

'Yes, when did you arrive in Ashdown?' Corbett asked.

'Early spring of this year.' The hermit was now agitated.

'It may cross your mind to get up and flee. I would advise against that. If you have done nothing wrong you have nothing to fear.'

'What are you saying?'

'Here you are,' Corbett pointed out. 'A self-confessed hermit. A stranger in these parts. Why come to Ashdown? It's not a place of sanctity or holiness. St Hawisia's Priory is not the sort which attracts men dedicated to the service of God.'

'I have nothing to do with that place.'

'No, no, you haven't. But I wager you have a great deal to do with Brother Cosmas.'

'This is nonsense!' The Franciscan sprang to his feet. 'Sir Hugh, this is God's house and my church!' He went and patted the hermit gently on the shoulder.

'Would you mind taking the bandages off Odo's hands?' asked Corbett.

Brother Cosmas looked as if he was about to refuse so Ranulf went and stood over the hermit with his dagger drawn. He was surprised as anyone at what his master had said, but if the King's commissioner wished these bandages to be removed, then Ranulf would see it was done.

Odo sighed. He undid the bandages and dropped them slowly on the floor. Ranulf re-sheathed his dagger and took the man's hands in his.

'The skin is white and soft, isn't it?' Corbett asked.

'Unmarked, cleaner than the bandages themselves.' Ranulf gripped both hands and squeezed tightly. The hermit winced in pain.

'Who are you?' he demanded.

'He is the Owlman,' Corbett declared. 'Release him, Ranulf.'

Ranulf returned to his writing. The hermit now had his hands in his lap, head down. Brother Cosmas was staring at a point above Corbett's head, lips moving quietly.

'Don't be so nervous, Odo. It's no crime to wear bloodstained bandages on your hand. And, apart from a few arrows and cryptic messages despatched to me, Lord Henry and, last night, through a window at Ashdown Manor, you've committed no real crime. Well, the evidence so far shows. Shall I tell you how I know?' He paused.

Alicia Verlian had come up beside them, engrossed as the drama unfolded.

'The great Aquinas, echoing the words of Abelard, said a logical conclusion can be reached by two methods.' Corbett paused. 'The first is by evidence, and I have some of that already; the second is by logic. Let me explain.

'First, the Owlman is a recent arrival in Ashdown

Forest, as you are. Secondly, the Owlman must be someone who can move around with impunity. Ergo, he must be someone who lives in the forest and is acquainted with its paths. More importantly, he must be able to travel around undetected, not only because he's disguised, but also because of the help and succour another provides. You are that person, while your friend and helper is Brother Cosmas of the Church of St Oswald's-in-the-Trees. Thirdly, the Owlman is not a common outlaw, or even a poacher. He has the opportunity to slay Lord Henry, or at least wreak considerable damage, but he does not. He simply tells him to remember the "Rose of Rye". Fourthly, the chain linking Lord Henry to the Owlman is centred on that tavern. As far as I know, such a connection cannot be placed at the door of anyone I have met in Ashdown. There was one exception, Mistress Jocasta, but she has purged herself. Her relationship with Lord Henry was honestly explained.'

Corbett spread his hands. 'By simply eliminating what is possible from what is probable,' he pointed at Odo, 'you bore the brunt of my suspicions. You pretend to be a hermit, living out at Dragon's Mouth cave. You would find that easy. What are you really, master hermit? A Franciscan priest, a lay brother? Your role as a hermit would not conflict with this. You can hide behind such a charade. No one would suspect a devout man of God whose hands are so injured he can hardly lift a spade, never mind draw a bow. You leave your hermitage and go to a secret place where you keep a cloak, a mask, a bow, a quiver of arrows, quill, parchment and ink. Like all Franciscans, you are not an unlettered man.'

Corbett paused. The hermit kept his head down. Brother Cosmas had moved a little closer as if to offer reassurance and support.

'You had a grievance against Lord Henry,' Corbett continued. 'But you are not a killer at heart. You were acting like a priest. You didn't want to punish Lord Henry for his sin but to stir his soul, make him remember, perhaps excite his remorse and contrition. You did that by sending messages, which does not concern me. What I want to know is, did your patience snap? Did you become tired of playing a game and, instead of reminding Lord Henry of God's justice, decide to take God's vengeance? Are you a murderer, Odo? Are you guilty of Lord Henry's death?'

'You have no proof.' The hermit glanced up. 'True, I bandage my hands but that can be to excite compassion. If the truth be known, Sir Hugh, there are many in Ashdown with a grievance against Lord Henry.'

'I mean you no harm,' Corbett replied. 'Who you are or where you come from is not a matter of concern to me. But I can order your arrest, have you chained and taken into London. You can be lodged at Newgate, the Fleet or the Tower while the King's clerks do a careful scrutiny, close questioning of your superiors in London. Brother Cosmas here will have to join you and, in the end, the truth will come out.'

Brother Cosmas was about to protest but the hermit tapped him gently on the back of the hand.

'I saw you ride through the forest.' He half-smiled. 'The King's clerk and his assistant come to do justice because the great Lord Henry Fitzalan has been killed. I was angry. When a great lord of the soil is murdered the King makes his power felt. However, when a young woman hangs herself, and her husband out of grief follows, it causes as little stir as a sparrow falling from the sky. I shot those arrows out of anger as well as to divert your suspicions.' He waved a hand. 'No, no, that's not the full truth, God forgive me. When Lord Henry was killed, I almost believed that I was responsible. In a way, I would scarcely object if the guilt was laid at the Owlman's door.'

'But that's not true!' Brother Cosmas broke in harshly.

The hermit gazed at him in surprise.

'It's not true,' the Franciscan repeated softly. 'Odo, you could not kill anyone. I shall tell you the truth.' The Franciscan hurried on as if anxious to divert Corbett's attention. 'You know about the story of the Red Rose of Rye? A tavern on the outskirts of the town and the fate of its owners, Alwayn and Katherine Rothmere?'

Corbett nodded.

'Odo was their young son. After his parents' death, he was sent to kinsfolk in Essex. He was raised by people very similar to those who live in Ashdown. He became a royal forester, later a soldier. Only as a young man did he learn the full truth behind the tragic death of his parents.'

'At first I swore vengeance.' The self-styled hermit took up the story. 'But my kinsfolk were kindly people. They raised me to fear God and the King. Since my youth I had a vocation to become a Franciscan. I entered the House of Studies at Canterbury where I met Brother Cosmas. We became firm friends: true brothers in every sense of the word. He told me about his soldiering days. I recounted my past. How I'd love to take vengeance on the Fitzalan family. Brother Cosmas was like some potion you take to ease the pain of an old wound. I became a Franciscan priest.' He fought to keep his voice steady. 'I worked for God's poor, travelling from parish to parish, preaching the crucified Christ. You see, Sir Hugh, I felt a deep sadness at the way my parents had died. The Church's teaching on suicide is very bleak. And my mother . . .' His eyes filled with tears. 'Let's be honest, clerk, my mother committed adultery, which brought about her death and that of my father. I thought by living a life of penance, I might atone for their sins. That Christ would purge them, lead them into Paradise. But, sometimes, at night, or when I saw a powerful lord ride through the town, banners and pennants flying, trumpets shrilling, I'd think of Lord Henry Fitzalan, the true cause of their sin. I heard how he waxed fat and rich, favoured by both King and Church. I travelled back to our house in Canterbury. It must have been a year last Easter. Cosmas was also there. He told me how he was working in Ashdown Forest.'

'We had a friendship,' Brother Cosmas broke in. 'Now bonded by a hatred of Lord Henry Fitzalan and all he stood for. Believe me, clerk, he was a wicked man.' Cosmas glanced at Alicia. 'He was cold and selfish. When you talked to him you felt his soul, behind the mask, was mocking you.'

'I persuaded my superiors that I go preaching in the shires south of London,' Odo continued. 'God forgive me, I came here to kill Lord Henry. I pretended to be the hermit. I was trained in archery and venery. Brother Cosmas showed me the paths and trackways of Ashdown Forest. He gave me food and sustenance.' Odo breathed in noisily. 'He also begged me not to exact the vengeance I wanted. I tell you this, Sir Hugh. Time and again I had Fitzalan in my sights. Time and again I could have put a shaft through his heart.'

'And did you?' Corbett asked. 'That morning in Savernake Dell? Did your lust for vengeance overcome your call to grace?'

'I was nowhere near Savernake Dell,' came the sharp reply. The hermit's eyes glowed. 'But I shall confess to you, royal clerk, and may Christ have mercy on me, I danced when I heard he had been killed.'

'And the arrow last night?' Ranulf asked. 'The one which shattered the window at Ashdown Manor?'

The hermit chuckled. 'Believe it or not, clerk, it was my farewell. I would have stayed a week, ten more days and taken my leave. Sir William is of the same rotten stock but I do not hold him guilty of any sin against me.' He sighed. 'I am sorry for loosing the arrows at you.'

Corbett scrutinised both the hermit and Brother Cosmas. On the one hand he felt the hermit was telling the truth but, on the other, he felt a slight unease. What if Brother Cosmas was the killer, using his friend as a pretext, a catspaw? Like many friars, both were practical men. Strong, vigorous, with a passion for justice, could this have clouded their priestly training?

'What now?' Brother Cosmas asked.

Corbett glanced at Ranulf but he seemed distracted. He was drawing something on the side of the piece of parchment, which Corbett recognised as the capital 'A'. Corbett got to his feet. He was aware of Alicia standing behind him while Verlian, sitting deeper in the sanctuary, must have also heard everything.

'I'll be honest,' Corbett began. He pressed his fingers on Ranulf's shoulder, warning him to keep silent. 'All four of you are suspects.'

'But I've told the truth,' the hermit gasped.

'I've said before,' Corbett reminded him, 'evidence or logic, or both, prove a hypothesis, verify a conclusion. I know you are the Owlman, that you were helped by Brother Cosmas. Logic and evidence also provoke suspicion against the Verlians, both father and daughter. So, if I empanelled a jury, it would note that each person in this church has a case to answer.'

'We are clerics,' Brother Cosmas protested.

'You could still be murderers,' Corbett replied softly. 'One of you, two of you.' He felt the nape of his neck grow cold. 'Indeed, all four of you could have been involved. Let me explain.' He sat down on the bench. His eye caught the gargoyle on top of one of the pillars: a grinning demon, cowled like a monk, its forked tongue slipping out between thick lips: the long-dead carpenter must have been ridiculing some priest. Corbett wondered if the two clerics in front of him were mocking him.

'Three people have been murdered in Ashdown Forest,' he continued hurriedly. 'Lord Henry and an Italian physician, Pancius Cantrone. Then we have this young woman, killed by an arrow, her body stripped and buried in a shallow grave but, for some strange reason,' he watched the hermit intently, 'her corpse was dug up and placed at the postern gate of St Hawisia's priory. Now, Odo, you expressed a deep desire to put an arrow deep into

Lord Henry's heart, and that happened. The other two were killed by an arrow to the throat.'

'What are you saying?' Odo became agitated. 'I – I – simply used a turn of phrase.'

'A jury might think it significant. It might wonder if we have two killers: one who slew Lord Henry, and a second who killed the other two victims.' Corbett paused. 'Tell me, Brother Cosmas and you, Odo, have you ever seen anything untoward in the forest? If you wish I can put you both on oath. Let me help you. A young woman was killed by an arrow to the throat. The assassin stripped her, for God knows what reason, and buried the corpse in a shallow grave. It was meant to stay there. Now, if anyone else had discovered that corpse, let's say a wolfs-head, he'd probably leave it where he found it. If Brother Cosmas had found the corpse he would have carried it to St Oswald's for honourable burial. One of the forest people would have raised the hue and cry while Master Verlian, or one of his verderers, would have taken it to Ashdown Manor.'

Ranulf's pen was now racing across the page, squeaking as he briefly summarised Corbett's statement. Corbett pointed at Odo.

'You discovered the corpse, didn't you? You are a priest and, for all my suspicions, a man of tender heart. You dare not raise the hue and cry because people would ask what this anchorite was doing wandering around the forest. You could not bring it to Brother Cosmas, that might arouse suspicion. So you took it to St Hawisia's priory. Your conscience clear, your duty discharged. I am correct, sir?'

Odo nodded.

'The morning Lord Henry was killed,' he replied, 'I knew about the hunt. I went to see if I could do any mischief: loose an arrow, scare the game. I slipped and fell where the earth was soft.' He shrugged. 'I found the corpse. The rest is as you say. I later came to St Oswald's to tell Brother Cosmas but I glimpsed Verlian's daughter in the cemetery, so I went back to my cave.'

Corbett turned, swinging one leg over the bench, and called Verlian and his daughter over.

'This is what I am going to do. Everyone shall stay where they are. Brother Cosmas here in St Oswald's. You, Odo, can act the hermit until this business is resolved. However, you will take me to where the woman's corpse was found.'

Odo agreed.

'Master Verlian, I have one question for you,' Corbett continued. 'On the night before the hunt, Lord Henry and his guests moved to Beauclerc hunting lodge some distance from Savernake. Why was that?'

The verderer, now sitting on the altar steps, spread his hands.

'That was the custom. Lord Henry always moved out of the manor. The dogs were brought there, the huntsmen and verderers given their instructions.'

'And you were present?'

Verlian's face paled.

'I understand that Lord Henry became ill, pains in the stomach, that he had to vomit and spend some of the night on the jakes purging his bowels?'

'He drank late,' Verlian answered. 'He and his brother. They opened flasks of wine. Lord Henry was always very proud of his wine.'

'And that wine?' Corbett asked. 'It was brought from the manor?'

Verlian wiped the sheen of sweat off his upper lip.

'Come,' Corbett insisted. 'You were chief huntsman. Your duty was to prepare the lodge, provide game, ensure it was cooked well for Lord Henry and his guests?'

'I'm not sure what you are saying.'

'And whose duty was it to serve the lords their wine? I mean, they were away from Ashdown, the usual servants and retainers would be left there.'

'I did,' Verlian cried, getting to his feet, rubbing his hands on the side of his robe. 'I served the wine.'

'And anything else?' Corbett asked. 'You are a forest man, Master Robert, you treat the dogs and horses. I wager you know as much about the plants and herbs as the woman Jocasta. Did you put something in the wine? Something to loosen Lord Henry's bowels, keep his mind away from lechery? Or was it an act of revenge or even an attempt to poison him?'

Verlian refused to meet his gaze. Ranulf was

gaping open-mouthed; he quietly vowed that, next time his master left the bedchamber early in the morning, he would follow him down. Corbett's brain had proved as sharp as a razor.

'Well, did you?'

'I did.' The chief huntsman waved his hand to silence his daughter. 'It wasn't poison, just a purgative. I saw him sitting there, face oiled, eyes mocking me. The rest of the guests had withdrawn. He asked for a special flask, one brought specially from Bordeaux. I opened the seal and sprinkled some powders in: not poison, Sir Hugh, but something to keep the humours of his belly busy and his mind free of lechery. You can't act the rutting stag when your bowels are loose! Nothing stronger than any apothecary would recommend. He never suspected. I returned to my own house and came back later on. In the morning Lord Henry, who had a strong constitution, was better; he'd purged his stomach, the potion had done no real damage. We assembled in the yard ready for the hunt. I was fastening the straps of his boot and he gently tapped me. "How is the fair Alicia?" he mocked. "Nothing like a day's hunting, is there, Robert, to stir the fires in the belly?" ' Verlian licked his lips. 'I became frightened. I wondered if Fitzalan would leave the hunt so I went to warn Alicia but she had already left; the rest is as you say.'

'And did Sir William drink of this?'

'A little, though he mixed his wine with water.

Lord Henry always made him act as cup man. He liked nothing better than to drink his brother under the table but Sir William had learned his lesson.'

Corbett got to his feet and picked up his cloak. 'I'm finished here.'

As he swung the cloak around himself he watched Ranulf busily clear away his writing implements. He shook a little sand lightly over the parchment, then blew this off, rolled the parchment up and tied it with a piece of green ribbon. That and the quills, knife and pumice stone went back into the chancery bag.

'We are on foot.' Corbett smiled at Odo. 'We left our horses at the Devil-in-the-Woods and the day has proved a fine one. Brother Cosmas, would you bring a mattock and hoe?'

The friar agreed and hurried off, the hermit following. Verlian went back into the sanctuary. Ranulf was shuffling his feet. Corbett decided not to be too harsh but walked down the nave, leaving the lovelorn man to make his own farewells. He went out and stood on the steps. The front of the church was now quiet and deserted. Sir William had taken his party, including the corpse, back to Ashdown Manor. Corbett stood and closed his eyes, listening to the birdsong. The fragrance of the forest, crushed grass, flowers and newly turned earth, assailed his senses. He wondered how Maeve was progressing at Leighton. Would she be safe? Was she well? He was always anxious that she would do too much but then he recalled that her uncle, Lord Morgan Ap Llewelyn, who had come as a house guest years ago and decided to stay, would shadow her everywhere, clucking like the busy old hen he was. He heard the door open and close behind him.

'Are you well, Ranulf? And Mistress Alicia?'

Ranulf's slightly flushed face told him everything. He opened his hand and Corbett espied the little locket he'd seen round Alicia's neck.

'A token of affection, eh, Ranulf?'

His manservant's face became grave. 'She thinks you are a very dangerous man, Sir Hugh.'

Corbett shook his head. 'You've read St Augustine? He defines murder as the supreme chaos and that chaos, Ranulf, must be resolved by logic, evidence and the enforcement of royal justice.' He tapped his clerk playfully on the side of the cheek. 'And murder comes in many guises. For all we know, Ranulf, we may have spent the morning in the presence of a cruel assassin. Remember the proverb: "Of the two brothers Cain and Abel, Cain was the comeliest and smiled the most." '

Chapter 12

After some searching, the hermit found the place where he had crossed the trackway. It was now about noon; clouds were closing over the sun and the first cool winds of autumn were making themselves felt. Gold-brown leaves whirled in the wind, laying down a carpet across the rutted track. The forest was silent apart from the occasional call of the birds and the incessant cawing of the rooks. Corbett noticed how the trackway curved and bent.

'A corner,' he said. 'The best place for an ambush, or so my lord of Surrey is always telling me.'

He and Ranulf followed the hermit and Brother Cosmas down the bank to the narrow grave from which Odo had dug the woman's corpse. Corbett knelt down and, with gauntleted hands, pulled away the leaves and twigs which had amassed there. The soil was soft, easy to dig; it must have taken only a short while for the assassin to slip the corpse in and then hide it under a layer of muddy soil.

'What are you looking for?' Brother Cosmas asked.

Corbett pointed back to the trackway. 'I suspect this young woman was coming from the Devil-in-the-Woods. She was travelling either to the manor or to the priory or, perhaps, north to London. She turned that corner. The assassin must have stood somewhere near here, arrow notched. There's a well-known outlaw's trick. You throw a stone in the air and let it fall on the trackway.'

'And the victim naturally looks up?'

'Yes, presenting his throat as a suitable target.'

'The archer must have been a good marksman?' the Franciscan insisted.

'We do not know how close he was,' Corbett replied. 'But he was definitely skilled with the bow and he fully intended to kill. You served in the wars, Brother. Do you recall a man suffering a throat wound and surviving? Anyway, the assassin steps on to the trackway and drags the corpse down here where it's stripped and buried. The poor unfortunate's clothing, smock, dress, boots, belt and cloak.' He paused, watching a squirrel scamper up the trunk of a tree.

Ranulf looked at Corbett curiously. His master stood, mouth half open, brow furrowed.

'Master, you were talking of the corpse being stripped?'

'Of course,' Corbett breathed. 'Why strip a corpse?'

'Because you need the clothes?' the hermit half-joked.

'No, no.' Corbett shook his head. 'The assassin was no common thief. He was waiting for this young woman. I doubt if she came upon him by chance. It has all the hallmarks of a well-plotted ambush. Our archer can afford a good bow, a quiver of arrows. So, why should he be so keen on some poor woman's clothes?' He punched Ranulf on the shoulder. 'Come on, Clerk of the Green Wax, clear your wits! Remember that corpse, the cropped hair, the sinewy body.'

'A man!' Ranulf exclaimed. 'The woman was travelling disguised as a man! That's why the clothes had to be removed. If you go back to the tavern and ask, as we have, "Can you remember a young woman?" the answer, of course, will be "No!" '

'In life as in love,' Corbett observed, 'the truth's always the same: very obvious to those who search for it! Brother Cosmas and Odo, I beg you a favour. Would you mind digging round this shallow grave?'

Brother Cosmas stared truculently back.

'I asked you as a favour,' Corbett added evenly. 'I will do my share as well.'

At this Brother Cosmas picked up the spade and

mattock. He gave the latter to Odo and they began to dig while Corbett led Ranulf away.

'How well do you know these woods, Ranulf?'

'Not at all.'

'Very well. Go back to the Devil-in-the-Woods. Search out young Baldock: he is now groom and Master of Horse to Sir Hugh Corbett, King's Commissioner. Sir William won't object. Tell him I'll draw the indentures up tonight before we go to Rye.'

'Rye!' Ranulf exclaimed.

'Yes, Rye. Baldock has two tasks. First, he's to take you to Savernake Dell and, when you're finished, to bring you back to the tavern. Afterwards he's to go and ask Sir William for a letter of release from his service.'

'What am I looking for in Savernake Dell?'

'Well, any sign of Sir William being ill.'

'Sir Hugh!'

'More importantly, see how long it takes to run from where Lord Henry was killed to the other side of the dell and back. Baldock will help you, he knows where everybody stood.'

Ranulf left. Corbett joined the others. They'd dug into the grave but only unearthed a silver button, no bigger than a groat.

'Would the assassin have hidden the clothes here?' Brother Cosmas asked. 'If he took such pains to strip the corpse?'

'True.'

Corbett squatted at the side of the pit, eyes half-closed, listening to the sounds of the forest. Brother Cosmas had led the digging and the clerk was suspicious. The Franciscan was an intelligent man. He had made no attempt to search elsewhere: like some menial servant, he had literally followed Corbett's orders, digging deeper, not accepting the logic that the assassin would scarcely have dug a deep grave only to bury the clothing, cover that up and place the corpse on top. Odo was also sullen, distracted. Corbett's hand travelled to the hilt of his dagger. He had acted arrogantly! Here he was with two strangers, both of whom were under suspicion, yet he was alone in the forest with them where any accident might occur. He got to his feet, quietly promising that he would not turn his back on this precious pair.

'I have shown you,' Odo protested. 'And I have dug. Apart from a button, we have found nothing.'

Corbett looked along the bank. Were these two men guilty of the murder? Had Odo brought him here because he had no choice? Corbett drew his dagger.

'The corpse was dragged down here,' he began. 'The assassin moved quickly. The corpse is stripped and swiftly buried.' Corbett looked to his left and pointed to the thick gorse and undergrowth which sprouted along the side of the bank. 'The assassin would wish to be away from here as swiftly as possible. He hurriedly put the clothing in a bag.'

Corbett walked to the far side of the freshly dug pit. 'Then up, across the trackway, and into the forest.' He crouched down and sifted with his dagger among the brambles and leaves. 'Let us hope he dropped something.'

The two men didn't join him. Corbett continued his search, using his dagger to scrape away the grass and weeds which clung so tenaciously to the soil. He carefully divided the ground into small squares, moving along the bottom of the bank and then up. Now and again he glanced at Brother Cosmas and Odo. They had drawn aside, whispering to each other. Corbett was about to ask them to join him but he decided it would be safer if they kept their distance. He was also unsure what they would do if they found anything untoward.

He was halfway up the bank when he found two small loops of cloth, luxurious in texture, now stained with grass and mud. Each had golden twine running round the centre and was more than an inch in circumference, the stitching small and precise. Corbett put these in his wallet, continued his search but found nothing else.

When Corbett clambered back on to the trackway, he pulled out the two pieces of cloth and studied them intently; two minute, costly pieces of needlework.

'You've found something, master clerk?'

Brother Cosmas and the hermit walked over.

'I think I have.' Corbett stretched out his hand.

'But I can't guess what they signify.' He put the items back in his purse. 'I have one last favour.'

'I must be getting back to my church!' Brother Cosmas announced. 'I have other duties, sir, apart from being host to a royal clerk and a digger of ditches!'

Corbett fished in his purse for a coin but the friar shook his head.

'Keep your silver, sir. Let's have done what you want.'

'Just lead me to St Hawisia's,' Corbett asked. 'I must have words with Lady Madeleine.'

A short while later the friar, still surly and withdrawn, left Corbett at the main gate of the priory and walked away without a by your leave. Corbett watched him and Odo go. He felt his suspicions were, perhaps, unworthy but, then again, they had deceived him. Both lived in Ashdown and both certainly had the motive and means to kill Lord Henry. He sighed and pulled at the bell rope. The small postern door in the main gate opened and an exasperated Sister Veronica waved him into the courtyard.

'I knew it was you!' she rasped. 'I looked through the grille and saw you coming with that precious pair!'

'Sister, for the love of Christ, don't you have any charity?'

'More than you, sir. But it's up to me how and when I dispense it!'

She took him through the rose garden towards the priory buildings.

'I would like to see Lady Madeleine.'

'Well, I know you haven't come to see me. You'll go, like the rest, to the guest house and wait for her there.'

Corbett plucked at her sleeve. The little nun stopped and peered up at him.

'What is it, clerk?'

'Why don't you take me to the prioress?'

'Lady Madeleine has her own house,' Sister Veronica explained slowly as if Corbett was dim in wit. 'She has her own house,' she repeated. 'Garden, stable and kitchen. No man is allowed in there.'

'I'll remember that.'

'What do you mean?'

'Nothing. But, Sister Veronica, one more question? You remember the corpse of the young woman left at the postern gate?'

'Of course I do. I heard the bell ring. I opened the gate and it was lying there.'

'Naked?'

'Oh no, wrapped in a grey blanket or cloak, I forget which.'

'And who looked after it?'

'Well, first, I sent a message to Lady Madeleine.'

'And?'

'She ordered the corpse to be brought into our death house. It's a small building in our cemetery. One of the labourers picked it up and put it there.

When our prioress graciously agreed to have it buried here, I washed the corpse and put it in one of our gowns; a short while later it was buried. Any more questions, master clerk?'

'No, no, I haven't.'

Sister Veronica strode on. She took Corbett round the church to a small, pleasant, two-storied building, through the wooden porch and into a large, whitewashed chamber. The guest room was stark and sparsely furnished. A large, black crucifix was fixed to one side of the window and a carving of St Hawisia to the other.

'This is our rest room,' she explained. 'The prioress will probably see you here.' Sister Veronica gestured at a stool before closing the door. 'Sir down. I'll bring you something to eat and drink.'

A short while later Sister Veronica returned with a jug of mead and a small dish of sugar-coated pastries.

'Lady Madeleine will see you when she can.'

Corbett wanted to question her further but Sister Veronica, despite her age, almost ran from the room, slamming the door behind her, so he picked up the jug of mead and went to the window to look out across the yard. He tried to make sense of everything he had learned this morning but he knew he would need Ranulf's help to untangle the different strands. He was pleased with what he had found but now conceded he had made little progress. He knew who the Owlman was but how much closer was he to unmasking the murderer? Or was it a group of assassins? People who lived in Ashdown, hated Lord Henry and plotted together to destroy him? And, of course, there was de Craon and his party. But how could he question them? De Craon was an accredited French envoy who would be only too delighted to refuse to answer Corbett's questions. Even if he did, Corbett mused as he sipped from the tankard, de Craon would scarcely tell him the truth.

'You are here yet again, royal clerk.'

Startled, he turned round. Lady Madeleine had quietly opened the door and slipped into the room. He could tell he was not welcome from the way her fingers tapped the side of her white gown while the other hand played with the medallion round her neck.

'More questions, clerk?'

Corbett slammed the jug down on the table.

'Yes, my lady, more questions! Piers Gaveston has, by royal decree, been exiled from this kingdom. He has been banished under forfeiture. It is a serious violation of the law to offer such an exile refuge and security. So, don't act the high lady with me. You, and Sir William, are guilty of a very grave offence. I believe your brother brought Gaveston from the coast. He allowed the exile to shelter in disguise at the tavern. Gaveston was later allowed into these grounds, yes, even into your own house.'

Lady Madeleine's eyelids fluttered. She swallowed hard.

'I am protected by Holy Mother Church!' she rasped.

'Don't be ridiculous! I haven't come to arrest you but I speak the truth. You sheltered Gaveston here, didn't you? He came here on two occasions. He was seen entering your private chambers.'

'Gaveston's more woman than I!' she retorted. 'Everyone knows that!' She sat on the bench. 'The arrogant fool! He came across the grounds, like some troubadour. Who saw him?'

'It's best if I don't tell you!'

Lady Madeleine sniffed noisily.

'In our youth, Sir William and I were playmates of the young prince. Edward asked for Sir William's protection and help and he gave it. I was drawn into the intrigue. The Prince of Wales sent a letter under his private seal, saying that when he became king he would not forget my help and assistance or that of the Blessed Hawisia's shrine.' She smiled thinly, took a string of Ave beads from a pocket in her robe, and threaded them through her fingers. 'I told him how to come,' she continued as if talking to herself. 'You've seen my house. It's built into the curtain wall of the priory with its own stables and yard. He could have arrived stealthily. But, oh no, Gaveston the young cock comes striding through, spurs clinking. He thought it was so amusing!'

'And when the Prince came here?'

'They met in the church; the Prince locked the door behind him. They were both in disguise. I told the good sisters they were stone masons, come here to look at possible building work. Edward then left, and shortly afterwards Gaveston followed.'

'How many times?'

'As you've said, clerk, twice he was seen, wasn't he? And what are you going to do now? Send letters to Westminster?'

'No, madam.' Corbett pulled a stool across and sat down. 'I'd like a mite more courtesy and co-operation.'

'Over what?'

'Your brother's death.'

'I know nothing of it. Henry was an arrogant fool.'

'And the death of that young woman?'

'I've told you all I know. Her corpse was left at our postern door, and I gave it Christian burial.'

'Do you know she was probably travelling disguised as a man?'

Lady Madeleine shrugged. 'What is that to do with me? We found her naked, we shrouded her, we buried her.'

'Except for the cloak wrapped around her,' Corbett added.

'God knows where that is now, master clerk!'

'And Pancius Cantrone?' Corbett demanded. 'The Italian physician. You know he has been killed? An arrow to the throat. His corpse was found on the edge of a marsh. He must have been murdered shortly after he left here.'

Lady Madeleine sighed noisily. 'Sir Hugh, look at this priory. It's an oasis of calm, of holiness: sure protection against the cruel world of Lord Henry and other men.' She spat the words out. 'I rarely leave the grounds. I am sorry for Cantrone's death but how can I help?'

'But you summoned him here?'

'Yes, he was a very good physician. Sister Fidelis' knuckles were swollen. I have told Lady Johanna the choir mistress to be more temperate in her dealings.'

'Can I see Sister Fidelis now?'

'If you wish. But why?'

'When Cantrone left here,' Corbett continued, 'did you notice if he was carrying anything?'

'Sir Hugh, I hardly knew the man. He came into the priory at our behest. I introduced him to our novice mistress, Lady Marcellina. She took him down to see Sister Fidelis. He examined her hands, recommended her treatment and, as customary, we gave him something to eat and drink, then he left. If you wish to speak to Lady Marcellina and Sister Fidelis I can arrange that. But there is little more I can say.'

Corbett scratched his head; he was tired and nothing made sense.

'And Seigneur de Craon?' he asked. 'The French envoy, has he ever come here?'

'He made two visits to our shrine. I met him on one occasion. I did not like his impudent eyes, but I know nothing of his dealings with my brothers.' She rose to her feet. 'But you wished to see the sisters I have named?'

Corbett made to refuse.

'No, I insist!'

And, without a word, Lady Madeleine left the room. A short while later the harsh-faced Lady Marcellina, together with a smiling Sister Fidelis, her fingers wreathed in bandages, came into the room. Corbett questioned them. Sister Fidelis was subdued but smiled at him with her eyes.

'Oh yes,' she declared, glancing sideways at Lady Marcellina. 'My knuckles began to swell like small plums. I showed this to Lady Marcellina and she told our prioress.'

'And the physician was sent for?'

'One of the grooms must have brought him,' the novice mistress said.

'You don't have a leech and an apothecary here?'

'Sir Hugh, we are nuns, not physicians. Sister Fidelis' fingers did alarm Lady Madeleine. Moreover, the Italian had been invited here on a number of occasions to treat certain of our sisters. He was a man skilled in the use of physic.'

'Was?' Corbett queried.

Lady Marcellina forced her face into a sympathetic smile.

'Lady Madeleine has told us the terrible news of

how the poor man was murdered after he left here.'

'Did he say or do anything untoward?' Corbett asked.

He heard the door open beside him and Lady Madeleine returned.

'All I know,' Lady Marcellina said in exasperation, 'is that I was summoned to the prioress's chamber. She introduced the physician and told me to take him to Sister Fidelis. He examined her knuckles, pronounced the swellings were deep bruises under the skin. He recommended a herbal poultice.'

'And then what?'

'Sister Veronica brought him some food and drink. He ate, drank and left.'

Corbett gazed at the young nun, who listened round-eyed to her superior, all the time nodding her head in agreement.

'He did seem distracted,' Sister Fidelis offered. 'Oh, he was kind and patient but it was as if his mind were elsewhere.'

'If there's nothing else, Sir Hugh?' Lady Madeleine murmured.

'No, my lady, there's nothing else.'

'Well, stay there a while, I will send some food and drink. You must refresh yourself before you leave. Please.' Lady Madeleine smiled. 'I feel, Sir Hugh, as if I have been discourteous. I would like to give you a gift before you leave. Our honey is famous throughout Sussex. Sister Veronica will bring you a jar. In the meantime let our kitchens refresh the inner man.'

Corbett was about to object but he realised he was being churlish so he agreed. The three nuns left. Corbett finished the mead. He heard the bells of the priory calling the sisters to prayer.

'I'll be back in the tavern by late afternoon,' he murmured to himself. 'I'll put down everything I've learned today. Study it, look for the gaps.'

The door opened and Sister Veronica came in bearing a small platter with roast hare, covered in a thick wine sauce, a goblet of wine and a small bowl with a manchet loaf cut up, the portions covered in butter.

Corbett ate the food hungrily. It was delicious and reminded him of Maeve's skill in the kitchen. When Sister Veronica returned, now silent and morose, she gave him a small leather bag containing two jars sealed with parchment and twine.

'You'll not find better honey in the kingdom,' she declared.

Corbett pushed away the trauncher, grasped the bag and rose.

'Then, Sister Veronica, all I can ask of you is to show me out and I'll be gone.'

The little nun led him from the guest house, through the grounds and out by the side postern door.

'And, before you ask!' she snapped. 'Yes, this is where the corpse was found!'

Before Corbett could make a reply, she slammed the door shut in his face. Corbett tied the leather bag to his war belt, eased the strap, pulled his cloak around him and walked across the heathland into the trees, following the path which would lead him down to the trackway and the Devil-in-the-Woods. The day was drawing on. He was distracted by the birdsong, and by crashing in the thicket; he stopped to watch two stoats scurry across the path into the undergrowth on the other side. Now and again he'd pause, looking around to ensure all was well. He felt uncomfortable and, once again, realised he had made a mistake.

'You never think, Hugh!' Maeve had scolded. 'You're that busy, lost in your own thoughts, you wander into danger and don't realise it! Please!' She had grasped his face between her hands. 'Promise me you'll never be alone!'

Corbett drew a deep breath.

'God forgive me, Maeve!'

The birdsong had fallen silent, or was that his imagination? He undid his war belt, as the jars were weighing heavy, and re-hitched it tighter. Holding the leather bag in one hand, his dagger in the other, Corbett walked on quickly. The forest reminded him of the heavy wooded valleys of Wales. He recalled the advice of a master bowman, a scout responsible for leading the King's troops.

'Remember,' he had warned. 'Look to your left and your right. Ignore your imaginings. Listen to the sounds of the forest. If you hear anything strange, move faster, never stand still. A running man is much harder to hit.'

Corbett walked quickly. He felt a pang of pain high in his chest from the wound he had received in Oxford. Memories flooded back. He controlled his panic, listening carefully, watching the trees on either side. A bird broke free from the branches crying in alarm. Corbett again quickened his pace. A twig snapped to his right. Something hit the trackway as if a stone had been thrown. Corbett didn't wait any longer but, body hunched, head down, he broke into a run; moving from side to side, he felt the arrow whistle by his face. He was tempted to stop, throw himself down. The assassin must be somewhere to his right so, leaving the trackway, he plunged into the undergrowth, using the trees as a barrier. He thought he was free but then an arrow thudded into a tree; it quivered with such force, the assassin must be close. Corbett ran on. He tried not to move in a straight line. Branches caught his face, nettles and briars stung his legs. He stumbled and this probably saved his life as another shaft went whirring above his head. Corbett glanced to his right. He must keep the trackway in sight, he must not become lost.

He dropped the leather sack and ran, the pain in his neck intense. He found it hard to breathe. At last he was forced to stop; leaning against a tree, coughing and retching, Corbett scanned the woods and behind him. He could see no sign of the assassin. He looked at his scarred hands, took the gloves from a small pouch in his cloak and put them on. Then he pushed through the undergrowth, back on to the trackway, sure he had left the assassin behind. Whoever it was must have realised pursuit was too dangerous. Ahead of him Corbett heard the creak of a cart. He unhitched his cloak, ignoring the stabs of pain in his belly and the soreness where the branches had caught his skin, and stumbled on, round a corner to the crossroads. The carter, a peasant with his family in the back, gaped in surprise as Corbett grabbed the side of his cart.

'Don't worry!' Corbett gasped. 'I am Sir William Fitzalan's guest, a royal clerk.'

The man continued to register amazement.

'The Devil-in-the-Woods tavern?'

The man nodded his head. Corbett took a coin out of his purse and pushed it into the man's callused hand.

'Take me there!'

Without waiting for an answer, Corbett climbed up beside the driver. He smiled reassuringly at the family, a mother and four children, staring owl-like at him. The farmer snapped the reins.

'The Devil-in-the-Woods you want, sir, then the Devil-in-the-Woods it will be. But, by the looks of you, it seems you've already met the devil!'

Corbett relaxed as the farmer, loudly chuckling

over his own joke, urged his horse on. Corbett glanced over his shoulder into the green darkness. He quietly vowed that he would use all his power and skill to bring his demon to justice.

Chapter 13

'So, you found nothing?' Corbett asked, dabbing his face with the salted water the taverner had given him.

Ranulf, seated on his bed, shook his head.

'Nothing untoward, no sign of any hidden weapons.'

'But could Sir William have gone round the other side of Savernake Dell?' Corbett persisted. 'Taken a hidden bow and a quiver of arrows then killed his brother?'

'It's possible.' Ranulf was secretly wondering how he could explain the sudden brutal attack on his master to Lady Maeve. 'It would only take a short while, a few minutes.'

Corbett winced as he dabbed at his face again.

'Do not tell Lady Maeve what happened.'

Ranulf lifted one hand. 'Oh, on that master, you have my word!'

'So.' Corbett ate a few mouthfuls of rabbit stew a pot boy had brought up and sipped from a blackjack of ale.

'Chapter and verse, Ranulf, what do we have?'

'First, Lord Henry was murdered by an arrow to the heart. The culprits could include his brother, the Owlman who we now know to be the hermit Odo, Brother Cosmas, Robert Verlian and, yes master, even Alicia.'

Corbett smiled at the soft glow in Ranulf's eyes.

'We could include,' he continued, 'the woman Jocasta or an assassin, paid by any of the people we have mentioned. Nor must we forget Seigneur Amaury de Craon.'

'Or the Lady Madeleine,' Corbett added.

'I don't think that's possible.'

'She could have left her convent,' Corbett pointed out. 'Gone to one of the hollowed oaks, taken out a bow and an arrow and shot her brother dead.'

'But why?' Ranulf asked. 'What grudge did she have against her brother? Alive or dead he meant nothing to her. And the other deaths? Moreover, I can't imagine Lady Madeleine riding through the forest, shooting an arrow and hurrying back to her convent walls. She would be fairly distinctive in a nun's gown. Finally . . .'

Corbett lowered his blackjack of ale. Ranulf smiled in triumph.

'All good archers are right-handed. You know that. A left-handed archer is always clumsy. Remember poor Maltote? He couldn't pick a bow up without hurting himself. When we were in the priory I noticed Lady Madeleine was left-handed, the way she held a quill.'

Corbett agreed.

'What else do we have, Ranulf?'

'We have the murder of that young woman, killed by an arrow to the throat. If your conclusion is right, she travelled to Ashdown as a man which was why her corpse was stripped. The clothes probably lie at the bottom of some swamp. Did you find anything?'

Corbett took out from his wallet the two pieces of fabric he had found.

'These, they're braided cloth loops.'

He handed them to Ranulf who went to the window to get a better view, holding each up as if it were a coin.

'They are small fillets,' Ranulf exclaimed. 'Hair bands. Lady Maeve uses the same to braid her hair at the back. She slips it through similar ones to keep the plaiting tight.'

'But the corpse had short hair,' Corbett mused. 'Cropped and close like that of a man? I wonder who she was? I must have words with our taverner. Go on, Ranulf.'

'The Italian physician Pancius Cantrone, also killed by an arrow to the throat. He was coming from St Hawisia's. We know that there was some connection between him, Lord Henry and Amaury de Craon.'

'Yes, that's right. Cantrone may have sold or given Lord Henry some great secret which the French were frightened of. Cantrone may have been killed by outlaws, or by one of de Craon's men to shut his mouth once and for all. Now, we can't question de Craon. He'll claim diplomatic status and send a fiery protest up to Westminster. In the end, Ranulf, we have three murders. Are they separate or are they connected? Is it one assassin, two or even three? Lord Henry's is simple. Everybody hated him. But Cantrone, and that of our mysterious young woman, we cannot fit them into the puzzle.'

'Did you believe the hermit Odo?' Ranulf asked.

'Yes and no. He and Cosmas are still waters which run deep. On the one hand they are priests, basically good men. However, both of them, Odo in particular, nourish deep grievances against the Fitzalans.'

He paused at a knock on the door and Baldock shambled into the room.

'You always wait for Sir Hugh to call you in!' Ranulf told him.

Baldock grinned and shuffled his feet.

Corbett studied the young ostler from head to toe. He had attempted to make himself clean, patting down his hair with water, washing his hands and face, though as a result he had simply pushed the dirt up around his ears.

'What's your first name?'

'Baldock, sir. I've only got one name, Baldock.' He thrust the piece of parchment into Corbett's hand. 'My letter of release, sir.'

'For God's sake, stand still!' Corbett demanded.

'I'm sorry, sir, I'm just excited.'

'Ranulf here tells me you are skilled at throwing a knife. And even better with horses?'

'I sleep with them, sir.'

Corbett glanced warningly at Ranulf. He didn't want his manservant making any quip or joke. Baldock had an innocent face; the cast in one eye gave him a vulnerable, rather innocent look. It was obvious how much the young man wished to join them.

'Have you ever been in trouble, Baldock?'

'Never, sir.'

'Never been taken by an officer of the law?'

'Ah.' Baldock shuffled from foot to foot. 'I've done a bit of poaching, sir. Been chased by verderers, more times than I'd like to count. But I'm a good, loyal servant. I've never stolen from my master.'

Corbett held his hand out. 'Go on man, clasp it.'

Baldock did. His grip was warm and strong.

'Master Baldock, that handshake means everything to me. You are my man in peace and war. You will look after me. I will look after you. You are now an officer of the law, a clerk of the stables.

Where I go, you follow. My home is yours. You will answer to Master Ranulf, who will draw up an indenture this evening. You will be paid well. Share our food, carry sword, dagger and a crossbow. You will be given robes, three times a year, payment once a week with special gifts at Easter, Christmas and midsummer. You will never tell anyone what you hear me say. Do you understand?'

Baldock nodded.

'Good man! Now go to the stables. I want the horses ready for Rye tomorrow morning. We'll leave before first light.'

Baldock fairly skipped from the room.

'Oh!' Corbett shouted after him. 'And tell the taverner I wish to see him now.'

'There goes a happy man,' Ranulf said as Baldock clattered along the passageway and down the stairs. 'But when you have time, master, you must hear him sing. He'd fair frighten Lady Maeve. I'm pleased he's joined us,' he added wistfully. 'I miss old Maltote. I'm glad I killed his assassins.'

Corbett mopped his face again with a rag. He put it back in the bowl at the knock on the door.

'Come in!'

The taverner sidled in wiping blood-streaked hands. He stood in the doorway, fearful of this sharp-eyed clerk and what the gossips in the tap-room were saying about him.

'I was in the fleshing-house, sir. You wanted to see me?'

Corbett took a silver piece from his purse and held it out.

'Go on, take it!'

The taverner wiped his fingers then snatched the coin from Corbett.

'Do you know,' Corbett continued, 'the old proverb: "Always ask the taverner"? Tavern masters have sharp eyes and good memories.' Corbett gestured at a stool. 'Sit down, Master Taybois. Do you remember me asking you about a young woman coming here by herself?'

The taverner nodded.

'I think she did stop here. But she was disguised as a man.'

At this the taverner narrowed his eyes.

'She must have come here,' Corbett shuddered inwardly as he recalled the corpse, 'within the last month, travelling by herself.'

The taverner was now decidedly nervous, rubbing his hands on his apron, swallowing hard.

'Of course,' Corbett exclaimed. 'You know full well what I am talking about! Ranulf, we should have this man arrested!'

'I beg your pardon?' the taverner protested.

'You are a horse thief,' Corbett declared. 'This woman wasn't from Ashdown or the local villages. She must have ridden here. Where's her horse?'

'I don't know what you are talking about, sir.'

'I think you do! You know full well what happened. Let me guess. A young man came here. He probably arrived, how far is it from Rye, a few hours? He stabled his horse, had something to eat, stayed overnight, then left the tavern but he never returned. Days turn into weeks and you, master taverner, are left with a horse and harness. Now, do you remember?'

'What makes you think she came from Rye?'

'A good question, taverner: it's a guess on my part. I believe this mysterious woman had business with Ashdown Manor. There is a strong link between the Fitzalans and the town of Rye so I suspect she came from there.'

The taverner coughed nervously.

'I wouldn't lie,' Ranulf advised him. 'My master gets into a fair rage with liars. Especially those who waste the time of royal clerks!'

'It's true what you say,' the taverner stammered. 'A stranger came here. He talked, well, as if he was foreign but he said he was from Rye. He arrived late in the afternoon. He ate and drank in the taproom, hired a chamber and then he left early the following morning, taking his saddlebags with him.'

'Saddlebags?' Corbett queried.

'Small panniers which he slung over his shoulder,' the taverner explained. 'In the taproom he acted strangely, keeping the cowl over his head. He didn't say much, really no more than a whisper. You know how it is, sir, there's interest in strangers but this one wouldn't be drawn. He had some chicken pie, a tankard of ale and kept to himself.'

'Why did he leave his horse?' Corbett asked.

'I don't know, sir. But he must have been travelling somewhere nearby, the manor, the church, the priory or some place in the woods.' The taverner smacked the heel of his hand against his forehead. 'Ah, that's it, sir! On the morning he left, he was most interested in what hour it was. He ate and drank slowly. Now and again he'd get up and examine the hour candles on either side of the fireplace.'

'And what time did he leave?' Corbett asked.

'I think it must have been an hour before midday. I thought he would return. After all, he'd left his horse, a saddle, some harness though nothing else.'

'He didn't rent a chamber for a second night?'

'No sir, but he said, just before he left, that he might need one that evening but he would settle with me on his return.'

'And you weren't curious when he didn't?'

'Master clerk, I run a tavern. I do not ask people to come and go. Yes, I kept the horse and harness. I fed that stranger's mount for a full week then I sold it to a chapman.'

'And you never thought of alerting Lord Henry or anyone else?'

The taverner just shook his head.

'I'll tell you what happened, sir,' Corbett began. 'The young man who came here was really a woman in disguise, probably French. She travelled up from Rye for a meeting here in Ashdown. Some time around the hour of eleven, on the day following her arrival, she walked down the trackway leading to Ashdown Manor only to be killed by an arrow to the throat.'

'And that was the corpse left at St Hawisia's?'

'Yes sir, it was.'

The taverner spread his hands beseechingly.

'Sir Hugh, I didn't know. Customers often leave . . .'

'It doesn't matter. You've looked after us well, while the stranger did owe you money for the stabling. You could have been more helpful when I first asked though you can make up for that now. Is there anything else you wish to tell me? Such co-operation will not be forgotten.'

The taverner put his face in his hands.

'Ashdown,' he mumbled.

'What was that?' Ranulf asked.

'I asked the stranger if he, or she, knew anybody in the area. "Lord Henry" was the reply and that was it. The stranger smiled. I think it was said to impress me or to lull suspicion.'

'And Lord Henry never came and made enquiries about this mysterious stranger?'

'Nobody did. I did not know what to do, sir. A stranger comes to my tavern then disappears. What happened if the finger of accusation was pointed at me? True, I sold the horse and harness but what could I do?'

'Never mind.' Corbett gestured at Ranulf. 'Let

him go. Keep the silver I have given you, sir. Buy yourself a tankard of ale.'

After the taverner had left Corbett lay down on the bed, staring up at the ceiling.

'This is a tangled mess, Ranulf. The day is drawing on but I think we should visit Sir William again.' He felt his body jerk as he relaxed. 'Do what you want,' he murmured. 'But don't travel far from the tavern.' He propped himself up on one elbow. 'I mean that, Ranulf, the assassin can hunt you as well as he can me.'

Corbett lay back down on the bed, his mind drifting back to that murderous assault in the forest. Who could it be? But, there again, as the taverner had said: everyone now knew of him, who he was and where he went. Ruefully, he reflected that the forest trackways of Ashdown were more dangerous than any alleyway or runnel in London. Yet again he tried to separate the threads one from another. Lord Henry was definitely going to betray Cantrone, hand him back to the French, make a settlement once and for all over the secret he held. But what was that secret? And this mysterious stranger? Why did she travel in disguise? Who was she going out to meet? What was she carrying? And those small hair bands? Why should a woman, whose hair was cropped closer than his own, carry them? Or did they belong to the murderer? Or were they just two items totally unrelated to the matter under investigation?

Corbett sighed and rolled over on his side. Tomorrow he would travel to Rye. He would ask the town council if any whore or brothel-keeper had disappeared. But what would that prove?

Corbett's gaze drifted to the small grille built into the wall to allow air to circulate into the room. Through the grille he could see parts of a tree trunk and, as he moved his head, what he saw was changed, disjointed by the grille. It reminded him of that picture . . . Corbett swung himself off the bed so quickly, Ranulf, penning another poem to Alicia, started and cursed.

'For the love of God, master! I thought you were asleep.'

He watched curiously. Corbett went over to his writing bag, muttering to himself. He took out the Book of Hours given to him by Sir William and opened it at the small parchment picture of Susannah facing her accusers where the eyes of each figure had been cut out. Corbett placed this on the pages at the back of the Book of Hours where Lord Henry had written his own personal memoranda.

'What are you doing, master?'

'I knew I had seen this before, Ranulf! What you do is write out something innocent like a letter with vague sentiments or items of gossip. However, if you impose a picture like this, on top of the writing, it picks out a secret message. The problem is, which way up do you place it? And which of these entries contains the cipher?'

Ranulf leaned over Corbett's shoulder and watched as the clerk applied the picture to each page.

'No, no, that means nothing.'

Corbett tried again.

'And the same that way. All we have is a jumble of words which mean nothing.'

'Are you sure, master?'

Corbett pointed over his shoulder at the grille in the wall.

'I was lying there, looking through that grille. I was half-dozing when I noticed how the small iron bars twist what you see.'

'But are you sure Lord Henry would use such a cipher?'

'It's possible. It certainly explains why we have a small picture, a scene from the Old Testament, where Lord Henry has carefully removed the eyes of each figure.'

Corbett continued to leaf over the pages, Ranulf went back to his poem. The poetry of the French troubadours had greatly impressed him and now he tried to recall certain lines so he could use them to describe Alicia's beautiful blue eyes, the line of her face. Across the room Corbett was still muttering to himself.

The afternoon wore on. Corbett asked for candles and rush-lights to be lit. Now and again he would get up and stretch to ease the cramp. Ranulf thought of Alicia. If only Old Master Long Face would go to sleep, Ranulf could slip out. He wasn't frightened of the forest while a meeting with his loved one removed any fear of attack.

Corbett, however, was now deeply immersed in his studies. When Ranulf had finished his poem he hid it in a small pocket of his doublet. He went down to the stables but Baldock was fast asleep on a bale of straw and Ranulf didn't have the heart to wake him. Instead he walked into the yard and scanned the sky. The sun was now setting, the tavern was quiet and the forest across the pathway seemed more dangerous, more threatening as the shadows lengthened. He heard his master call his name and went back, running up the stairs. Corbett was sitting on the edge of the bed, grinning from ear to ear.

'I've found the secret!' He held up the Book of Hours. 'You remember that story about a saint Johanna Capillana?'

'Yes, the one Lord Henry described in the back of his Book of Hours.'

'I wager, Ranulf, a firkin of ale against a tun of wine, that there is no saint called Johanna Capillana.' He opened the Book of Hours and placed the picture against the text.

'Let me explain, Ranulf. *Capillana* is vulgar Latin for the head, it also stands for Capet.'

'The name of the French royal family!'

Corbett tapped a page excitedly. 'Two years ago Philip's wife, Johanna of Navarre, died rather suddenly. People thought it was a fever but, if you use Lord Henry's cipher, the story of Johanna Capillana becomes the story of Johanna Capet, Queen of France.' Corbett gestured at Ranulf. 'A piece of parchment and a pen!'

Corbett opened the Book of Hours. 'Now, write down the following: "*Johanna Capillana, regina occisa, mari, rex interfecit eam, non per gladum, sed vitrio secreto infuso, teste medico suo.*"

'You have that?'

Ranulf nodded.

'It's doggerel Latin,' Corbett explained. 'Each of these words are framed by a gap in the picture of Susannah and translated . . .'

Ranulf whistled under his breath.

'Johanna Capet,' he said slowly. 'The Queen was slain by her husband. The King killed her, not by the sword but by a secret infusion of poison. This was witnessed or known by her doctor.' Ranulf shook his head. 'Master, it can't be?'

'Clerk of the Green Wax, it can be! If I remember rightly, Gilles Malvoisin was physician to Queen Johanna. I met him on two occasions, a pompous man but a skilled practitioner.'

'But why should Philip kill his own wife?'

'I don't know. But he has a lawyer, a member of his secret council called Pierre Dubois, who has written a confidential memorandum in which he urges Philip to extend his power in Europe, not through war but by marriage.'

'Such as his own daughter Isabella to the Prince of Wales?'

'Precisely. Philip has three sons betrothed to different princesses whose marriage portions and dowries will strengthen the power of the Capets and extend the borders of France.'

'Flanders!' Ranulf exclaimed. 'The Count of Flanders has a daughter.'

Corbett tossed the Book of Hours back on the bed.

'Ranulf, your wits are not as lovelorn as I think. Two years ago Philip invaded Flanders only to be disastrously defeated at Coutrai. It's possible that our Spider King has designs on a Flemish princess though Edward of England would never allow such a marriage.'

'So what else?' Ranulf asked.

'Philip also has designs on the Templar Order. He has, ever since he came to the throne. You've met the Templars, Ranulf: a powerful order of fighting monks. More importantly, the Templars are bankers with houses throughout Europe. Their wealth in France alone totals more than all the receipts of the royal exchequer. Now, a few months ago, there were rumours that Philip himself had applied, as a bachelor, to join the Templar Order.' He glimpsed the puzzlement in Ranulf's eyes. 'Can't you see the path he's treading? Philip becomes a Templar, a fighting monk, dedicated to chastity. It harks back to his saintly ancestor Louis. How Europe would marvel at Philip Capet, king, Christian, warrior and monk. Yet that would only be the beginning of it. If the Templars accepted Philip, I would wager a gold crown that, within two years, he would be Grand Master of the Order.'

Corbett sat back on the bed.

'Can't you imagine it, Ranulf? Philip would not only be King of France but master of an order which spans Europe, from the cold wastes of Norway to the oases of North Africa. From Spain across the Middle Sea to Greece and Syria. He'd have access to their wealth, their power, their knowledge. Philip had everything to gain and nothing to lose by the removal of a wife who had served her days and purpose.'

'And her murder is the secret Lord Henry knew?'

'Yes, Ranulf. Pancius Cantrone was once an associate of Malvoisin the royal physician. Malvoisin died in a boating accident. He was probably murdered because of what he knew. Cantrone fled. Lord Henry provided protection, Cantrone revealed his secret and our sly lord hinted to Philip of France what he knew.'

'In other words Lord Henry was blackmailing him?'

'Yes he was: a few gifts, trinkets, but eventually Lord Henry demanded payment in full.'

'That's why Philip of France asked for him to lead the English embassy to France?'

'Of course. Lord Henry would go there for the

betrothal negotiations. He would receive some lavish reward in return for which he would give up his secret.'

'And poor Pancius Cantrone?'

'Cantrone was to be drugged, bundled aboard a ship and handed over to French officials. Our King could not object. Cantrone was not one of his subjects. Lord Henry would have some suitable story prepared to account for his actions. Amaury de Craon was sent to England, not only to conclude these marriage negotiations but to bring Lord Henry back and ensure he fulfilled his bargain.'

'And what sort of reward would Lord Henry be looking for?'

'I don't know,' Corbett replied. 'Possibly bullion. Whatever, Lord Henry would become one of the richest men in the kingdom. Philip would have silenced Cantrone and the murder of his wife would remain his secret, allowing him to pursue his nefarious designs.'

Ranulf pulled his stool closer. 'But that's dangerous, master.'

'Yes, I know what you are saying,' Corbett mused. 'But let's keep to the main line of our argument. I think Lord Henry knew that Sir William had helped Gaveston, that's why they quarrelled. Lord Henry did not want anything to occur which might prevent him travelling to France with de Craon. Now, let's address the problem you've raised, Ranulf.' He tapped the Book of Hours. 'This is only a story, a rumour, a scurrilous allegation. Philip could reject it out of hand. Secondly, Lord Henry must have realised that travelling into the spider's web was highly dangerous. Which means what, Ranulf? How would Lord Henry protect himself in France?'

Chapter 14

Corbett stood outside the two-storied house in the narrow, cobbled lane which ran from Rye market-place. The houses on either side were of stone and half-timber; glass glinted in the windows. The woodwork was painted a gleaming black and russet brown, its plaster limewashed in white or pink. The sewer down the middle of the street was clean and filled with saltpetre, which made his nose wrinkle. Baldock, holding their horses at the far end of the street, was sneezing at the acrid smell. Ranulf had his hand across his nose. Corbett glanced over his shoulder at the sheriff's man.

'You are sure this is the place? It looks more like a rich merchant's house than a brothel.'

The man pulled back his hood and scratched his balding pate. His lined, wrinkled face broke into a smile, showing the one tooth his mouth boasted.

'When the rich take their pleasures, Sir Hugh, they like to do so discreetly. Clean chambers, crisp linen and the softest flesh, be it from the fields of England or France.'

Corbett looked up at the house. On either side of the door hung shiny brass hooks carrying lantern horns. Above these black iron rods protruded from which flower baskets hung, exuding the sweetest fragrance. The clapper on the door was shaped in the form of a jovial friar, bagpipes in hand, the usual sign for lechery.

'The street's quiet,' he observed.

'It's only noon,' the sheriff's man replied. 'And on Thursdays there's no market.'

'What are we waiting for?' Ranulf asked. 'Master, why not just knock?'

'You can't enter, until the mayor's commission arrives.'

'We carry the King's warrant!' Ranulf snapped.

'The law is,' the sheriff's man repeated ponderously, 'in a royal borough the King's writ must be shown to the mayor before it is executed.'

Corbett winked at Ranulf.

'It will come and I am awaiting it.'

Corbett walked back up the street towards Baldock, gesturing at the other two to follow.

'I don't want the ladies within to be warned.'

Corbett had arrived in Rye just as the bells were sounding for morning Mass. He'd gone to the town hall where the mayor and leading aldermen had been hastily summoned. Corbett had wasted no time. He demanded if they knew a whore, hair cropped short, a lily branded on her shoulder, who had disappeared recently from the town. Of course, there were the usual head-shakings, murmurings and lowered glances. However, Corbett knew that these venerable city fathers could help, despite their assurances that they knew nothing of such women. Corbett loudly wondered whether the royal justices should be summoned to assist. Memories were stirred and a name had been given. Françoise Sourtillon, a courtesan and joint keeper of a discreet house of pleasure in Friar Lane.

'We know nothing of this woman,' the mayor insisted. Except that, how can I put it, her "sister" who lives in the same house, one Roheisia Blancard, has petitioned the city council regarding Françoise's disappearance.'

'And what did you do?' Ranulf demanded.

'We organised a search.' The mayor spread podgy hands. 'But where such women go is not our concern.'

Corbett had thanked them but the mayor had insisted that they wait for his writ before demanding entrance. Corbett replied he would tarry no more than half an hour and he sincerely hoped that, when he entered the house, he would find no disturbance.

'You are not saying we would warn them?'

'Of course not. But I tell you this, sirs, if anyone did, a visit to the Marshalsea prison in London is an experience they'd never forget.'

'Here he comes,' Ranulf said.

A tipstaff was hurrying along the lane, white wand of office in one hand, in the other a scroll tied with a red ribbon. Ranulf didn't wait for Corbett to take it but went to the door and brought the clapper down with a resounding crash. Corbett looked up at the windows. He suspected the ladies inside hadn't even risen for the day. As Ranulf had caustically pointed out, they worked so late at night. Ranulf was now enjoying himself, bringing the clapper up and down until a voice shrieked: 'We have heard! We have heard!'

There was a sound of locks being turned, bolts being drawn. The door swung open. A tall, grey-haired woman, a fur-lined gown over her shoulders, peered out heavy-eyed at them.

'The *Dulcis Domus*,' she told them, 'is closed until dusk.'

'Oh, is that what you call it?' Corbett pushed the door aside. 'The House of Sweetness! And you must be Roheisia Blancard?'

'If you are sheriff's men,' Roheisia answered, glaring at the little official behind Corbett, 'we have paid our dues, as members of the corporation who visit here could attest!'

Corbett surveyed the passageway, quietly marvelling at the comfortable opulence. The air was fragrant with beeswax candles, pots of herbs and the savoury smells of cooking. The paved floor was covered with woollen rugs; the wooden linen-panelling gleamed like bronze.

'Roheisia Blancard?' he said quietly.

'Yes, and you?'

'I am the King's clerk, Sir Hugh Corbett. This is Ranulf. I think you know the gentleman who accompanied us.' Corbett tapped the sheriff's man gently on the shoulder. 'Now you may leave.'

Ranulf almost pushed the protesting official out of the door back into the street. He closed it and pulled across the bolts.

'Now, madam.' Corbett walked closer. 'I carry the King's warrant. I want the truth from you. Or I'll send to Arundel Castle, have you all placed in carts and transported to London for questioning.'

'There's no need to threaten.'

'I am not threatening, madam. I'm promising. Françoise is dead, murdered in Ashdown Forest.'

'I see. I see,' Roheisia said. 'Then you'd best come with me.'

She led them off the passageway into a small parlour, a well-furnished room. The fire in the grate had already been lit. On the walls hung gaudy paintings, garish, not well done but purporting to show scenes from the Old Testament and the classics. They all had one motif in common: plump young wenches in various stages of undress. Roheisia pushed two chairs up in front of the fire while she sat on a bench alongside the wall.

'Do you want something to eat or drink?' she mumbled, clawing her grey hair away from her face.

'No, madam, just the truth and the quicker the better.'

'Françoise came from Abbeville,' she began. She fought back the tears and lifted her face. 'She had been mistress to a nobleman who turned her out so Françoise stole a considerable part of his treasure and fled to Rye.' She shrugged. 'Like is drawn to like. I met her and we decided to share our resources. We bought this house and keep it well stocked with plump, fair flesh.'

'And why did Françoise leave?'

'I don't know.' She saw the warning look in Corbett's face. 'Truly, sir, I don't. A month ago, she took a horse from the stables, filled some saddle-bags and said she would be away for two or three days but she'd come back a wealthy woman. Now, you can take me to London, you can burn and tear my flesh but that's all I know.' She leaned back against the panelling and looked up at the ceiling. 'How did she die?'

'An arrow to the throat. Her corpse was stripped and buried in a shallow grave. We suspect she was disguised as a man.'

Roheisia laughed deep in her throat. 'That's the way Françoise always dressed when she travelled.' Her eyes became wary. 'Françoise, how can I put it, she did not like men though she liked to act the part herself. She could swagger and curse with the best of them. If she was in Ashdown then she must have been travelling to see Lord Henry Fitzalan.'

'Do you know he's dead as well? Killed by an arrow?'

The woman looked startled.

'No, no, I did not.'

'It will become common knowledge soon enough. But what makes you think she was visiting Lord Henry?'

'Because he always visits us and he's the only person in Ashdown Françoise knew.'

'Lord Henry often came here?'

'Oh, a true cock of the walk our manor lord.' Roheisia grinned. 'But, before you ask, Françoise shared her bed with no man. She entertained him, mind you. She allowed him to peep into the chambers when others were there and allowed him the choicest wench.'

'Why?'

'Oh, not because Françoise liked him. If the truth be known, Françoise hated him. For what he was, for his wealth, for the way he didn't care. A man, how did she put it? Yes, that's it, deeply in love with himself. I'm a whore, master clerk. A strumpet, a bawd. But I fear God and I do not pretend to be what I'm not. If Françoise was to be believed, Lord Henry Fitzalan feared neither God nor man.'

'You do not grieve over her death?' Ranulf asked.

'I will grieve in my own way! And in my own time and place. So you, sir, with your cat eyes and sharp face, ask your questions and be gone for I can help you no further!'

'Which of your ladies did he favour the most?' Corbett asked.

'He favoured them all. Variety is the spice of life, he would boast. Sometimes he'd take one, sometimes he'd take two or three together.'

'Would any of them know?' Corbett paused. He had to be careful how he asked this question.

'Would who know what?' she asked angrily.

'Why, madam, one of the other ladies? Did Françoise have her favourites? Someone she confided in?'

'I know what you are saying, clerk. However, as long as the girls keep themselves clean, cause no disturbance and make themselves available, what they do is a matter for them.'

'So you cannot help us?'

'No, I cannot.'

'In which case,' Corbett took the warrant out of his pouch, 'I want the entire house roused. I want to meet all your ladies.' He opened his purse and tossed a gold piece at the woman, who caught it deftly. 'I want it done now.'

Roheisia left without demur. Corbett sat back in the chair and listened to the house being roused, the clatter of feet above him; shouts, a cry of protest, footsteps on the stairs. Roheisia swept back into the room and gave the most mocking curtsey.

'My lord, the ladies of the house are assembled in our hall. If you would like to favour them? You've paid for your introduction. But, if you touch any of the merchandise, you must pay.'

Ranulf was about to reply but Corbett held his hand up. Roheisia, who had now fastened her gown tightly around her, pushed back the door.

'They can only hold their eagerness for so long.'

'Do they know who I am?'

'A King's man. But still a man.'

Roheisia swept out of the room, leading Corbett and Ranulf down the passageway to a long, dark, wooden panelled room at the back of the house. The tousled ladies were assembled around a long dining table. Most of them wore cloaks, or robes, about their shoulders. A host of pale faces, heavy eyes, confronted the two men. About a dozen in number of different sizes, ages and, Corbett suspected, nationalities sat there. A few were beautiful. Some, who looked raddled, didn't even bother to raise their heads when Corbett and Ranulf entered the chamber. A few looked boldly at him; one pursed her lips and blew a kiss in Ranulf's direction. Corbett saw his embarrassment as he tapped the table with his fingers.

'Ladies, accept my apologies for this rude awakening. I am the King's clerk, I need to ask you certain questions. A member of this . . .' He paused. 'This community, Françoise Sourtillon, was murdered in Ashdown Forest.'

Their smiles and giggles disappeared.

'Do any of you know why she should go there?'

'The Fitzalan lord.' A fat, red-haired woman spoke up.

'Did she say as much?' Corbett asked.

'If Françoise told me little,' Red Hair replied, 'she would tell even less to my sisters here.'

'Do any of you know?' Ranulf barked. He felt uncomfortable. The brothel brought back memories and this made him uneasy as his heart was now set on the chaste and beautiful Alicia.

'We know nothing,' Red Hair retorted boldly.

Her reply was greeted with nods and murmurs of agreement.

'The one who could tell you,' said a young, flaxen-haired woman at the end of the table, 'is Cecilia.'

'And where is she?' Corbett asked.

'Gone,' Roheisia said. 'Lord Henry removed her from the house.'

'Why?'

'We don't know. We heard rumours that she had been lodged in a tavern in the town and then sent abroad.'

'And why should Lord Henry do that?'

'I don't know. He bought her from Françoise, paid for her services in good gold. Cecilia left and that's the last we heard of her.'

'So she could be in Rye?'

'It's possible.' Red Hair spoke up. 'But Mistress Roheisia is correct. Lord Henry had a fancy for the girl. He lay with her on a number of occasions and then she was gone.'

'Is this customary?'

'If a lord likes a wench, he can buy her indentures and rent her a private chamber for his own personal pleasure.' Roheisia shrugged one shoulder then winked at Corbett as a sign that she wished to say more but not here. 'So,' Roheisia said as she got to her feet. 'If, sir clerk, you have no more questions for my sisters, they need their rest.'

Corbett looked round the different faces but could detect no sign or gesture that these ladies of the night were prepared to help him. He thanked them, handed two pieces of silver to Roheisia to buy each a goblet of wine and followed her back into the parlour. Roheisia closed the door behind him and stood, clicking her tongue.

'I am sorry.' She smiled. 'But your silver has just jogged my memory. Françoise was close to Cecilia but, like any of us, would never stop one of her sisters' advancement. To become the mistress of a manor lord marked the beginning of a prosperous career.'

'But?' Corbett asked.

'Cecilia left about two months ago. One evening I found Françoise here, in the parlour, in a terrible rage. She wouldn't tell me what had happened except what you learned in there: how Lord Henry had bundled Cecilia aboard a ship and sent her to foreign parts.'

'Why?'

'I don't know. But Françoise declared she had made careful searches among the different ships which berth at Rye. Apparently she learnt from a captain of a cog what Lord Henry had done.'

'And?'

'All Françoise said was that she'd teach that reprobate to treat Cecilia as he had. I asked what she meant by that, she didn't reply.'

'Did Françoise leave any private papers?' Ranulf asked. 'Documents, letters?'

Corbett took out a pure gold piece from his purse. Greed flared in Roheisia's eyes.

'Françoise could write and read her letters.'

'And could Cecilia?'

'It's possible.'

'What did this Cecilia look like?' Corbett asked.

'Oh, young, slender, very beautiful, hair like spun gold. It fell down almost to the floor, very proud of it was Cecilia. Françoise used to comb it for her. Very popular with the lords was our young Cecilia. Françoise made them pay heavily for her favours.' She looked at the gold coin. 'I'll see what I can do.'

She left the parlour, asking if they wanted refreshments, but Corbett refused. A vague suspicion stirred in his mind.

'What do you make of this?' Ranulf asked once Roheisia had gone.

'I don't know. But let's see what our lady of the night can find for us.'

'We should go after her,' Ranulf urged. 'Search this place from garret to cellar.'

Corbett shook his head.

'First, Ranulf, that would only alienate our good ladies. Secondly, Françoise has been missing for a month. I am sure the good Roheisia has already been through her documents and papers. She knows there is something which might interest us and she's gone to find it. If we start stamping our feet and rattling our swords, I don't think it will be handed over to us.'

Roheisia came back, a sheaf of greasy-edged parchment in her hand. She thrust these at Corbett but held on to them until he handed across the gold piece. By the light of a candle he quickly went through the different pieces of parchment. One or two were items of purchase, one a letter, enigmatic and curt: Corbett suspected it was a message to one of her clients, or at least a draft that had never been sent. He glanced up. Roheisia was watching him closely.

'Don't play games, mistress,' he warned her. 'I don't pay gold for an empty cup. You knew all this when we first arrived!'

'Oh, there's something there,' she admitted. 'Not much.'

Corbett continued searching through the papers and then he found it. A draft of a letter to Cecilia

Hocklewell at the Chambard tavern in Dieppe. Corbett felt slightly guilty. Françoise had written it as if she were Cecilia's lover rather than her friend, vowing how she missed her, that she would return. He noticed the phrase, 'when your glory has been restored'. He glanced at Roheisia.

' "When your glory has been restored", Mistress Roheisia? What on earth does that mean?'

She stared blankly back. Corbett rolled up the piece of parchment and put it in his wallet.

'Madam, I come here as the King's officer. You know full well that Françoise has been murdered in the same forest where Lord Henry was killed. Now, there's more to Lord Henry than being a client of your house. He and Françoise shared a common bond, Cecilia. Lord Henry took her out, ostensibly as his personal mistress, but then he bundled her abroad. Françoise makes careful searches. She finds Cecilia but she apparently refuses to come back until what Françoise calls "her glory" is restored.' He gripped Roheisia's wrist. 'Now, madam, an explanation!'

Roheisia swept across to a chair and sat down on it. She sat like a queen, hands dangling down the side. 'I hate men. I hate them because they are hypocrites, because they believe they can buy what is precious. They strut in here full of wine, mouths bleary, cocks hard, as if this is nothing more than a barnyard. I liked, even loved Françoise but, as the years passed, this grew cold. It was

Françoise who brought Cecilia into our house. A Kentish girl. I never knew whether she loved Cecilia as her daughter or as a man would a maid. Françoise distrusted Lord Henry but allowed him to take Cecilia out. When Françoise discovered that she had gone missing, she became demented. The management of this house, the pleasuring of our clients were forgotten. Lord Henry came here and she confronted him. I heard nothing of their bitter words, only Lord Henry laughing, mocking her as he often did. Françoise became determined. She became a constant visitor to the harbour. She would go out visiting this place or that. Sometimes she was absent for days. She'd curse Lord Henry and said both he and his family would pay for what they had done. *Ça ira*, that's all I know.'

'And Cecilia's glory?' Ranulf asked.

'She must be referring to the girl's face. What Lord Henry did, I am unsure: in his cups he could be vicious. There are men, master clerk, who like to beat women, see them bleed before they can take their pleasure with them.'

'And you think this happened?' Corbett asked. 'That Lord Henry beat Cecilia so badly, he sent her to Dieppe to hide any scandal?'

'It's possible.'

'So, Cecilia wouldn't return until these wounds were healed?'

'Again that's possible. It's also possible that Françoise travelled to Ashdown to confront Lord

Henry but, to do that, she was very foolish. After all, who cares if an arrow slits a whore's throat?'

'Are there any other letters?' Ranulf asked.

Roheisia threw her head back and laughed. 'Françoise was like myself, young sir. Our correspondence? Let me put it this way, good whoring and letters do not go together. A love note received on Monday can be dangerous by Friday. Françoise was no different. Before she left she either burned her letters or took them with her. I only found those by mistake. She'd left them in a pocket of a robe hung on a peg in her chamber. Master clerk?'

Corbett was sitting, eyes closed. 'I wonder,' he murmured, 'Ranulf, I really do, what Lord Henry did to that girl?'

In the priest's house, a narrow, two-storied dwelling built just behind the church of St Oswald's-in-the-Trees, Alicia Verlian filled a goblet for her father and placed it on the table in Brother Cosmas' clean-swept kitchen. Outside darkness was falling, the silence broken by the sounds of the forest as it awaited the night. The verderer sipped from the cup and glanced across at his daughter.

'It will be good to get back,' he said.

'We should leave now,' Alicia replied. 'You have nothing to fear and Sir Hugh will protect us against Sir William.'

Verlian shook his head. 'It's best to wait.'

Alicia looked at her father pityingly. He had aged

in the last few days, nervous, unsure of himself. He was even frightened by the shadows in the church. Brother Cosmas had kindly agreed that he could move into his house. Indeed, since Corbett's questioning in the church, the Franciscan had grown very preoccupied. He had left early in the afternoon, saying he wished to have words with Odo.

'But make yourselves comfortable,' he had offered. 'I have some wine, dried meats and freshly baked bread. Build the fire up. Alicia, if you wish, you can stay, sleep in the church or make up beds for both of you on the kitchen floor.'

With that he had taken his cloak and cudgel and left them. Alicia had repaid his kindness by tidying up the sanctuary and sweeping the floor. She promised herself that, tomorrow, she would return to her own house and bake some pies, recompense for this gruff priest's kindness.

'Do you think it will end soon?' Her father broke into her thoughts.

'Sir Hugh is a good man. He will execute the King's justice without fear or favour. However, he keeps his thoughts to himself. I suspect, Father, there's more to this man than you and I can ever imagine.'

'And the other one?' her father teased, trying to lighten his mood. 'Who walks and looks like a cat? He is much smitten by you, Alicia.'

'And I by him,' she admitted.

'Would you become handfast to such a man?'

Alicia glanced away. 'And what would you do then, Father?' She tugged at the Franciscan robe he wore. 'Become a priest?'

'I don't know what I will do,' Verlian said. 'But, when this is all over, I am finished with the Fitzalans!'

'And now you want to marry me off?'

'He's an ambitious young man.' Verlian grasped his daughter's wrists. 'Alicia, you don't favour him because you have something to hide?'

She blushed. 'I have nothing to hide, Father. Ranulf-atte-Newgate is a personable young man. I have never met his like before. Oh, some of the forest people are kind but Lord Henry was really no different from the rest, except he had the power and the wealth to pursue his lust.'

Alicia studied her father's face. She loved him so deeply. He was gentle and kindly, being both mother and father to her. A man who loved the forest, he'd taught her everything she knew. Even as a little girl he would take her out to show her a badger's sett or a fox's lair, even climb a tree to study the thrush's eggs. How could she tell him about her secret?

'You wouldn't become a nun?' he teased. 'Not one of Lady Madeleine's ladies?'

'I don't know, Father.'

Verlian's heart sank. He'd meant it as a joke but she didn't object as he had expected.

'I have . . .' She stumbled over her words. 'I know

what I do not want to be. I . . . I wish . . .'

'Do whatever you want, child,' he reassured her.

Alicia was going to reply when there was a loud rapping on the front door. She made to rise but Verlian, embarrassed by his own fears, shrugged a shoulder and got to his feet.

'Stay there, daughter. It will only be one of the forest folk looking for Brother Cosmas.' Pulling the cowl over his head, Verlian limped towards the door and opened it. 'Who's there?' he called.

Outside a cold breeze had sprung up, setting the fallen leaves whirling like lost souls. Verlian smelt the fragrance of the forest; his anger curdled to be locked away from it. He walked out on to the porch. Behind him the door swung open. Verlian stepped forward, then realised he had made a mistake. No one was about and he was a target against the light behind him. He turned but, even as he did, the arrow caught him full in the heart.

Chapter 15

Corbett contemplated the corpse laid out in its Franciscan robe. The coffin was no more than a wooden casket, probably an arrow box; thick, white bandages bulged over the dead man's chest. These closed the wound, yet death was never presentable: two coins kept Verlian's eyes closed but the face was sunken, unshaven, the mouth slightly open. The man's hands lay across his chest clasping a wooden crucifix. Corbett heard the sound of weeping. He went and stood in the entrance in the rood screen of St Oswald's-in-the-Trees from where he saw that Ranulf sat on the bench with Alicia.

The young woman's grief over her father's murder was uncontrollable. Her eyes were red-rimmed with crying, her face pallid, her beautiful hair fell into tangles to her shoulders. She sat head forward, hands clasped in her lap. Ranulf had one hand on her shoulder, whispering to her, but she seemed not to listen to what he was saying. Corbett went over and knelt down.

'Mistress Alicia, I am truly sorry. I am also sad that there's nothing I can say, or do, to ease your terrible grief.'

'My father was murdered.' Alicia brought her head up. 'He was a good man, clerk. It was so sudden,' she gasped. 'We were sitting in the priest's kitchen. There was a knock on the door. Father went on to the porch, he called out then I heard him fall. I ran out but no one was there, nothing but the forest.'

Corbett patted her gently on the hands before returning to put the lid on the coffin. He glanced across at Brother Cosmas kneeling at the prie-dieu before the Lady Chapel.

'Why?' the Franciscan grated, getting to his feet. 'Why do such murders occur, Corbett? Why didn't Christ send one of his angels?'

'You know the reason,' Corbett said. He pointed to the wall where an artist had drawn a crude but vivid picture of Satan, depicted as a hare, chasing foxes with human faces. The hare had a demonic mask, its long ears were horns, its eyes fiery red and in its sharp claws it carried a net. 'Christ called Satan the first killer. We are all assassins, Brother. Here.' He tapped his chest. 'In our hearts we wish to kill and destroy. Didn't you ever want to lift a sword, a club against Lord Henry? God forgive me, Brother, but the Frenchman, Amaury de Craon, I would love to finish matters with him! Pay a reckoning which has increased over the years.' Corbett walked towards the priest. 'But I tell you this. I am going to take my net and trap this killer. Our only defence, our only protection against these sons of Cain, who put their murderous lusts into action, is the law.'

'And the justice of God,' the Franciscan added.

'Aye and there's the mystery. God's justice depends on us. You should pray, Brother.'

'I always do.'

'No, you should pray for Verlian and for yourself.'

Brother Cosmas looked puzzled.

'I don't believe the killer intended to slay Verlian,' Corbett explained. 'I think he intended to kill you!'

The Franciscan's fingers went to his lips. '*Jesu miserere!*'

'Think about it, Brother. A knock on the door at night, Verlian answered it . . .'

'Of course, he was dressed in one of my robes! Alicia told me the cowl was up!'

'The killer didn't know Verlian was sheltering in your house, that you had gone to see Odo.'

The Franciscan nodded.

'The assassin would only have a short while, a few seconds. In the poor light Verlian would look like you. An arrow is loosed and so is the poor man's soul.'

'So, who could it be? Who would want me dead?'

'I don't know yet, brother, though I have a suspicion. And you know the true irony? I think the assassin, even if you had been killed, would have made a mistake. But now I must go.'

Corbett went through the rood screen and saw that Ranulf was still sitting next to Alicia. The young woman was talking softly, earnestly. When Ranulf looked up, Corbett had never seen him look so stricken, no longer the roaring boy, the street fighter, Jack the lad with his sardonic smile. Ranulf looked younger, like a child who has learned a hideous secret.

'I'll be at the tavern,' Corbett told him. 'When you are ready, join me.'

Corbett nodded to the priest and walked down the church. He collected his horse, still weary and mud-spattered from their hasty ride from Rye, and slung himself into the saddle. As he was about to spur into a gallop riders broke from the trees. Corbett's hand went to his sword but he reined in as he glimpsed the Fitzalan livery. Sir William rode up, pushing back the hood of his military cloak.

'I thought you'd gone to Rye, Corbett?'

'I did. We left there before dawn.'

Sir William nodded at the church.

'Another killing, poor Verlian.'

'Aye, poor Verlian.'

Sir William searched Corbett's face for sarcasm. 'He was a good verderer, very skilled in forest law.'

'He was also a good man and a loving father,' Corbett said.

'I know. I know,' Sir William replied testily. 'I came here last night to pay my respects.' He shifted in the saddle. 'Sir clerk, I admit, we Fitzalans have done great harm to that family. I will ensure Verlian gets proper burial.'

'And his daughter?' Corbett asked.

'Why, sir, hasn't she told you?' Sir William didn't wait for an answer. 'She has a kinswoman, a prioress at Malmesbury. I have agreed to provide Mistress Alicia with a proper dowry . . .'

'She's to enter a convent!' Corbett exclaimed. 'She will take vows?'

'She will enter a convent,' Sir William affirmed, leaning down and patting his horse's neck. 'But whether she takes vows is a matter for her. Last night I swore an oath and my word is good. She will receive a dowry and an annual pension.'

He gathered his reins but Corbett held out a restraining hand.

'Sir William, why did you leave the hunt the morning your brother was killed?'

'I've told you. My belly was weak, my bowels like water.'

'No, they weren't,' Corbett said, pushing his horse alongside. 'You drank very little wine the night before, even though it was tainted.'

'How do you . . .!'

'Never mind! Why did you leave the hunt and go into the trees? Was it to be away from the marksman? The assassin hiding on the other side of the forest dell?'

'Don't be ridiculous!'

'Don't threaten me, my lord! Tell me this. You Fitzalans are hunters, aren't you? You were all born to the chase?'

Fitzalan's anger was replaced by puzzlement.

'What has that got to do with it?'

'Never mind. Now, if Lord Henry, who drank the tainted wine, could recover, why not his brother?'

'I'll tell you, Corbett. On the morning of the hunt there was nothing wrong with my belly or my bowels. But, as I waited in Savernake Dell, my brother threatened me over my help for Gaveston. You didn't really know the Lord Henry, did you? He was a man who drank deep of power, particularly over other people. If he had the knife in you, he'd turn it until you screamed.'

'Like he did with the King of France?'

Sir William looked shocked. 'What? What?' he stammered.

'Just tell that to Amaury de Craon,' Corbett murmured. 'But you were talking about your brother?'

'Once I realised he knew about Gaveston,' Sir William's shoulders sagged, 'I knew I would never hear the end of it. Not as long as he lived. I went away, frightened and humiliated, to be sick. I puked like some little boy. I couldn't stop trembling. Can you imagine it, Corbett, living at the beck and call of someone like Henry?'

'Is that why Lady Madeleine became a nun?'

'I confess this, Corbett and, if you ever repeat it, I'll drive my gauntlet into your face. Madeleine hates men and can you blame her? Years ago, every time Henry had the opportunity, he had his hands up her skirts as if she were some tavern wench.'

Corbett drew back his horse, shocked at what Sir William had told him.

'So, I bid you adieu, clerk.'

Sir William was about to ride on but Corbett caught the reins. Sir William's hand fell to the pommel of his sword.

'Hush, my lord,' Corbett said. 'Just remember to tell Seigneur de Craon exactly what I said to you about Henry and his master!'

'He'll be gone soon, thank God! He's away to Eltham for an audience with the King.'

'And Gaveston?'

'Why, clerk, I am now a manor lord. The King's most faithful subject. Gaveston is well beyond the seas.'

Sir William rode on into the small yard in front of the church, his horsemen clustered about him. Deep in thought about what Sir William had said, Corbett dug his spurs in.

Once he had reached the tavern, Corbett went up to his own chamber where he cleared the small table, took out a piece of parchment, quills and pumice stone and wrote down everything he had learned. A scullion brought up a trauncher of food and some ale. Corbett absentmindedly thanked him and went back to his writing.

He listed the names of the victims who had been killed in the forest, all slain by an arrow, then looked up and tapped his quill against his cheek. Somewhere on the edge of the forest a wood pigeon cooed rhythmically time and again. Corbett felt a twinge of pain in his neck and nursed the scar left by the assassin in Oxford. And the secret? Fitzalan's blackmailing of the French king. Where was the proof? Sir William didn't know anything about it. Was de Craon involved? He wrote down 'Pancius Cantrone the Italian physician', then laughed softly.

Of course there were no hidden manuscripts! Cantrone was the proof! He had been physician to the royal court in France: that's how the pact was to be sealed! Philip would be only too pleased and pay heavily to have his hands on such a man. Once Cantrone was gone, Lord Henry Fitzalan could say nothing. True, Corbett reflected, Lord Henry might have left some cryptic message with his brother but, 'Oh, the beauty of it all!' he murmured. Of course, Philip would have Cantrone but Lord Henry would have gold bullion despatched by Philip's bankers. The French king would effectively silence

Fitzalan: how could an English lord explain to his King how he became so rich at the hands of the French? He might even be accused of treason! It was like a game of chess. Philip and Lord Henry would have checkmated each other.

Corbett heard a sound on the stairs and Ranulf slipped into the room. He sat on the edge of the bed, a woebegone expression on his face.

'I talked to Alicia.'

'Does she love you?' Corbett asked. 'I am sorry to be so abrupt but that's what it's all about. Not power, money or influence. Does she love you? For, as the poet says, "What is love if it is not returned?" '

Ranulf put his face in his hands. 'She doesn't know,' he muttered. 'She cannot say, she will not tell.' He stamped one foot. 'But she's intent on entering a nunnery, a house near Malmesbury, and her mind will not be changed. I asked her why. She said she wants peace, a time to think and reflect.' He raised tear-filled eyes. 'But I know, once she enters, she'll never come out. And when she's gone I've lost her for ever. I didn't think it would be like this, master. Kiss them and tease them! But this emptiness.' He got up and walked to the door. 'I'll be across the trackway.' Ranulf didn't turn his face. 'You are close to the killer, aren't you?' he asked. 'I can see that in your eyes.'

'Yes, I'm close.'

'You have the evidence?'

'No, Ranulf, I don't. This is going to be a mixture of logic and trickery. I want to go through Fitzalan's Book of Hours again.' He paused. 'Ranulf, where I take you and Baldock, I want your word, no violence.'

'You have my word, master. No violence.'

Ranulf closed the door. Corbett sighed and turned to his parchment. Again he listed all the victims. All the items he had learned. 'What is common to all of these?' he asked himself. 'What is the single factor which answers each question?'

Corbett scribbled down a name and then, putting the quill down, recalled all that had happened, putting himself into the mind of the assassin, watching that dark shape slip through the trees meting out death without pity or remorse. Killing and killing again for what? Corbett got up and fastened on his war belt.

'It's best done now,' he said out loud to the empty room. 'If de Craon is returning to Eltham, I must be there when he meets the King!'

Corbett took his cloak, went down the stairs and out into the stable yard shouting for Baldock. They led out Ranulf's horse and found him sitting on a fallen log across the trackway.

'It's time, isn't it?'

'Yes, Ranulf, it's time.'

On reaching St Hawisia's priory, Corbett was in no mood for the moans and barbed comments of Sister Veronica.

'I wish to see the lady prioress!' he demanded. He

thrust the King's commission into her face. 'And I wish to see her now, alone in the priory church! She'll know where to meet me.'

The little nun scuttled off, now quite frightened by this grim-faced clerk and his attendants. Corbett walked up the path, through the rose garden and in by a side door. The church was quiet, calm; the air still rich with the smell of incense and beeswax candles after the midday service.

'Ranulf! Baldock! Stay at the back!' He grasped Ranulf's arm. 'Promise me! You will do nothing!'

When Corbett plucked both Ranulf's sword and dagger from their sheaths Ranulf didn't demur and Corbett walked up into the side chapel. He placed both sword and dagger on the great oaken sarcophagus and stared through the tinted, silver-rimmed glass at the beautiful golden hair which lay coiled on its silken couch.

'Blasphemy and sacrilege!' he whispered.

The far door opened but Corbett didn't look up until Lady Madeleine stopped at the tomb before him.

'You've come to venerate our relic, Sir Hugh?' Her voice was soft.

Corbett glanced up. 'Why should I do that, Lady Madeleine? Why should I venerate the hair of a whore from the town of Rye?'

Lady Madeleine gripped the tomb more tightly and swayed slightly. Corbett grasped her elbow and took her over to the small stone plinth which ran along the wall.

'Why do you say that, Sir Hugh?' Lady Madeleine's face had paled, her eyes were watchful. 'What nonsense is this?'

'Lady Madeleine Fitzalan,' Corbett replied. 'Daughter of a noble family, half-sister to Lord Henry and Sir William. A woman who was raised in the noble tradition, an accomplished horse-rider, huntress and archer. In your golden days, before life turned sour, you played in Ashdown Forest. You and your brothers came to know these woods better than any of the forest people, particularly Savernake Dell and the hollow oaks.'

Lady Madeleine had her head down, hands resting in her lap.

'But life changes,' Corbett continued. 'As the heart grows older it comes on colder sights. The harshness of age begins to freeze the joy of youth. You grew to hate your brother Henry. And why not? Perhaps you had good cause. A lord who feared neither God nor man. However, the Fitzalans used their influence to make you prioress at St Hawisia's: this became your castle, your fortress against the world of men. A community of women, devoted to the memory of a woman who had been killed by her own family.' Corbett paused.

'Are you going to say I killed my brother?' Lady Madeleine asked coolly. She lifted her face. Corbett could see she had regained her wits.

'Yes, you are a murderess,' he replied. 'You have the blood of many people on your hands: Lord

Henry, Pancius Cantrone, Robert Verlian, as well as the whore Françoise Sourtillon.'

'And pray, clerk, how did I murder these? And why should I?'

'You don't deny it,' Corbett noted. 'And you know of Verlian's death.'

'Gossip spreads quickly in Ashdown.'

'Aye, it does. Let me go to the beginning.' Corbett pointed at the tomb. 'Your patron saint Hawisia is the cause of all these deaths, isn't she? I learned how this shrine had been closed for a while.' He gazed round the pink-washed walls. 'Refurbished, wasn't it?'

'Stop your questions, clerk, and come to the point!'

'Lord Henry came here,' Corbett continued. 'While you were away collecting your rents, acting lady of the manor. He brought that Italian physician Cantrone with him. Lord Henry was a cynic, constantly ridiculing you about your shrine and its sacred relic so he opened the glass case to examine the hair more carefully, or rather Cantrone did it for him. The glass case is fixed by clasps. A man skilled as Cantrone could loosen these and take the hair out. He examined its texture. He wanted to please his lord and prove that this was no relic. I don't know what really happened but the hair decayed. Perhaps some contagion in the air? They put the hair back but it began to wither and rot. You returned and realised what had happened. The relic had been violated. Lord Henry returned to the priory. Did he come back to bait you? Rejoice in what he had done?'

'Do you have proof of this?' she asked. 'Such blasphemy, such sacrilege would cause both uproar and outcry.'

'I don't think so, my lady. You had come back to St Hawisia's. By your own admission you go away as rarely as possible. You hear your brother had been here, locking himself in the church. You recall his baiting, his cynical attacks upon your relic. The first thing you do is go and check. At first you see nothing disturbed, nothing out of place. But a day, maybe two days later, you notice the hair decaying. The shrine is closed and Lord Henry is immediately invited here. You are furious but you want to keep the matter secret. After all, the relic is a source of revenue as well as status. I can imagine Lord Henry's malicious glee. How did you threaten him, eh? What happened during that furious, hushed row between brother and sister? Lord Henry must have realised the danger he had placed himself in. After all, if the relic was destroyed, you could claim it was due to sacrilege, a blasphemous act. Holy Mother Church does not like such actions. If the scandal reached Canterbury, Lord Henry could face excommunication. Now, for a powerful lord, one who hopes to lead an embassy to France on behalf of his King . . .' Corbett paused and let his words hang in the air.

Further down the church he could see Ranulf sitting with his back to a pillar. Baldock sat beside him, whispering in his ear, and Corbett realised that Ranulf had found a new friend. He could tell by Baldock's face that the groom was doing his best to console his new-found patron. Corbett glanced round. Lady Madeleine now had her hands folded as if in prayer. As she looked at him, her face smooth, eyes wide, he caught a glimpse of the beauty she must have been as a young woman but he also saw the glint of obsession, the gleam of a fanatic in her eyes.

'Lord Henry must have sobered up,' Corbett went on. 'What he'd done as a jibe against his pious sister had gone terribly wrong. So he offers reparation, something which can please you both. The shrine will be sealed off for refurbishment; the walls repainted and gilded at his expense. This will hide the damage to the relic while he tries to look for a replacement.'

'And I accepted this, clerk?'

'You had no choice. No relic, no pilgrims, no royal status.' Corbett paused. 'I wondered how you could be drawn into Sir William's petty meddling with Gaveston and the Prince of Wales. You did it for one reason. Not because of any childhood friendship. No, help the Prince now and, when he became King, St Hawisia's would become one of the most famous shrines in all of England. You couldn't lose that.' Corbett tapped the oaken sarcophagus. 'Anyway, the shrine is sealed off. Workmen are not brought in till Lord Henry has fulfilled his side of the bargain. Unknown to you he goes to Rye. He buys the beautiful golden hair of a whore. He pays her off and bundles her aboard a ship to France. Her golden locks, her glory, are brought here, probably by Cantrone, a skilled physician. The hair is dressed in certain potions and unguents which will keep it fresh and supple. If decay occurs again it can always be replaced. The hair is brought secretly to the shrine. You open the glass case and replace the relic. The rest of the shrine is repainted and refurbished and, once again, opened to receive the prayers of the good nuns and the pious faithful. Now that should have been the end of the matter!'

Corbett sat down beside her.

'With any other man it would have been the end. Lord Henry had fulfilled his side of the bargain, but he had some control over you. He must have reminded you about that. How, if matters between you ever became bitter, he could deny his sacrilege but, perhaps, let it be known the true origins of your famous relic. Did he then tell you where it came from? Did he hint? Did he think that it was amusing and mock you with his revelation?'

'As you said, sir clerk.' Lady Madeleine turned her face. 'Lord Henry feared neither God nor man.'

'Unfortunately for both of you,' Corbett continued, 'someone found out what had been done: a brothel mistress from Rye. She had a special affection for the young whore Cecilia whose hair had been sacrificed. She made careful enquiries. She discovered that Cecilia had been sent abroad, so Françoise comes to Ashdown. Now, I doubt if Lord Henry would have told her why he plucked Cecilia's golden tresses. However, Françoise Sourtillon was a woman of the world, wasn't she? I suspect she came here to St Hawisia's and visited the relic. One among many pilgrims. Françoise knew Cecilia's hair, she had combed it often enough, she realised the truth behind your relic. Did she confront you? Or would the great prioress refuse to see her?

'So, François writes you a letter. At first glance an innocent-looking missive but you would read between the lines. Did she threaten you with blackmail or public ignominy? You, of course, sent a sweet, innocent note back. Why shouldn't Françoise come up and discuss these matters? Perhaps she could stay at the Devil-in-the-Woods tavern? Françoise, full of anger, would accept this. She wanted reparation. She wanted justice.'

'And I left my priory and rode out and killed her?' Lady Madeleine taunted.

'I think it's possible. You have your own house, kitchens and stable. There is a side gate leading from there into the forest. You answer to no one. You can issue an order that you are not to be disturbed and go riding. Dressed in a cloak and cowl who would suspect this was the prioress? You have fixed the date and time when Françoise should meet you. I checked with the taverner. Françoise stayed there one night, then the next morning she left the tavern. She walked along that lonely trackway to be at the prearranged meeting place at the appointed hour. It would be some lonely spot, not far from the tavern, a dell or a clearing? Perhaps you even offered to meet Françoise on the trackway?'

'To send such a letter would be dangerous.'

'Would it? Unsigned? Unsealed? Especially if you told Françoise to bring it for identification.'

'She could have told someone else.'

'Why should she, if blackmail was intended?'

Lady Madeleine glanced away.

'Meanwhile,' Corbett continued, 'you had left the priory by a secret route. Your bow and quiver of arrows were already hidden away. You'd be there in good time. You did the same as you did to me, threw a pebble on the track. Françoise stopped and looked up, the arrow shaft took her in the throat. You make sure the way is clear and you hurry across. You roll the body down the bank, take her purse and saddle panniers, strip the corpse then bury it. You were calm enough to go through her personal possessions. I suspect Françoise brought a strand of Cecilia's hair.' Corbett opened his wallet and took out the two cloth clasps. 'That lock you took away but dropped these in your hurry. Disguised, you creep back along the trackway, mount your horse, throw Sourtillon's possessions into a marsh and return to St Hawisia's.'

'An interesting tale, clerk.'

'God knows what happened next,' Corbett went on evenly. 'Did your brother, who visited the brothel in Rye, discover Françoise was missing? Did he threaten you? Or did he continue his secret taunts about your sacred relic? Enough was enough: Lord Henry was the cause of all your trouble. You heard about the hunt. You went to that dell, where you had played as a child, the afternoon before the hunt took place. You put a bow and quiver in the hollow of an oak tree. The next morning, cloaked and cowled, you left the priory. This time you'd silence your brother's taunts about the relic and possible jibes about Gaveston for good. You could settle, once and for all, your longstanding grievances with this hated man.'

Lady Madeleine put her head down.

'A fine, sunny morning,' Corbett remarked. 'Lord Henry would prove a good target, this time not to the neck but an arrow straight in his heart. Even as he fell to the ground, you'd be hurrying back to your horse, bow and quiver hidden away, and return to St Hawisia's.'

'But why should I kill my brother?' Lady Madeleine lifted her head. 'If, as you say, the Italian physician Cantrone already knew?'

'He was a stranger. A foreigner. What proof could he offer? Who would believe him or the whore Cecilia now Françoise and Lord Henry were dead?'

Corbett paused. 'In a few months,' he continued, 'what could Cantrone say? But, you were committed to the hunt and Cantrone was an easy victim. So why let him go? He'd dared to threaten you, not realising how vulnerable he made himself. However, Lady Madeleine, when you kill, you not only trample lives but become immersed in other plots, other schemes. Cantrone didn't give a whit about the relic. He and Lord Henry were involved in other stratagems, very dangerous to himself. Cantrone simply wanted to flee. His patron was dead and the French wanted to get their hands on him. He needed gold and silver, didn't he? You didn't send for him. He came to the priory demanding to see you. He mentioned the relic and insisted that you buy his silence. Some gold and silver for his journey, he would be gone and that would be the end of it. Cantrone really meant that but you didn't trust him.'

'But I was here when he left!'

'No, Lady Madeleine, you are cunning. You probably paid him then remembered little Sister Fidelis. She would be your excuse, the reason for his visit. You gave out some story that you'd sent for him. Cantrone would accept that. He'd be a little puzzled but,' Corbett shrugged, 'what was that to him? Or that you offered food? Ashdown Manor was in uproar following Lord Henry's death. Servants and retainers were departing. Cantrone would be hungry. You order him to be taken to the refectory, given something to eat. In the meantime you once again left the priory as you did with me. Ashdown, particularly for a stranger, is a death trap. There's only one road out to the manor. I, Cantrone, Françoise Sourtillon, must take that trackway or become lost in the trees.

'By the time Cantrone had reached it you were waiting. Again an arrow to the throat. His wallet and purse are taken. A slender, light man, you'd put Cantrone's corpse across the saddle of his horse, take it deep into the woods and hide it in a marsh.'

Corbett stood up and glanced down the church where he noted that Ranulf was still sitting at the foot of the pillar.

'Finally, madam, we come to a death, a murder that need not have occurred! The death of Robert Verlian!'

refectory, given something to eat. In the meantime you once again left the priory, as you did with me. Ashdown, particularly for a stranger, is a death trap. There's only one road out to the manor. Cantrone, François Sourdillon, must take that trackway or become lost in the trees.

By the time Cantrone had reached it you were waiting. Again an arrow to the throat. His wallet and purse are taken. A slender, light man, you'd put Cantrone's corpse across the saddle of his horse, take it deep into the woods and hide it in a marsh.'

Corbett stood up and glanced down the church where he noted that Ranulf was still sitting at the foot of the pillar.

'Finally, madam, we come to a death, a murder that need not have occurred. The death of Robert Verlain.'

Chapter 16

'His death,' Corbett continued, 'was the quickest and easiest to plan, or rather that of the person you really wanted to kill. You went to the priest's house, knocked on the door and hurried into the shadows of the trees only a few yards away. You believed Brother Cosmas was there. You'd noticed the light in the window. The friar would answer the knock; you would loose an arrow and that would be it. What you didn't know was that Brother Cosmas was absent, gone to see his friend Odo.' Corbett sat down beside the prioress. 'You know the hermit was the Owlman?'

'What!'

For the first time since Corbett had begun questioning her, Lady Madeleine showed genuine surprise.

'Oh yes, he hated your brother as much as you do. An ancient sin, one curled up like a poisonous snake. The fruit of your brother's lusts and lack of care for anyone else.'

'Why should I kill a Franciscan?' she asked sharply.

'Let us go back to the death of Françoise Sourtillon,' Corbett replied. 'You'd killed her, buried her corpse and you thought that was the end of the matter. True, the grave was shallow. One day the body might be unearthed but the corpse would be simply regarded as a casualty of some outlaw attack, or even the infamous Owlman. My suspicions were first provoked by your generosity. Lady Madeleine, you may be consecrated to Christ but, to be honest, you manifest little of His teaching. You are locked in your own private heaven where the male and the brutish things of life are kept carefully at the gate. Yet you immediately offer to bury a stranger's corpse. Why?'

'An act of compassion. It is one of the Corporal Works of Mercy.'

'You don't understand the meaning of the word!' Corbett snapped. 'You buried her corpse to get it out of the way, hidden in the soil as quickly as possible. If it had been any other corpse, you would have sent it to St Oswald's-in-the-Trees for interment in the common plot. I did wonder why the great Lady Madeleine manifested such speedy and merciful measures? You kept well away from the corpse but you made careful enquiries. Perhaps this is where God's hand makes itself felt; for you became very suspicious why the corpse of your victim was left at your priory gate. Was someone pointing the finger of suspicion? Had your attack on poor Françoise been seen? Was this a reminder? Now, and this is a series of coincidences, on any other day you might have thought it was your brother. One of his subtle tricks to prick your memory. But, that particular morning, it couldn't have been. He was preparing for his great hunt in which he was later killed.'

'So?' she asked, a touch of humour in her voice.

'You went down to the death house, where the corpse had been placed in a habit. You carefully studied the cloak in which it had been wrapped when it was left at your postern gate. I would wager a tun of wine that you recognised that cloak, one your priory had given to Brother Cosmas.'

'Where is this cloak?' Lady Madeleine asked, eyebrows raised.

'Oh, madam, I am sure it's gone now. You would, perhaps, recognise the distinctive stitching and draw the logical conclusion that the corpse had been left by Brother Cosmas. What you didn't know was that Cosmas, in turn, had given that cloak to the hermit, Odo, who was also the Owlman. Odo had come to this forest in search of justice against Lord Henry.'

'And so it was he who found the corpse?' Lady Madeleine asked quietly.

'Yes he did and he's confessed to it. He didn't

want to carry the corpse to St Oswald's-in-the-Trees, that might create suspicions. The corpse was that of a woman, so he left it at the priory.'

Lady Madeleine abruptly rose to her feet. Corbett's hand dropped to the dagger on his belt. She moved to stand beside the oaken sarcophagus but kept well away from Ranulf's sword and dagger lying on the top. For a while she stood caressing the dark polished oak. Then, going round the side, she stared squarely across at Corbett.

'This is a beautiful shrine, Corbett,' she said, staring up at the ceiling. 'And I am its keeper and prioress. There's no one here to witness what I say.'

'Except God, his host of saints and all the heavenly force.'

'In which case, clerk, they already know the innermost workings of my heart!' She leaned on the tomb and half-smiled. 'Now, sir, you've walked into this shrine and laid serious allegations against me, one of the Lords Spiritual of Holy Mother Church. Yet what proof do you have? Where are the witnesses? Where is the documentation? How can you prove that I left the priory to go murdering in the forest?'

'I have very little proof, madam. I said that from the beginning. But there's a logic to it. You wanted your brother dead. You had to kill Françoise. Cantrone had to be silenced and Verlian's murder was the work of your tortuous, twisted soul.'

Lady Madeleine stood back as if Corbett had struck her in the face.

'How dare you!' she hissed. 'How dare you come swaggering in here!'

'You are a demon.' Corbett grasped the sword and dagger and pulled them away. 'You are a demon, Lady Madeleine, dressed in the clothes of an angel. God knows what you worship here but it isn't God. You talk of proof. I could go searching for that. Where is the cloak in which the corpse of Françoise was left? Shall we summon Sister Veronica? I am sure that she'll find it has disappeared and wonder why. Or Sister Fidelis? Or the other nuns? We will certainly establish just who did send for Cantrone?' He paused. 'Which of your servants took the message? Which peasant? Did anyone at Ashdown remember such a message arriving? Then, of course, I could go across to your lodgings, make a careful search for the dark cloak and cowl you probably wear when you ride out. Perhaps examine the harness and saddle of your horse? Inspect the trackway which lies outside the gates leading from your private quarters? Or shall I just prove where you actually were when your brother, Cantrone and Verlian were killed?'

Corbett tapped his finger against the polished oak.

'Ranulf said you were left-handed so you'd make a poor archer but you're gifted, I've noticed that, in the use of left or right. Do you still have the bow and quiver of arrows?' He raised his hand. 'You nearly killed me, you devil in flesh! You're a consummate archer who'll do anything to defend this shrine. Now Henry, Françoise and Cantrone are gone who can really challenge you?'

'Yes, clerk,' came the curt reply. 'Who can? Will you, with your meagre evidence?'

Corbett spread his hands. 'Perhaps I can have the royal searchers seek out this young prostitute, Cecilia. Have her brought back to England and closely questioned. Or shall I offer a reward to the chapmen and tinkers who ply their trade between Rye and Ashdown? See if anyone brought a message from Françoise Sourtillon to the prioress?' Corbett held up Ranulf's sword as if it were a cross. He could tell by Lady Madeleine's face that he had struck his mark. 'You are an assassin. I don't know whether you are just evil or mad or both. And all this.' Corbett banged the wooden sarcophagus with the sword. 'It's all mummery! The corpses of dead saints, relics of golden hair! You no more believe in the Lord Christ than the animals which dwell in the forest. At least they are true to their nature. You, Lady Madeleine, are true to nothing!'

And, turning on his heel, Corbett walked out of the shrine and down the nave of the church.

Edward of England lounged in a high-backed chair. He drummed his fingers carefully on the table as Corbett recounted what had happened at Ashdown.

The King, dressed simply in a brown tunic and leggings with high-heeled riding boots, played with the tassels of his war belt on the table before him. He picked up the jewelled goblet and stared at its engraving of a knight kneeling, hands clasped, in front of a crucifix.

'You are sure of this, Corbett?'

The King kept his face down so the clerk wouldn't catch his excitement.

'As I am that I sit here, my lord. Lady Madeleine is an assassin and, somehow or other, she should be brought to justice.'

'Oh, never mind that.' The King sipped from the goblet and stared over the rim at Corbett. 'I am interested that Piers Gaveston has the impudence to come stealing back into my kingdom like a riffler along an alleyway.'

'But, sir, you promised not to raise it with your son?'

'Oh, I won't do that.' The King scratched the side of his head and gazed sweetly on this, his most favoured clerk. 'I think I'll post rewards in every port and harbour. Gaveston will think twice before he sets foot in this kingdom again. No, no, it's more what you tell me about my beloved brother in Christ, Philip of France!'

The King hugged the cup to his chest, scraping back the chair. He stared at Corbett from under heavy-lidded eyes.

'Can you imagine it, eh? The descendant of St

Louis of France killing his own wife? We'd heard rumours, you know.'

Corbett kept his mouth shut. He didn't want to tell the King about Master Aidan Smallbone. After all, Smallbone was a veritable source of gossip and chatter. The King quickly crossed himself.

'Do you remember Simon Roulles?'

Corbett nodded.

'They found his mangled corpse on a muddy bank of the Seine. A few days earlier, they'd discovered the half-naked body of Mistress Malvoisin, a few yards further up.'

'The widow of the royal physician?'

'The same. Poor Simon was searching for what you discovered at Ashdown, and he may have even found it. What a waste! A good spy, a cunning clerk but not as good as you, eh Hugh?'

'You won't use it, sire?'

Corbett glanced sideways at Ranulf who sat tense, eyes watchful. Ever since they'd left Ashdown and journeyed up to Eltham, Ranulf had been obsessed with bringing Lady Madeleine to justice.

'What do you mean, I won't use it!'

'Sire, the treaty!'

The King's smile widened. 'Ah, you mean my beloved son's marriage to the Princess Isabella?'

'Sire, you know that marriage treaty has the support of the papacy, not to mention your Council and the Commons who recently met in parliament. If you break it, there'll be war within a month and

French ships will be helping the rebels in Scotland.'

Corbett studied his king. Edward was almost beside himself with glee yet Corbett, who had sat with the rest of the King's Council and negotiated this treaty which was to bring a lasting peace, knew how deeply Edward nurtured his hatred against Philip.

'Seigneur Amaury de Craon,' Corbett said, 'is now outside, in your antechamber. He is insistent on returning to France. You must name the lord who is to lead the English delegation.'

'Does he know that I know?' the King teased.

'He may suspect, sire, but what proof do we have? An entry in a Book of Hours, the corpse of a dead Italian physician?'

Edward put the cup down. He rubbed his hands together like a little boy who has won a game.

'In a short while, Corbett, de Craon will know that I know what Philip knows but, what he doesn't know,' the King laughed at the turn of phrase, 'is what I really know and where I have hidden the proof.'

'What proof, sire?' Ranulf exclaimed.

The King chuckled.

'Precisely, Ranulf! They'll always wonder just what proof I really have.' The King raised his hands as a sign that the meeting was over. 'I don't think you should stay, Sir Hugh, when I see de Craon.'

Corbett and Ranulf got to their feet and bowed. Edward rubbed his fingers along the top of the table.

'Do you know, Corbett,' he said thoughtfully. 'Sometimes I wonder if the game is more important than winning? I met Philip's wife Johanna. I often wondered how long Philip would tolerate her. I wonder what he really is after? Marriage to a Flemish princess? I'll stop that. And, as for the Templars? Soon it will be Christmas. Perhaps it's time I invited the Grand Master, Jacques de Molay, back to England.' Edward clapped his hands. 'Oh, Corbett, Ranulf, I think we'll celebrate the feast of All Saints at Leighton!'

Corbett smiled to hide his deep anguish at having to act as host to Edward and his cronies. They would sweep into his manor and all harmony would be shattered.

'Is there anything I can do for you?'

'When Lady Maeve's child is born,' Corbett replied quickly, because he knew the King loved such requests, 'if you could stand godfather at the font?'

'Done.' The King raised his hand. 'And, before you leave, Corbett, I have something for Lady Maeve. A necklace.' His eyes softened. 'Once worn by my Eleanor.' He opened the large wallet which hung from his war belt and tossed a purse of gold coins down the table. 'And that's for you, my Clerk of the Green Wax!'

Ranulf let it lie.

'Come! Come!' Edward drew his brows together. 'Do you refuse a prince's gift? What else do you want, Clerk of the Green Wax? Promotion? A bishopric?'

'Lady Madeleine dead!' Ranulf spat the words out, ignoring Corbett's hiss of disapproval.

'Pick the gold up!' Edward ordered. 'Pick it up, boy!'

Ranulf obeyed.

'I can't give you Lady Madeleine's head on a platter.' Edward drew his dagger, clasping his fingers round the hilt. 'But, I, Edward, King of England, Ireland and Scotland, give my solemn word: before Easter comes and goes, Lady Madeleine Fitzalan will join her brother before the court of Heaven. That matter's finished!'

Corbett tugged at Ranulf's arm. They bowed and walked out of the chamber. De Craon, lounging in a window seat, got up.

'Ah, Sir Hugh, your king is pleased?'

'My king is always pleased, Seigneur Amaury.'

De Craon pulled his face into mock grief and spread his hands.

'I hope His Majesty is in good humour. We were grieved to hear of the death of one of his clerks, Simon Roulles, a student of the Sorbonne. Such a dreadful death! Surely it proves Scripture, that we never know the time or the place of our demise?'

'My dear Amaury.' Corbett faced him squarely. 'None of us know the time and place. But the good Lord be my witness. If there is a time and place when I can settle accounts with you,' he held his hand up in a gesture of peace, '*pax et bonum*, my dear Amaury.'

The French envoy bowed, stepped aside and swept into the royal chamber.

'My dear, dear Amaury!' Edward of England half-rose from his seat, then slouched back as if the effort was too much. He gestured at the chair Corbett had vacated. 'I understand you have been enjoying the air of Sussex?'

'I am grieved, sir.' De Craon took a seat.

Edward offered his cup. De Craon took it and sipped, pleased at this mark of favour.

'At the death of Lord Henry and, of course, Signor Cantrone. Now I bring you official news of the death of Simon Roulles. Sire, accept my condolences as well as those of his most gracious majesty the King of France.'

'God only knows your grief,' Edward replied. He gestured at a sheaf of documents in front of him. 'And I have similar bad news: Pierre Rafael?' He raised one eyebrow. De Craon tensed. 'A French student in the Halls of Oxford,' the King explained. 'A man, indeed, who seemed to spend most of his life in study. Pierre often journeyed to our eastern ports, he appeared very interested in shipping . . .'

'What happened to him?' de Craon asked quickly.

'Unfortunately he was drowned,' the King replied. 'His body was fished out of the Thames. My own clerk, Master Aidan Smallbone, was in the vicinity at the time. He examined the corpse most carefully, a boating accident.' Edward spread his hands apologetically. 'These students and their drinking!'

De Craon swallowed hard. He would miss Pierre. He wondered how Edward of England had discovered his spy's true identity.

'Simon often writes to his family in England,' the King continued.

'Sire, what has this got to do with the negotiations for the betrothal of your son and the Princess Isabella?'

Edward waved a hand. 'Oh, don't worry about that. My good friend, John de Warrenne, Earl of Surrey, will lead our embassy. You should be in Dover in three days and in France before the end of the week. Other lords and ladies will accompany him.'

'So, the betrothal will go ahead?'

'Of course!' Edward smiled. 'It is a sworn treaty, sanctified by the Holy Father in Avignon. However, there are one or two little clauses I would like to discuss with you.'

'What clauses?'

'Ah, that's why I mentioned Roulle's letters. He was a great gossiper, a friend of Lord Henry Fitzalan, not to mention Signor Cantrone and Lady Madeleine. Well, to cut a long story short, de Craon, I am deeply distressed at the malicious rumours that Queen Johanna of France did not die of natural causes.' Edward kept his face grave though he was gratified by the alarm in de Craon's eyes. 'Some say that she was poisoned. Isn't that dreadful?'

'They lie and my master will have their heads!' de Craon retorted.

'Quite right.' Edward scratched his head. 'These same scurrilous gossips also point to the sudden and unexplained deaths of Monsieur Gilles Malvoisin, Queen Johanna's physician, and Madame Malvoisin his wife, not to mention Malvoisin's assistant and close friend Signor Cantrone.'

De Craon licked his lips. Edward leaned forward.

'It grieves my heart, Amaury,' he said in a low voice, 'that these same gossips lay the blame for Queen Johanna's death at the door of my beloved brother in Christ, Philip. They tell fabulous tales, how Philip wishes to marry again, a Flemish princess! Or, even worse, that he wishes to become a bachelor, gain entry into the Templars and so dominate that Order.'

'These are lies! What is their source?'

'We'll come to that in a while.' Edward offered his goblet to de Craon. 'I merely tell you this out of friendship.'

De Craon took the cup.

'So incensed am I by these malicious rumours,' Edward continued, thoroughly enjoying himself, 'that I intend to write to the Holy Father and, indeed, all the crowned heads of Europe, to refute them.'

De Craon spluttered on his wine. Edward sprang

to his feet, pushed the cup away and patted him hard on the back.

'It's a good, strong claret,' he said. 'The best MY,' Edward emphasised the word, 'MY duchy of Gascony can produce.'

'There is no need to do that.' De Craon coughed. 'Please, sire, there is no need for that. By writing such letters the rumours would only spread.'

'Oh, I hadn't thought of that!' Edward admitted, retaking his seat. 'But they are terrible lies. I mean, if the King of France married a Flemish princess or tried to control the Order of the Templars which has houses, lands and treasure throughout all of Europe, England and its allies would regard that as an act of war. The peace treaty would be rescinded and there would be no marriage between my boy and the Princess Isabella.'

'Your Majesty jumps too far too soon!'

'You do not wish me to write such a letter? You want me to keep the matter secret and confidential?'

'Of course, sire. But, if you could tell us the source of such slander?'

'I will in due time.' Edward sat up straight in the chair. 'But there are a few,' he waved a hand, 'a few anomalies about this betrothal treaty.'

'Your Majesty?'

'I want the dowry to be doubled: six hundred thousand pounds sterling.'

De Craon blanched. 'I think that's possible, in the circumstances,' he stammered.

'Good! I want my sweet brother's assurance that all aid and sustenance to the rebels in Scotland will cease forthwith.'

'Agreed!'

'I want my sweet brother's confirmation that the duchy of Gascony and the city of Bordeaux are recognised as belonging to the English crown.'

'Agreed!'

Edward spread his hands. 'Then we are in harmony?'

'Nothing else?' de Craon asked suspiciously.

Edward pursed his lips and shook his head.

'My master the King of France will agree to these, but what assurances do we have that this malicious gossip will not be spread?'

'I sent Hugh Corbett to Ashdown,' Edward replied. 'He knows about these rumours. He is sworn to secrecy. However, you've met Lady Madeleine Fitzalan?'

'Half-sister to Lord Henry and prioress at St Hawisia's?'

'The same.'

'An arrogant woman,' de Craon said. 'I heard rumours . . .'

'Such rumours are correct, Seigneur Amaury. Lady Madeleine is a threat to the amity of both our kingdoms. She learned this malicious gossip from Cantrone and told it to her brother. Only she has the details.' Edward waved a hand. 'The time, the places, et cetera, et cetera. She refused to tell

Sir Hugh very much. We think she is the root and cause of it all and provided details to her brother. Of course,' Edward smiled, 'she is now the only surviving member of that unholy trinity! I believe Fitzalan's murder, and that of Cantrone, were over this malicious story and who should profit from it!'

'Thieves falling out?'

'Precisely, de Craon.'

'So what shall we do, sire?'

Edward caught the word 'we' and smiled.

'Yes, Amaury, what shall *WE* do?' He lifted his hand. 'Before you leave for Dover, I will take an oath on what I have said today.'

'On a book of the Gospels?' de Craon asked.

'On a book of the Gospels,' Edward confirmed. He picked up the cup, then remembered de Craon spluttering in it so he put it back on the table. 'This evening, Amaury, you can lodge here and you must attend the banquet tonight. I have a special choir. I've taught them a beautiful hymn. We'll have good roast beef and pledge eternal amity.'

'Lady Madeleine Fitzalan?' Amaury insisted.

'Oh yes, you will write to me, offering me your condolences on the death of her brother and requesting . . .'

De Craon's face split into a smile.

'That Lady Madeleine Fitzalan accompany us to France so my master can console her personally?'

'Amaury! Amaury!' Edward stretched forward,

clasped de Craon's hand and squeezed it viciously. 'I love our little talks.'

'A journey across the Narrow Seas,' de Craon mused as he nursed his bruised fingers, 'can be fraught with dangers.'

'If anything happened to Lady Madeleine,' the King replied, 'I would not hold you or your master accountable.'

De Craon bowed. 'In which case, Your Majesty.'

He scraped back his chair and got to his feet. Edward did likewise, came round and grasped de Craon in a bear-like hug. They exchanged the kiss of peace. The French envoy, gratified, responded but stiffened as the King's embrace became vice-like.

'But Corbett,' Edward whispered in the Frenchman's ear, 'Corbett I regard as my brother. If anything should happen to him and I can lay it at your door or that of your master in Paris, God be my witness, dear Amaury, you will be able to measure your life span in a few heartbeats!'

Edward released the envoy and stood back.

'We have an understanding, Seigneur de Craon?'

De Craon gave the most ostentatious bow.

'In the pursuit of a common peace, sire, I and my master understand you completely!'

Author's Note

This, of course, is a work of fiction but it contains many strands of historical truth. In the Middle Ages relics were often forged and led to a brisk international trade which ran into literally hundreds of thousands of pounds. The best examples of a shrine making its possessors millionaires is, of course, St Thomas à Becket's in Canterbury or the phial, allegedly containing the Precious Blood, held by Hailes Abbey.

There was intense diplomatic activity between France and England over Philip's demand that his only daughter Isabella marry the Prince of Wales. Philip, aided by a lawyer, Pierre Dubois, dreamed of having a grandson on the throne of England. The marriage took place in January 1308. However, the best laid plans of mice and men go awry. All of

Philip's sons died without issue while Isabella's offspring, in turn, laid claim to the crown of France which marked the beginning of the Hundred Years War.

After 1303 Philip suddenly met with a fresh set of demands by Edward I. I have looked at the original in the Archive Nationale in Paris: Carton J 655 No. 25. One of these demands was for a massive dowry which, as Professor Elizabeth Brown maintains in her scholarly study, 'Customary Aids and Royal Finance in Capetin France' (Med. Academy of America 1992), almost bankrupted the French treasury.

The story that Johanna, Philip's wife, was poisoned, is contained in the *Chronographia Regum Francorum* edited by H. Moranville, Volume 1 (Paris 1891). The same source also repeats the rumour about Philip wishing to marry a Flemish princess and/or take over the Order of the Templars against which Philip launched his savage persecution in 1307.

Gaveston was a real historical figure. He was banished from England by Edward I but the favourite's insistence on slipping secretly into the kingdom led to well-attested, acrimonious disputes between father and son. On Edward's death in 1307 Gaveston was recalled only to meet violent opposition and murder in 1312.

Paul C. Doherty

The Quick and The Dead

Alison Joseph

Working in a hostel for the homeless, Sister Agnes had for a while, felt an unaccustomed contentment with her faith. But when Sam, a sixteen-year-old runaway, is forced to return to her family and then goes missing, Agnes's hard-won equilibrium vanishes.

Sam's friends recall her saying she planned to join anti-road protesters in their tree-top encampment at the edge of Epping Forest. Sure enough Agnes finds Sam there, amidst the beggars, travellers and anarchists, revelling in their fireside talk of apocalypse, though contemplating returning to live with the father who deserted her sixteen years earlier and who, suspiciously to Agnes's mind, has suddenly reappeared. For the moment however Sam seems secure at the camp, though its tents and tree houses can only provide a temporary bulwark against destruction.

But even that safety is illusory. Only hours after Agnes's arrival a body is found. Of a brutally murdered young girl.

'Enjoyable ... with a satisfyingly believable conclusion' *Glasgow Herald*

'Nice one that doesn't start with a bang and end with a whimper' *Newcastle-upon-Tyne Journal*

'A refreshingly different character' *Bolton Evening News*

'One helluva nun' *Hampstead and Highgate Express*

0 7472 5233 7

headline

The Quick and The Dead

Alison Joseph

Working in a hostel for the homeless, Sister Agnes had, for a while, felt an unaccustomed contentment with her faith. But when Sam, a sixteen-year-old runaway, is forced to return to her family and then goes missing, Agnes's hard-won equilibrium vanishes.

Sam's friends recall her saying she planned to join anti-road protesters in their tree-top encampment at the edge of Epping Forest. Sure enough Agnes finds Sam there, amidst the beggars, travellers and anarchists, revelling in their fireside talk of apocalypse, though contemplating returning to live with the father who deserted her sixteen years earlier and who, suspiciously to Agnes's mind, has suddenly reappeared. For the moment however Sam seems secure at the camp, though its tents and tree houses can only provide a temporary bulwark against destruction.

But even that safety is illusory. Only hours after Agnes's arrival a body is found. Of a brutally murdered young girl . . .

'Enjoyable . . . with a satisfyingly believable conclusion' *Glasgow Herald*

'Nice one that doesn't start with a bang and end with a whimper' *Newcastle-upon-Tyne Journal*

'A refreshingly different character' *Bolton Evening News*

'One helluva nun' *Hampstead and Highgate Express*

0 7472 5263 7

headline

Satan's Fire

P. C. Doherty

In 1303 the Old Man of the Mountain remembers back to when he nearly killed Edward of England almost thirty years before. He never forgets his prey – and now decides to release an imprisoned leper knight to avenge old grievances.

One windswept evening a few months later two nuns are hurrying to their mother house in York when they smell the sickly odour of burning human flesh. Rounding the corner, they confront the macabre sight of a man being hungrily consumed by a roaring fire.

News of this grisly death meets Edward I of England as he arrives in York for secret negotiations with the leaders of the military Order of the Temple. His unease deepens for, as he enters the city, a would-be regicide attempts to murder him. When the assassin, wearing the livery of the Templar Order, is found dead – having been engulfed by a mysterious fire – Edward immediately enlists the help of his Keeper of the Secret Seal, Sir Hugh Corbett, to investigate.

0 7472 4905 9

headline